The wounded man
staggered forward, then fell

Cheetah Luis knelt over the fallen fighter. "What happened to the others?" he demanded.

"Cannies took them all. The living and the dead. Dragged off into the swamp..."

"Did you see the live prisoners? Did you see them get taken away?" Ryan asked.

The dying man nodded, but as he did so, his eyes fluttered shut and his chest stopped heaving. Ryan leaned down and grabbed the man's chin. When he squeezed hard, the fighter opened his eyes wide.

"Did you see a black woman and a pale-skinned man? Were they taken prisoner?"

"Cannies took them both. Man's in bad shape."

**Other titles in the
Deathlands saga:**

JAMES AXLER

DEATH LANDS®

Cannibal Moon

A GOLD EAGLE BOOK FROM

WORLDWIDE®

TORONTO • NEW YORK • LONDON
AMSTERDAM • PARIS • SYDNEY • HAMBURG
STOCKHOLM • ATHENS • TOKYO • MILAN
MADRID • WARSAW • BUDAPEST • AUCKLAND

First edition March 2007

ISBN-13: 978-0-373-62587-1
ISBN-10:   0-373-62587-1

CANNIBAL MOON

Copyright © 2007 by Worldwide Library.

Printed in U.S.A.

...Late August,
I speed through the antiseptic tunnel where
the moving dead still talk
of pushing their bones against the thrust
of cure. And I am queen of this summer hotel
or the laughing bee on a stalk
of death.
—Anne Sexton,
"You, Doctor Martin" [1960]

THE DEATHLANDS SAGA

This world is their legacy, a world born in the violent nuclear spasm of 2001 that was the bitter outcome of a struggle for global dominance.

There is no real escape from this shockscape where life always hangs in the balance, vulnerable to newly demonic nature, barbarism, lawlessness.

But they are the warrior survivalists, and they endure—in the way of the lion, the hawk and the tiger, true to nature's heart despite its ruination.

Ryan Cawdor: The privileged son of an East Coast baron. Acquainted with betrayal from a tender age, he is a master of the hard realities.

Krysty Wroth: Harmony ville's own Titian-haired beauty, a woman with the strength of tempered steel. Her premonitions and Gaia powers have been fostered by her Mother Sonja.

J. B. Dix, the Armorer: Weapons master and Ryan's close ally, he, too, honed his skills traversing the Deathlands with the legendary Trader.

Doctor Theophilus Tanner: Torn from his family and a gentler life in 1896, Doc has been thrown into a future he couldn't have imagined.

Dr. Mildred Wyeth: Her father was killed by the Ku Klux Klan, but her fate is not much lighter. Restored from predark cryogenic suspension, she brings twentieth-century healing skills to a nightmare.

Jak Lauren: A true child of the wastelands, reared on adversity, loss and danger, the albino teenager is a fierce fighter and loyal friend.

Dean Cawdor: Ryan's young son by Sharona accepts the only world he knows, and yet he is the seedling bearing the promise of tomorrow.

In a world where all was lost, they are humanity's last hope....

Chapter One

Pistol in hand, Dr. Mildred Wyeth leaped through swirling, acrid smoke. Blistering heat seared through the back of her gray T-shirt and desert camouflage BDU pants. The junked Winnebago RV behind her was swallowed up in a thirty-foot-high pillar of flame. Over the roar of the blaze and the mad crackle of blasterfire, she heard children screaming as they were dragged away.

Cannies—as cannibals were called in Deathlands—loved babies.

And cannies were everywhere.

Dark, furtive shapes darted between the bonfires they had made of shanties, lean-tos, and wheelless, rusting RVs. Gunfire boomed from all sides of the ramshackle ville. Ricochets whined overhead. Somewhere in the maze of torched structures, the black woman's five companions fought shoulder to shoulder with the ville folk, dealing death to the invaders.

Mildred blinked her streaming eyes, every nerve straining. When the children screamed again, she zeroed in on the sound. For a split second she had a clear view of three cannies as they raced past the burning hulk of a station wagon. The two in front carried a squirming child under each arm. The cannie covering the hasty retreat clutched a remade Ruger Mini 14 rifle in both hands. Mildred snap-fired her Czech-made ZKR 551 target pistol, taking the only shot she had. She dropped the tailgunner with a single .38-caliber slug in the base of his spine. As she ran toward him, she got a last glimpse of the children's kicking legs and bare feet, then they and their captors vanished through a break in the log-and-earth defensive berm.

Mildred could no more wait for help from Ryan Cawdor and the others than she could will her own heart to stop beating. Unless she closed on the cannies quickly, unless she chilled them, they would escape into the night with their innocent prey.

Howling, the flesheater she had wounded dragged himself after his fellows, clawing the dirt with both hands, trailing his paralyzed limbs behind him. Mildred jumped over his prostrate body. She didn't bother shooting him in the head.

A cannie wasn't worth a second bullet.

At the edge of the berm, she struggled to pick up their direction of flight. Squinting hard, she could see perhaps sixty feet in front of her. The starlit world was a dim monochrome, varied shades of gray blotched with black. When she heard the faint sound of children mewling, she holstered her handblaster and broke into a run. The cannies were heading east, across the wide valley of the Grande Ronde river, probably making for a hidey-hole in the densely forested Wallowa Mountains whose craggy peaks loomed in front of her, blocking out the stars on the horizon.

In daylight, the high desert valley was a fairly easy traverse. On a moonless night, it was like crossing a vast carpet-bombed battlefield. The depressions were deeper and the rises were higher than they looked. The impact of repeated, misjudged footfalls racked Mildred's knee and hip joints. The sound of her own breathing roared in her ears. A burning pain stabbed her lungs, but she kept on running, full-tilt. She couldn't see the cannies, but she could hear them ahead, crashing through the stands of brush. Burdened by their struggling prizes, the flesheaters were gradually losing their lead.

From the darkness beyond the limit of her vision came nearly simultaneous thuds and yelps. Mildred's fingers closed around her holstered gun butt.

A moment later a pair of terrified little boys blundered into her path. As she reached out for them, they took to their heels, scattering to either side into the night. At least they had a chance now.

"Run and hide!" Mildred shouted over her shoulder as she raced on.

The fleeing cannies had each jettisoned a child to lighten the load and make better time. Carrying one small victim each, they quickly pulled away from her, their footfalls growing fainter and fainter. They weren't circling or splitting up, trying to throw her off the trail or to catch her in an ambush. Afraid of losing their way in the dark, they were beelining for the foothills. The only signposts were the stars overhead. Mildred guessed they had picked a constellation on the horizon and were running toward it. She did the same, determined to play out the hand she had been dealt, but with fast-fading hope. Ahead was a vast maze of potential escape routes.

The extreme northeast corner of Oregon had avoided the leading edge of Armageddon, the all-out U.S.-Soviet nuclear exchange of January 21, 2001. There had been no military installations or population centers to attract the nuke-clusters of Russian MIRVs. Since the mountainous, heavily forested area was three hundred miles from the Pacific Ocean, it had also dodged the great tsunamis, spawned by worldwide thermonuclear detonations that had devastated the coastline. Northeastern Oregon had drawn a pass for everything but the earthquakes and a terrible firestorm that had swept through mountains and valley, burning out the little towns in its path; and of course the nuke winter that had gripped the entire planet. Even before the end of civilization it had been a rugged place, thinly colonized.

A little farther to the east, the landscape got even tougher.

One hundred miles away was Hells Canyon, the deepest canyon in the world, deep enough to hide twenty battleships, stacked one on top of the other. Hells Canyon also hid a predark redoubt, a vast bunker and storage facility, complete with a functional mat-trans unit. The mat-trans network was intended to move people and matériel across vast distances instantaneously. It was thanks to that system that Mildred and her companions had emerged unscathed into the wilds of Oregon.

Most of the predark interstate highways in Deathlands led to uninhabitable ruination: miles-wide, nuke warhead impact craters, skeletonized cities, poisoned water, air and soil. Highway 84, which cut across northeastern Oregon, through the Grande Ronde valley, was an exception. Sections of its crumbling roadway still connected minor habitations and nowhere villes; out of necessity it had become a corridor of life and trade.

Where there was life in the hellscape, there were predators. Two-legged, four-legged, winged and slithering…

Running in the dim half-light, Mildred wished that Jak Lauren had been by her side. The ruby-eyed, white-haired, wild child could track a rabbit fart in a hurricane.

The base of the foothills stopped Mildred's advance. Above her the slope's blackness wasn't quite absolute. Faint starlight reflected off basalt bedrock, making it look wet. It was not. Ancient lava dikes and arches radiated trapped day heat like a furnace. Above the bedrock were densely treed slopes, fully recovered from the wildfires of more than a century earlier. If the cannies had climbed into the tree line, she knew she would never find them this night. And by morning it would be too late to save the children.

Mildred scanned the rocky flanks of the hills while her heart thudded in her throat. Come on, you bastards, she thought. Come on. Where the hell are you?

Then she saw something odd—a flicker of light bouncing off the black rock a couple hundred feet up the hillside. It was there, then it was gone. Not from the stars, because it was the wrong color. Pale yellow, instead of dead white. Had she imagined it? Were her eyes playing tricks?

Breathing hard, she watched. After a minute or two the light reappeared. Then vanished. It was real. The Wallowa Mountain basalt was riddled with caves. Some were little more than shallow dishes. Others were long and winding. A campfire set deep in a cave, perhaps around a bend or two, would give off that kind of weak light. Light that could be completely blocked by some kind of barrier.

At least she knew where they had gone.

Mildred started to climb, careful not to dislodge any loose bits of rock. If there was an established track to the cave, she couldn't see it. The sound of the gun battle was far behind her now. There would be no backup. And no going back.

The cave entrance, a low arch in the basalt slope, would have been hard to find even in the daytime. Without the intermittent flicker of light, she might have climbed right past it. No one stood guard outside. The cannies thought they had lost her.

Mildred brushed the sweat from her eyes with the back of her hand, then wiped her fingers dry on her BDU pants. By feel, she broke open her revolver, replaced the single spent shell, then softly clicked closed the 6-shot cylinder.

She didn't know how many flesheaters were in the cave. Cannies usually ran in hunting packs. They used footspeed and the cover of night to snatch away the weakest, the dumbest, the easiest chills. This night the no-name ville had been hit by multiple packs simultaneously, all competing for the spoils. Cannies didn't like to share. And when push came to shove they ate one another.

Mildred reached into her right pants' pocket. With her fingertips she counted four, full speedloaders. She took one out and palmed it in her left hand.

The ZKR ready to rip, she stooped to enter the cave. Inside the arch, the ceiling was eight or nine feet high. The walls were about that far apart, too. There was no guard on duty. Moving quietly, Mildred followed the faint light around a bend. Beyond it, the cave walls necked down and a ratty, brown-polyester blanket blocked her path. It hung from the ceiling to the dirt floor, leaking yellow points of light from a hundred holes and small rips.

From the other side, she heard voices. And soft whimpering.

Mildred stepped up and peeked through a hole in the blanket. It took a couple of seconds for her eyes to adjust to the glare of light, which came from a stone-ringed firepit in the middle of a wide chamber. She counted four cannies. She couldn't tell whether the cave went on or dead-ended. Strewed in a corner was a pile of fire-blackened human bones. From the angle she had she couldn't see the children, but the whimpering was definitely theirs.

With a sweep of her hand, Mildred pushed back the blanket, looking over the ZKR's sights. She caught the cannies flat-footed.

The Czech target pistol boomed deafeningly in the tightly enclosed space. The closest cannie, a tall man with a bushy, foot-long chin beard, took the up-angled round through his left eye-socket. His hair, skull and brain matter splattered the cave ceiling and he toppled over, rigid from head to toe with shock, like a felled tree.

Two others leaned over a boy and a girl who were huddled in a corner. The cannies whirled at the gunshot, the slivers of fileting knives flashing in the firelight. Unblinking, Mildred shot them both rapid-fire, placing one slug below each breastbone.

Heart shredders.

Muzzle climb was her old and trusted friend, and she rode it onto the fourth target who had grabbed up a blaster and was coming at her fast. As the cannie charged, he swung the side-by-side scattergun from the hip. The full-length weapon came around slowly. Way too slowly.

Center chest, point-blank, Mildred tapped him three times. As she pivoted away, the cannie's filthy cotton shirt and matted chest hair burst into flames. Dead on his feet, he dropped to his knees, then crashed in a cloud of dust at her boot tops.

With the ZKR aimed at the ceiling, she broke open the cylinder and flicked out the smoking empties. Muzzle down, her feet braced wide apart, her steady, deft fingers fitted the speedloader in place and twisted the cartridge release.

She felt a rush of breeze on her neck as the blanket over the entrance whipped aside. In the next instant, something heavy slammed into the back of her head. Her knees buckled under her. Everything went black. She didn't feel the ground when it flew up and hit her in the face.

WHEN MILDRED OPENED her eyes, the world spun madly around her. She had a splitting headache. She tried to focus and was overcome by a wave of nausea.

Shutting her eyes, she leaned back against what felt like a rough wooden post. It was wedged tightly between the cave floor and ceiling. Her wrists were lashed around the post behind her; her ankles laced to its base. The bonds were skillfully tied. There was no wiggle room, and no stretch whatsoever.

As she waited for the vertigo to pass, she recalled the seconds prior to her blackout. She had been pole-axed from behind, and that was the source of her throbbing headache.

Opening her eyes again, she looked up into a gaunt, unshaven face.

At that moment she realized that a possible skull fracture was the least of her worries.

The cannie's right cheek was marred by a burn scar, a swathe of shiny, pink, pockmarked skin where whiskers no longer grew. To Mildred, it looked like a near-miss from a close-range black-powder discharge. A victim fighting for his or her life had failed to hit the point-blank ten-ring. The cannie had no eyebrow or eyelashes on that side. His right eyelid was shriveled to nothing and the eyeball was milky-white, like a hard-boiled egg, cooked in its socket by a flash of Pyrodex. The bastard's breath stunk like a three-week-old corpse.

But that wasn't the worst of it.

Stalactites of gray hung glistening from both his nostrils. The thick discharge had smeared and crusted like a snail trail through the dark stubble that covered his upper lip and chin. He was infected with the scourge of Deathland's cannibal clans, a contagious, blood-born, inevitably fatal disease known far and wide as "the oozies."

Mildred looked past him. There were two more cannies. Live ones. The trio had entered the cave as she had started shooting, probably rejoining their running buddies for a share in the spoils. With no one covering her back, she had left herself open to attack.

The two kids were still alive, huddled in each other's arms on the dirt floor, crying softly. From stories told on their mothers' knees, they knew what was coming next.

The scarred one smiled down at her, showing off yellow incisors filed to points. He was the pack leader, the alpha. Without a word, he reached around her hip and groped her buttocks. Not in a sexual way. His interest was entirely culinary. Mildred tried to twist away from his powerful fingers. He squeezed harder, until she stopped struggling, then he let go.

"She's a tough one," the alpha said to his pals. "We've got to pit roast her. Slow fire, wrapped in wet leaves. Let her cook all day."

The other two cannies stepped closer. They had hollow-cheeked faces, skinny arms and legs. Bloated potbellies.

"Or we could slice her into steaks," the nearly bald one suggested. "Pound 'em flat with a rock. Quick-fry 'em in baby fat." The fringe along the sides of his head fell in long, greasy coils to his shoulders.

The third cannie licked his cracked lips. He had a narrow groove across his forehead where the bone had been crushed by a blow, perhaps by a tire iron or piece of rebar.

Mildred looked from face to grimy face. Gray pendulums of snot swayed from their noses. Gray discharge leaked from their filthy earholes. They were all goners. Terminal stage oozies.

There had been no such disease in the scientific literature when Mildred Wyeth had graduated from medical school. There had been no such disease when years later she had undergone a relatively minor surgical procedure and had experienced a negative reaction to the anesthetic. In a last-ditch attempt to save her life, her colleagues had put her in cryogenic stasis. That had been shortly before the cataclysmic events of January 21, 2001. After sleeping through the end of western civilization, and a century or so thereafter, she had been revived by Ryan Cawdor and the others, reborn into a strange and violent new world.

Medical science no longer existed. What information there was, was anecdotal and unsubstantiated. Rumors and lies. Lies and rumors. From her own limited experience over the years, Mildred had come to no conclusions about the true nature of cannies, or their fatal affliction. They didn't exhibit the gigantism or chimerism found in Deathlands other mutated species. Superficially at least, their flesh-eating seemed more like an addiction. One taste of human flesh and they were forever hooked. Oozie infection only seemed to increase their depravity, giving them a bottomless hunger.

In human history, cannibalism was almost always a ceremonial choice, Mildred knew. Eating one's fallen or captured enemies was a way of taking their physical and spiritual power; it was never the mainstay of diet. Epidemiological studies that might have answered the questions about cannies were no longer an option. That kind of research had vanished forever, along with the Centers for Disease Control.

Dr. Mildred Wyeth stood disarmed and helpless, facing a truly horrendous fate, but she wasn't thinking about herself, nor about how far she had come to die so miserably. She was thinking about the children. The only way she could protect them was by getting eaten first. There was still a remote chance her companions would track her to the cave before the cannies got hungry again.

"I did your packmates a favor when I blew them apart," she taunted her captors. "It was mercy chilling. You ought to thank me for easing their way to hell. Dying from the oozies is triple hard, as you boys are finding out. First come the uncontrollable hand tremors, then you start shitting yourselves. You can't digest human flesh anymore, but you can't eat anything else. You eat more and more but still you slowly starve, until you're too weak to fight off the blades of your own blood brothers."

"We've been final stage for over a year," Rebar Head bragged. "Still hunting strong. Took our medicine…"

In Deathlands, white-coated doctors and scientists had been replaced by raggedy charlatans riding from ville to ville in donkey carts, dispensing homemade potions and elixirs in recycled plastic pop bottles. They were miles away by the time their customers started dropping dead from the "medicine."

"There's no drug for what you've got," Mildred said. "It's turning your brains to pus. That's what's dripping onto your boots."

"You don't know shit about shit, Lamb Chop," Alpha said, his carrion breath gusting in her face.

"Let's eat the bitch first," the bald one snarled. "Pay her back for chillin' half our crew. The kids'll keep."

"Gotta much better idea," Alpha said. He pulled a long knife from a sheath hidden in the top of his lace-up boot. It was a predark Ka-Bar combat knife with a black Kraton handle. Alpha knelt beside the first cannie Mildred had shot. He lifted the dead man by the armpits, holding the torso propped upright. Using the knife's bluesteel pommel, he pulped the residue of brains left in the cratered skull. Mortar and pestle. When he was satisfied with the result, he tipped the man's head, slopping the lumpy mess into a tin plate.

"Old Tom, here, is gonna have his revenge," he said, shoving aside the corpse. "Open her mouth."

Mildred went rigid against the pole. She clenched her teeth with all her might.

Twenty filthy fingernails couldn't pry her jaws apart, four hands couldn't hold her head still.

Alpha broke the stalemate, sucker-punching her in the stomach. The others exploited her moment of weakness. Baldy pulled down her bottom jaw, Rebar Head forced a thick stick crossways, between her back molars.

Mildred couldn't snap the stick and close her mouth. She couldn't dislodge it by shaking her head. She flexed her throat muscles, shutting her gullet, her eyes wide with panic.

Then came the metallic taste of the plate on her tongue, followed by warm goo flooding her mouth. Before she could cough out the pureed brains, hard fingers pinched off her nostrils and a callused palm covered her mouth.

Mildred's stomach heaved violently, but she couldn't expel a single drop. The resulting explosion of pressure only drove it up into her sinuses.

"How do you like it?" Alpha inquired, pinning the back of her head to the pole and holding it there.

The taste of death was shrill, feral, fecal. The stench in her nose burned like battery acid.

With the hands shutting off her air, it was either swallow or suffocate.

She wanted to suffocate, but the choice wasn't hers to make. Her nervous system's hardwiring wouldn't allow it. Just before she passed out, she swallowed.

When Alpha released her, she gasped a breath, then projectile vomited across the cave floor.

The cannies brayed at her dry heaving, and her frantic coughing and spitting. "You been dosed good," Baldy said.

"You'll be hungry for long pig in no time," Alpha added, wiping his leaking nose on the back of his hand.

"The oozies might chill me, but it won't make me a rad-blasted cannie," Mildred said defiantly.

"You think cannies are born that way?"

The monsters laughed some more.

"Which came first, the cannie or the oozies?" Alpha asked her. "Guess you're gonna find out." Then he glanced over at the children, his good eye narrowed to a slit. "Throw some more wood on that fire," he told his packmates. "Let's get something cooking. I don't know about you guys, but I'm fuckin' starvin'."

Chapter Two

Ryan Cawdor followed in Jak Lauren's footsteps, trying hard to keep up, his SIG-Sauer P-226 blaster in hand. Behind Ryan in a tight single file was the remainder of the companions. Krysty Wroth, Ryan's red-haired, emerald-eyed lover, was wrapped in a long, shaggy black coat, and carried a Model 640 .38 Smith & Wesson revolver. John Barrymore Dix, Ryan's comrade since the days of riding with Trader's convoy, had his trademark fedora screwed down on his head; his military-style, M-4000 shotgun swung on a shoulder sling. Theophilus Algernon "Doc" Tanner, Oxford scholar circa 1881 and reluctant time traveler, brought up the rear in his tattered frock coat and cracked riding boots. In one fist he held a massive Civil War relic black-powder handblaster; in the other an ebony walking stick that concealed a rapier blade.

One of their number was missing.

They wouldn't rest until they recovered her.

Krysty had watched Mildred vanish into the night, chasing a pair of cannies who carried off two young children each. Pinned belly-down by withering blasterfire, the tall redhead couldn't go to her friend's aid, and in the deafening clatter of the exchange couldn't summon the others to help. It wasn't until almost half an hour later, until after the attack had been beaten back and the cannies driven out of the ville's berm, that Ryan and the companions had regrouped and begun the pursuit.

They had covered less than a hundred yards when Jak called a halt to the advance. Kneeling, he holstered his .357 Magnum Colt Python and carefully examined the narrow strip of churned-up ground.

"Cannies dropped kids," the albino announced.

"No bodies here," Ryan said as he looked around. "They must have been alive. Looks like they got away."

Jak walked on a few more yards. "Cannie tracks both heavy on one leg," he said.

"They're still carrying a kid each," Krysty said. "I saw them take four from the ville."

"I wonder why our Mildred did not stop to round up the escapees?" Doc asked.

"They probably hit the ground running," Ryan answered. "Even if she saw them she couldn't catch them in the dark."

"That way," Jak said, pointing due east.

The companions resumed the chase. They moved triple fast and triple quiet. There was only the soft hiss of their bootheels on sand as Jak led them across the valley, toward the dark screen of mountains.

As Ryan ran, he thought about the ville they had just left, and the dozens of bodies strewed in its rutted dirt lanes. How many of its folk had died fighting? How many had been carried off to meet a worse fate than a bullet? How many women and children had either been suffocated by smoke or burned alive in their underground hiding holes? The exact cost of victory was impossible to count until after daybreak, which was still hours away. The shambling shacks could be rebuilt, of course. The stacked logs and heaped earth of the defensive berm could be repaired, and its design much improved. But Ryan knew it would take years to restore the human population to its former size.

All the while with flesheaters hammering at the gates.

Taking the battle to the cannies, finding their dens and chilling them one by one, was the only way to tip the balance. It was a daunting task, given the mountainous terrain and their apparent numbers. Even before the attack there hadn't been enough ville folk to handle the job. Unlike Deathlands numerous mutated species, cannies were still essentially human beings. Humans gone psycho-renegade. They fought with blades and blasters instead of teeth and claws. This night they had been particularly well-armed with semiauto and full-auto centerfire weapons. Several of them weren't remades.

Over the years, after numerous skirmishes, Ryan had cannies pegged as cunning, cowardly adversaries. Their normal strategy was hit and git, like true pack-hunting predators. Cannies worked a vulnerable territory until it could no longer support them or until they were chilled or driven out.

Because they looked human, cannies sometimes infiltrated villes and mingled with norms, then struck without warning. Children and the dimwitted simply disappeared overnight. Cannies were blood traitors to their own species, universally despised and feared. The happy downside to the cannie lifestyle was the oozies, a horrible, wasting disease that ultimately claimed them, one and all. It was widely assumed that they got it from eating the infected brains of their own packmates.

No one knew their exact origins. From the time-honored campfire tales, it appeared cannies had been around since skydark, when nuke winter had forced the surviving humans to make awful choices about protein sources. Although the companions had come across isolated small bands that roamed Deathlands interior, Ryan had never seen or heard of cannies unleashing a coordinated, mass attack on a bermed ville. Their organization had always stopped at the pack level, the primary hunting group.

The hellscape was full of mysteries. Explanations, when they came, were usually incomplete.

Jak somehow picked out Mildred's trail in the weak light, leading the companions across the high desert valley on a near dead run. How the albino managed the feat was a puzzle to Ryan, especially after Mildred had explained her twentieth-century understanding of albinism to him. Before the Apocalypse it had been a well-documented genetic disorder, caused by a random mutation that stopped production of a chemical vital to normal development of skin pigmentation, eyes and brain. According to Mildred, predark albinos always had poor vision, were susceptible to sunburn and had blue-gray or brown eyes. Jak had exceptional eyesight. He never sunburned. And his eyes were ruby-red. The youth vehemently insisted that he wasn't a mutie—those with mutie blood were Deathlands untouchables, often chilled on sight—but the evidence said otherwise. Whether he was seeing the bootprints in the sand, or smelling out the track, or using some other extra-norm sense that had no name, Jak was bird-dogging. The pace he set was grueling, but no one complained, and no one asked for a rest.

Ahead, the impenetrable black of the mountain crags loomed larger, the landscape tilted underfoot, and the companions began to climb the gradual incline of the valley side. As the physical effort increased, body heat built up. Sweat peeled from Ryan's hairline, down his forehead, burning into his good eye. The other socket was an empty hole, covered by a black leather patch. A livid scar divided that eyebrow and split his cheek, a secondary wound from the knife slash that had half blinded him. Ryan ignored the growing ache in his thighs, pushing the pain aside as though it belonged to someone else.

Mildred Wyeth was more than a treasured friend, more than a trusted comrade in arms; she was a resource the companions couldn't afford to lose. Mildred had been a physician; she understood the workings of predark science and technology. She had come from a time not only with different knowledge, but very different values.

Would any of the other companions have taken off on their own to rescue the children?

Mebbe.

Mebbe not.

When the five reached the base of the mountains,

they paused for breath, faces upturned, searching the black vastness above.

"Where'd she go?" J.B. said softly.

Jak tugged on Ryan's sleeve.

"There," the albino teen said. "Cave mouth."

Above them, weak firelight flared against bedrock, then it was gone. They all saw it.

"How can you be positive that's where Dr. Wyeth has gone?" Doc asked.

"Can't," Jak said.

"That fire didn't start itself," Krysty said. "Got to be cannies hiding inside. Nobody else would be out in the bush around here."

"Nobody in their right mind," J.B. added.

"We need to have a look-see," Ryan told the others. "Spread out, take it slow, make sure of your footing. We don't want any rockslides on the approach."

The companions climbed the mountain flank, closing in on the cave entrance with blasters raised, safeties off. They saw no movement and met no resistance. The cannies weren't expecting company. Probably because they considered themselves well-hidden and figured no one would try to hunt them down before dawn.

As Ryan neared the cave mouth, he smelled wood smoke, charring meat and burning hair. His stomach twisted into a knot.

Not Mildred, he thought. For nuke's sake, not Mildred…

He ducked under the low arch, entering the outer chamber, where the trapped smoke and stench hung like an evil fog.

When all companions were inside the arch, he led

them through the smoke, toward the source of the flickering yellow light. Around the cave's bend, they spread out on either side of the blanket that served as a door, weapons aimed, fingers resting lightly on triggers.

Holding the SIG-Sauer braced against his hip, Ryan leaned forward and peered through a rip in the fabric. He saw two men, one bald and the other with a badly scarred face, crouched on the far side of a roaring fire. There had to be a vent in the ceiling, he thought, a fissure in the rock drawing most of the smoke up and out. The cannies were eating with their bare hands, pulling greasy strips of charcoaled meat off the shoulders of a human corpse. They had removed the dead man's clothing but hadn't bothered to cut up his body. They had simply shoved it into the fire like an oversize log, burning it at one end, flame-roasting the head and upper torso.

A third cannie stood with his back turned to the entrance, urinating torrentially against the cave wall. When Ryan saw Mildred tied to the post, the weight on his shoulders lifted. She was still alive. The children were huddled in a corner. Still alive, too.

Ryan turned to the companions and held up three fingers. Three targets.

"Mildred?" J.B. whispered.

The one-eyed man gave the thumbs-up.

At his signal, Krysty ripped down the tattered blanket. Ryan and J.B. burst into the death chamber, shoulder to shoulder.

Before the bald cannie could stand, J.B. blasted him full in the face with a load of double-aught buckshot. The cannie jerked violently backward, a plume of skull and brains flying; J.B. cycled the M-4000's action and fired again. The scar-faced cannie was already moving sideways, lunging for a nearby weapon. J.B.'s buckshot missed its intended target by a foot. Instead of taking off his head, the blast slammed the cannie in the left shoulder, bowling him over as a cloud of dirt and rock dust rained from the ceiling. The creature landed hard and stayed down.

The remaining flesheater lunged toward the children through the swirling dust, his knife blade drawn. Leading him, Ryan squeezed off two shots with the SIG-Sauer. And hit the ten-ring. A pair of tightly spaced, 9 mm rounds in the head blew the cannie off his feet before he could cut throats. He crashed into a pile of bones at the base of the wall, and lay there, twitching.

Doc rounded the firepit and covered the wounded cannie with his double-barreled LeMat. Krysty gathered up the children, who were bawling with relief.

Drawing his eighteen-inch panga from its leg sheath, Ryan stepped over to Mildred. There was blood on her chin. The glistening stripe ran down the front of her neck and onto her T-shirt, which was speckled with pink bits of bone. She reeked of vomit.

As Ryan cut her bonds he said, "Are you okay?" When she didn't answer, he added, "Are you wounded?"

Mildred shook her head minutely, but she wouldn't meet his gaze.

Ryan had fought side by side with this woman in countless pitched battles. Under fire, Mildred was intense, determined, fearless. He had never seen her like this in the aftermath of combat. Numbed. Shell-shocked. What had the bastards done to her?

He wasn't the only one who noticed the change.

There was concern on J.B.'s face as he returned Mildred's revolver to her. "You did good," he assured her. "It all worked out."

Mildred holstered her revolver. She let her arms drop to her sides. Then she slumped back against the wooden post, utterly deflated.

"Mildred?" J.B. said. He stared helplessly at the dazed, blood-smeared physician.

"For nuke's sake, Jak," Ryan snarled over his shoulder, "drag the chill out of the fire. Stop that rad-blasted stink."

The albino grabbed the corpse by the heels and pulled it from the blaze. Then he kicked dirt on its smoldering head.

"Who was he?" Ryan asked the woman. He put his hand on her arm and gave it a gentle shake. "Mildred?"

"Cannie I shot," she replied in a barely audible voice. "The others decided not to let him go to waste."

Doc loomed over the sole cannie survivor, holding the LeMat's shotgun barrel against his temple, and down angling the load of bluewhistlers so as to empty his cranial vault, top to bottom. As the old man cocked the black-powder blaster's hammer, Alpha twisted his head around so he could look his executioner in the face.

"Prepare to meet your maker, Devil spawn," Doc said.

The wounded cannie pursed his lips and blew Doc a juicy, gray-smeared kiss.

Suddenly, Mildred came to life. "No!" she cried, lunging forward with arms outstretched. "Don't chill him!"

Chapter Three

"Forgive me, my dear," Doc said, decocking his antique weapon. "I didn't mean to presume. You will, of course, wish to do the honors yourself." As he stepped away from the wounded cannie, he made a sweeping gesture with his ebony swordstick, gallantly inviting her to have at her revenge.

Mildred advanced on the monster with gun drawn.

Ryan was gratified to see her back in action.

His relief was short-lived.

"When you gonna tell 'em, Mill-Dred?" cannie said, sneering at her. "When you gonna tell 'em our little secret?"

Instead of immediately shooting the cannibal through the head as Ryan and the others expected her to do, Mildred braced her feet, and, grunting from the effort, started pistol-whipping him with the barrel of her ZKR 551. She literally beat the evil grin off his face, in the process knocking out several of his filed teeth, and cutting deep slashes in both his cheeks with the Czech blaster's front sight.

No one said a word. Her longtime companions looked on in astonishment. In the space of a couple of minutes, Mildred had gone from devastated to near-demonic, and in the process, turned her physician's oath on its head.

"Get him up on his feet!" she shouted to J.B. and Jak.

The two men scrambled to hoist the cannie from the cave floor.

Raising her arm, threatening to continue the beating, Mildred backed the monster against the post. "Tie him tight, Jak," she said.

The albino teen cinched wrists and ankles to the rough-hewn pole.

When the cannie was immobilized, Mildred's fury seemed to ebb. She viewed the blood on her gunsight with deep, deep disgust; she scooped up a dead man's rag of a shirt and quickly wiped the muzzle clean.

"I need to talk to Ryan," she told the others.

"So talk," J.B. said.

"I need to talk to him alone."

"We'll wait outside the cave, then," Krysty offered.

"No," Mildred said. "Ryan and I have got things to do here, just the two of us. It's going to take a while, and it's going to get loud before we're done. I don't want the children to hear and be scared all over again."

Jak stared at the battered, bound cannie, his ruby eyes glittering with menace, certain that rough justice was on its way.

"Take the kids back to the ville, Krysty," Ryan said. "Find their parents, if they're still alive. Jak, Doc, J.B., go with her."

"Not a good idea for you two to stay here by yourselves," J.B. said.

"I concur most emphatically," Doc said. "We either should all go, or all remain, for safety's sake."

"We've got plenty of ammo," Ryan said. "Daybreak's not far off. We'll be fine. We'll catch up with you in the valley."

The companions didn't like leaving them behind, but there were no more protests. Mildred had earned herself a private face-to-face, and private payback, if that's what she wanted.

"We'll see you back at the ville, then," J.B. said. With a wave of his arm he led the others out of the cave.

Krysty touched Mildred on the hand as she herded the wide-eyed children past her. "You saved them," the redhead said. "You saved them, and you survived. You did great, Mildred."

After the companions had filed out, Ryan threw another hunk of wood on the glowing coals and watched it slowly ignite. "What's going on, Mildred?" he said.

"Something real bad."

"Figured that."

"I wanted to tell you about it first," she said, her voice tight, her words clipped. "I need you to make me a promise. I need you to give me your word on something."

"Of course."

"Before you and the others got here," Mildred said, "the bastards force-fed me cannie brains."

Ryan felt the bottom drop out of his stomach. The puzzle had been solved, albeit horrifically. Now he understood why she had acted with such uncharacteristic savagery.

"They were infected brains, Ryan," Mildred said. "Terminal stage oozies. Three of them ganged up after they had me tied to the post. They made me swallow a plateful. Afterward I vomited up as much as I could, but chances are I'm infected."

Ryan reached out to comfort her, but she backed away.

"I don't know how long it'll take for the oozies to manifest," she told him. "I don't know what will happen when the infection starts to spread through my brain."

"You didn't have to keep this from the others."

"Yes, I did," she insisted. "We've been together too long. Covered too much ground, been through too much hell. I trust every one of them with my life, Ryan, but not with my death. I'm afraid they might wait to do what needs to be done, out of friendship or love or misplaced sympathy. I won't risk that. I don't know how long I can fight off the disease. I may not know I've lost the battle until it's too late for me to do anything about it. What I'm saying is, I may be too weak or too crazy to eat my own gun. Ryan, I want you to promise me you'll do the job when the time comes. Without hesitation or mercy. Will you do that for me?"

It wasn't a deed Ryan wanted on his conscience, it made his head reel to even contemplate it, but he couldn't refuse her. He concealed his reaction behind a mask of stone, looked her straight in the eye and said, "You got it, Mildred."

"And there's something else. It's the reason I stopped Doc from chilling that one."

"I wondered why you stepped in like that," Ryan

said. "After what the bastard did to you, why you didn't shoot him yourself?"

"When they had me tied up," Mildred said, "the cannies started talking about their 'condition.' They claimed they had medicine for the oozies. They didn't elaborate on what it was or where it came from. They said it kept them alive, even though they had been in final stage for over a year."

Ryan turned and addressed the filthy, scarred man tied to the pole. "Is that true?"

The cannie cackled and spit a big crimson gob in the dirt.

"It probably was idle talk," Mildred said. "Something they made up to mess with my head. Or maybe they came across some carny show snake oil, drank it down and are hoping against hope. On the other hand, it just might be something real. Ryan, I know it's a hell of a long shot, but I've got a short list of options. I'm looking at a triple nasty ride on the last train west. It's a journey I surely don't want to make."

Ryan said nothing. He'd seen a few victims of end-stage oozies in his time. Based on that experience, if he'd been the one infected, he knew he'd have been grasping at straws, too.

"I'll tell you everything," the cannie offered, "if you just snip off one of them nice, crispy ears and pass it over to me."

"Shut up," Ryan said, "or I'll saw off your rad-blasted foot and make you eat that, boot and all."

The one-eyed cannie grinned back, showing off the bloody slivers of his fractured incisors. "You can't do anything to me that I won't purely enjoy."

"You're wrong there," Mildred assured him. "If we do absolutely nothing, you're going to purely hate it, and sooner or later you'll tell us everything we want to know."

The cannie spit again.

"You got a name, shitbag?" Ryan said.

"I got two names. My born name and my hunting name."

"Take it from me," Ryan said, "your hunting days are done. What name were you born with?"

"Georgie Tibideau Junior," the cannie said. "From the Siana line of Tibideaus, though if you asked my ma and pa about me, I suppose they would deny I was ever born."

"You're a long way from home, cannie," Mildred said.

"Been walking the Red Road for years."

"What road?" Ryan asked.

"You never heard of the Highway of Blood? It's the path all cannies take, the path we make. It stretches from here to there."

"'There?'" Cawdor said.

"The homeland."

"And where might that be?" Ryan asked.

Tibideau squinted his good eye up at Cawdor's face, then said, "You know, I should get me a patch like that. Got some style. Bet it keeps dirt and crap from falling into the hole, too." Having delivered a transparent compliment, the cannie tried to reap an undeserved reward. "You know you folks broke in before I could finish my morning snack," he told them. "Come on, brother, use that big, sharp blade of yours and hack me off a hunk of one them dead 'uns. Don't let that good meat go to waste."

It was Ryan's turn to hawk and spit.

Interrupting the cannie's calorie intake was the whole idea.

Ryan and Mildred took seats on flat rocks near the fire and propped up their boots, settling in for an extended rest.

At first, Junior Tibideau remained sullenly quiet. Unable to backhand away his nasal excretions, he let them trickle down his unshaved upper lip; when they spilled over onto his mouth, he spit.

Ryan and Mildred didn't have to discuss the interrogation strategy. They both saw the same weakness in their enemy, and the same way to exploit it. When infected cannies neared death, they reaped so little energy from their food that they had to eat almost nonstop. No matter how much they ate, they were in state of perpetual near-starvation.

Junior Tibideau was a tough nut. He didn't buckle under the psychological pressure, the anticipation of the terrible agonies to come. It took almost six hours on the post for his hunger pangs to become unendurable. Mildred and Ryan watched him sweat, squirm, shiver head to foot; they listened as his high-pitched whimpers turned to guttural moans. And when Junior couldn't stand it anymore, it was like a dam breaking. The cannie started talking, fast and furious, chatter-boxing like a jolt addict coming off a two-week binge.

"Do you really think this is how I dreamed of ending up when I was little?" Junior said. "Tied to a pole in a stinking cave with my shoulder shot and my belly on fire? Mebbe I deserve to die triple hard because of what I've done, but I had no choice. I didn't wake up one day and decide to be a cannie. I woke up and I already was one. Mebbe you don't want to believe it, but I'm as much a victim as the stupid bastards I've made my meat."

Although Ryan and Mildred didn't respond to his plea for sympathy, Junior pressed on. "That very first night, years ago," he said, "when cannies came through our swamp, they could've butchered me on the spot, but they didn't do me that favor.

"I was night fishing by myself down by the river. I'd just set my snag line when I heard them sneaking through the mangroves along the mud bank. It was too late to get away. I can't swim a stroke. They had me sandwiched, all of them with blasters and long blades ready. I thought for sure they were going to eat me then and there. But that wasn't what they had in mind. Turned out that they needed another hunter to fill out their crew. If I'd said no to joining the pack, they would have sundried strips of my flesh on the bushes and turned me into jerky.

"I didn't taste human being that night, though there was plenty of eating going on. I ran with the pack, hanging back a little and watching what they did. How they hunted the tiny, shit-scrabble farms on the edges of the swamp, how they swept through the ramshackle buildings, chilling as a team. Some cannies ate way more of the bounty than others. They were the sick ones.

"I was back in my bed in my folks' shanty before

sunup, with no one the wiser. It was triple hard getting to sleep. All I could think about was running free and wild. I'd seen a different world through different eyes. I woke up feverish and dripping sweat the next morning. Through the heat of the day my whole body throbbed. It felt like it was going to explode. I just laid there on my straw and panted like a dog. The coolness of evening eased my fever but not the pressure inside me.

"At dark, when the cannies came back for me, I was shivering I was so ready to join the hunt. When they asked about easy pickings close by, I told them about a little dimmie boy I knew who lived with his pa on the other side of the swamp. I told them the dimmie was blond-haired and freckled—a couple weeks later I would've just called him a 'hundred pounder.' That's gutted, hanging weight.

"I tricked the dimmie boy into coming out of his shack by standing at his window and calling his name real soft. He knew me from night fishing, so he didn't suspect anything. I got him over to the edge of the woods and when his head was turned I whacked him on top of the head with a steel hatchet. I split his skull wide open with the first blow, before he could yell for help from his pa who was sitting in the shack, sipping joy juice, not fifty feet away. The dimmie was still twitching a little when me and the others dragged him deep into the thicket. We picked at his bones until dawn.

"One taste of long pig and I had to have more. I never went back home. Never saw my kin again. I've been on the Red Road ever since, with this pack and that."

"Along the way looks like somebody managed to royally fuck you up," Ryan said.

"Brother, the way you look, you must've pissed somebody off, too."

Ryan shrugged.

"I got this face three years ago," Junior said. "Dirt farmer heard our pack coming through her corn field and took her kids down in the root cellar to hide. We shot holes through the wooden door until we figured we must've nailed her. When I opened the hatch everything was quiet below, so I jumped down for a looksee. About then her oldest son cut loose with a black-powder handblaster. He got off one shot before I had hold of him. His pistol ball missed my head by a gnat's ass, but the muzzle-flash caught me square in the peeper. Felt like hellfire burning into my brain. I screamed, but I didn't let go. The others had to pry my fingers off the kid's busted neck so they could fry him."

"Maybe I should just go ahead and kill this filthy bastard," Mildred said through gritted teeth.

"That's your call," Ryan said.

"Brother, your woman there isn't telling you the whole story," Junior informed him.

"About what?" Ryan said.

"The oozies."

"Mildred, what's he on about?"

"According to Junior, the oozies does more than chill," she replied. "He claims it turns norms into cannies. The infection comes first, then strict cannibalism, and finally the array of debilitating symptoms leading to death."

"Either of you ever see a norm with the oozies?" Junior added.

Ryan couldn't say that he ever had. "Is that even possible?" he asked Mildred.

"Hypothetically, I suppose it is. If the oozie virus permanently alters the brain chemistry of its victims, it could affect sensory perception, ideation and ultimately behavior."

"Nukin' hell!" Ryan exclaimed as he followed that premise to its logical conclusion.

"You got it," Mildred said. "If what Junior says is true, sooner or later, and long before I'm dead, I'll end up just like him."

"Not going to let that happen," Ryan said. "No fucking way." Rising to his feet, he unsheathed his panga. He leaned over one of the dead cannies and smeared the heavy blade with congealing blood.

"This what you want?" he asked Junior as he waved the bloody knife under his nose.

Whining, Junior craned his neck as far forward as he could. He opened his mouth wide and started to drool. The look on his face said he would have eaten his own hand if had he been able to reach it.

"Where did the oozie medicine come from?" Ryan said.

"For a lick, brother. I'll tell you all about it for one little lick."

"Answer the question, then mebbe I'll give it to you."

"Got the medicine down in the homeland. From La Golondrina."

"What's La Golondrina?"

"Who. She's a who. Gimme my lick…" Junior thrust out a gray-coated tongue. Stretching. Stretching.

When Ryan pulled back the glistening panga, the cannie started to shake violently from head to foot. "Stop playing games, shitbag," Cawdor said. "And spill it."

"La Golondrina's a freezie," Junior hissed. "As far as anybody knows, she was the first case of the oozies. She came down with the sickness before the nuke-caust. She was the very first cannie, too. Did some hunting on her own down in southern Siana until the predark law caught up with her. Law turned her over to the whitecoats for testing. They couldn't cure her, and they were afraid the disease might somehow get out and spread. The legend says they put La Golondrina into some sort of deep sleep when she was in the last stages of dying. She was frozen, sort of. She woke up about a year ago, after there was some sort of malfunction. She still had the oozies, but it was too weak to chill her."

"What's that got to do with the medicine you took?" Ryan said.

"One drop of her precious blood keeps a hundred of us alive, brother. The word about La Golondrina's healing power spread from pack to pack all across Deathlands. Cannies started pilgrimaging from the farthest corners to find her and be saved from the Gray Death. They're still coming."

Ryan turned and gave Mildred a dubious look.

"There had to be a Patient Zero, Ryan," Mildred said with conviction. "An initial human case. If this woman survived, whether because of the freezing or thawing process, or the duration of her cryosleep, or some other unknown factor, she had to have produced antibodies to the disease. If oozie-infected blood can kill, blood with oozie antibodies can save."

"Do you have to take the medicine more than once to be protected?" Mildred asked Junior. "Does its effect wear off over time?"

"Don't know. I've only taken it the once. Four months ago. I haven't gotten any worse."

"It may not be a complete cure," Mildred said. "In low concentrations, it could be just a temporary treatment, a palliative that has to be repeated to keep the final stage at bay."

"How do we find this freezie?" Ryan asked the cannie.

Junior cackled, sensing a sudden turn of fortune. "You don't," he said. "Not without me to guide you."

"Yeah, right."

"You need me, brother. If what we did to you norms down in the valley was hell, the homeland in Siana is hell on wheels. You'll never get close to La Golondrina without my help."

"Let's talk outside a minute," Mildred told Ryan.

As they left the cave, Junior's shrill pleas echoed against their backs. "Feed me! You promised you'd feed me!"

Squinting at the bright morning light, Mildred and Ryan stared across the wide river valley. They could see fires still burning out of control in the no-name ville.

"What happens to me is no longer the issue," Mildred said gravely. "I don't matter anymore."

"What do you mean?"

"There's a much bigger problem, Ryan. Until now the oozies kept a lid on the population and spread of cannies. Until now it was one hundred percent fatal. If there's a treatment that lifts that lid, there's nothing to stop the disease and cannies from overrunning the continent. Every norm in Deathlands is a potential new cannie or cannie victim."

"How can we follow a stinking bastard who'd eat his own mother if given the chance?"

"We don't have any choice, other than hiding our heads in the sand. We've got to turn off the spigot once and for all, or every night is going to be like last night—or worse. We've got to find La Golondrina and kill her."

"Jak's gonna take the news about Siana triple hard," Ryan said. "And the whole crew is gonna to be mighty unhappy if we bring Junior back alive."

"Ville folk aren't going to like it much, either. We have to convince them that he's too valuable to chill."

"Tough sell all around."

As if to underscore his point, a familiar cry echoed in the cave behind them. "Feed me!"

"Junior won't survive the journey unless we let him eat a little something," Mildred said.

"Little is what he's going to get. If we keep the bastard hungry, we keep him honest."

Chapter Four

Naked to the waist except for her Army-issue bra, Mildred squatted beside the creek, sloshing her T-shirt in a shallow pool. She washed off the crusted vomit and gore, then wrung it out and pulled it back on, still wet and clinging. No way she could wash the smell from the inside of her nose. The cannie cave's greasy pall of melted fat and burned flesh clung to her skin and hair, as well. Inside and out, she felt soiled, contaminated.

She inventoried her physical state with as much professional detachment as she could manage. In the wake of the forced feeding and projectile vomiting, her stomach ached like she'd swallowed, then expelled, a five-pound cannonball. There was no evidence of fever, though. According to Junior Tibideau, he had come down with symptoms overnight, after his first contact with the Siana pack. No flesh-eating on his part.

"Woke up cannie."

An unlikely outcome, Mildred knew.

If oozie virus was inhaled or absorbed through the skin, it would take several days, perhaps even a week or two, to build up to the point where increased production of white blood cells would cause his body temperature to rise to the fever point. She also knew that brain lesions and radical changes in behavior didn't happen suddenly in the absence of violent head trauma. Mildred concluded that Junior was flat-out lying, trying to deflect the blame for his vile actions, which were more voluntary than he wanted to let on; this in order to minimize or eliminate punishment. The wretched, weak-willed bastard didn't want to admit that he had been so easily seduced by the cannie lifestyle.

Junior had proved himself a liar, so how could she believe him about the existence of the oozie medicine?

He wasn't the only source of that information. The cannie with the caved-in head had bragged about it before Junior had dosed her, while they were still in complete control of the situation. So it couldn't have been a lie calculated to keep the miserable bastards alive, or to make her a compliant member of the pack by dangling survival under her nose.

Before they left the cave, Mildred and Ryan had decided that she would have the only close contact with Junior. They couldn't be sure how contagious the infection was; and she was already exposed to the max. Mildred checked his shoulder and found a superficial flesh wound, which she cleaned, but didn't bother to stitch.

Then at blasterpoint they turned him loose for a couple of minutes on the dead 'uns.

It was triple hard to watch him go at it. He fed like

a ravening animal on his own, downed packmate. Mildred couldn't help but think she might be looking at her own future, and even more horrifying, the future of her companions. She had driven Junior off the charred corpse with a sharp blow of her pistol butt on the top of his head and a single, barked command. "Enough!"

She picked up her gunbelt and rose, still dripping, from the creekside.

Thirty feet upslope, Ryan guarded the cannie with his SIG-Sauer. Junior's wrists were tied behind him. A thick, four-foot length of tree limb was thrust between his back and crooks of his arms. This served to keep the prisoner bent slightly at the waist, off balance; he couldn't run five steps without falling on his face. Which made him much easier to handle. They didn't have to keep him on a short leash.

Under a clear blue midday sky they continued across the Grand Ronde valley. In the distance, the ville's dirt-and-log berm was still burning, sending up clouds of brown smoke and soot. As they neared the encampment's perimeter, they could hear sounds of weeping, coughing and the intermittent crunch of shovels gouging the stony earth. When the blinding smoke shifted, it revealed a line of women, children and oldies digging a long communal grave in the hardpan.

On the other side of the trench, more than twenty bodies were lined up on the ground, shoulder to shoulder. Young, old, male, female. Hacked. Shot. Incinerated. They had manned the barricades and defended the rutted lanes with their lives. Some had died trying to escape the cannie wolf packs. Mildred knew there were many more ville folk missing. On their descent of the valley, she and Ryan had come across numerous sets of tracks in the sand, twin, parallel tracks made by bootheels, the last impressions of unconscious victims as they were dragged away.

Downwind of the diggers, a wide, shallow pit belched low flame and coils of black smoke. Doused with gasoline, the heaped cannie dead were burning like garbage on a midden.

Mildred visualized ten thousand such narrow Pyrrhic victories. Adding up to an unwinable war against an implacable, ever-growing foe. After the long, valiant struggle up from the radioactive ash heap of Armageddon, it was the end of humanity's hope. With considerable effort, she drove the awful images from her mind.

"Stop right there!" someone shouted from behind the berm. "Stop or we'll fire!"

Blaster barrels poked over the berm's ridge, and here and there through crude firing ports. Every sight was trained on them.

"Who you got there?"

Even at a distance Junior Tibideau's identity was obvious from his filth, his disfigurement and his overwhelming carrion stench.

"That's a cannie!" one of the grave-digging women cried, pointing at him with her shovel. "They caught a cannie!"

"Chill the bastard!" another woman shouted.

"Pulp his fucking head!" shrieked an oldie.

The column of gravediggers surged forward, waving shovels, clubs and pickaxes.

Mildred and Ryan drew their blasters but held fire. They had no cover. Shooting the diggers would only bring a withering response from the blasters along the berm.

For a second it looked as if they were going to be overrun and surrounded, perhaps summarily clubbed down by the mob. Then blasterfire chattered, freezing the crowd's advance. The ville folk craned their necks to locate the source of the shooting.

J.B. stepped out of the berm gate with a smoking AKS aimed in the air. Mildred figured he had picked up the assault rifle from a dead attacker or defender. Jak, Krysty and Doc followed him with their blasters out and ready. They quickly formed ranks around Mildred, Ryan and Junior. Shoving, kicking, threatening, they made the diggers retreat toward the gate.

The companions regarded the trussed-up cannie with surprise and displeasure.

"What in dark night are you doing, Ryan?" J.B. asked.

"Why he not dead?" Jak demanded, aiming his .357 revolver at Junior's heart.

The mob cheered his question.

"Hang him high," someone in the rear of the throng shouted.

"Skin him first," a haggard, blood-stained woman countered.

Junior grinned nervously from around Ryan's back.

"Let us have him," the woman said. "Let us punish him, and no harm will come to any of you."

"Can't do that," Ryan told her. "We need him alive for the time being. He's ours. We're not going to give him up."

"Then you're going to die, too, cannie lover."

"Mebbe they've all gone cannie?" someone cried. "Chill 'em all!"

The crowd picked up the chant. "Chill 'em all! Chill 'em all!"

"How soon they forget," Doc chided, sweeping the twin muzzles of his Le Mat over the crowd of mostly women, children and geriatrics. He shook his head. "This, dear friends, is an abomination."

"We saved your rad-blasted bacon last night!" J.B. hollered at the belligerents. "Wasn't for us there wouldn't be one of you ungrateful bastards left!"

The truth silenced the mob for a moment.

"Too many good folks have died here, already," Ryan told them. "Don't make us add to it."

"We don't want you here no more," an oldie brandishing a pickax informed him.

The ville folk shouted in agreement, spreading out and blocking the gate with their bodies and grave-digging tools.

"Don't matter what you did or didn't do for us last night," said the haggard woman. "We can't trust you today. Take your pet cannie and make tracks out of here. That's all the thanks you're going to get."

One of the children picked up a stone and chucked it at them. Another did the same. Soon the companions were being pelted with showers of rocks, large and small.

"Nukin' hell!" J.B. growled, touching off another clattering air burst, emptying the weapon's 30-round magazine. The stone throwers scattered for cover. J.B. tossed the AKS aside as the companions rapidly backed out of range. There was no pursuit, no long-blaster fire from the berm. The ville folk were content to see them gone.

"We have been cast out, like lepers," Doc said.

"Like what?" J.B. said.

"The accursed, the afflicted, the unclean."

"The misunderstood," Mildred added.

J.B. scowled at what were to him unintelligible pre-dark references. He turned on Ryan, scowl intact. "We want an explanation," he said.

Mildred provided it. In clipped, emotionless terms, she described exactly what had been done to her.

The companions stood stunned as their battlemate read out her own death sentence.

Then J.B. swung his 12-gauge pump to hip height and advanced on the prisoner with murder in his eye.

Mildred blocked his path, pushing the wide barrel aside.

"Don't," she said.

"Couldn't we catch it, too," Krysty blurted, "just from being around him?"

She didn't add, "And around you."

She didn't have to.

The companions were incensed, sickened, grief-stricken, but deep down Mildred knew what they were thinking.

That death walked among them.

Horrible, lingering death.

"If you could catch it that way," Mildred said, "you've already got it, Krysty. We were all in the cave, in the confined space, all breathing the same contaminated air."

"Why haven't you chilled that unspeakable degenerate?" Doc demanded.

"Because there might be a cure, Doc," Ryan replied. "And he's the only one who knows where to find it."

Mildred recounted the story to the companions. She told them about the supposed existence of the freezie Patient Zero, the putative first victim and the first survivor of the oozies. She told them about the supposed ability of La Golondrina's blood to prolong the lives of the terminally afflicted. She didn't have to explain the double downside of cannie longevity and the resulting spread of infection.

Because she owed nothing less than the whole truth to her friends, she also told them about the possibility that the disease and the cannie lifestyle were linked.

"Turn cannie on us?" Jak said in disbelief.

"Not if the medicine really exists," Ryan countered at once.

"If it does exist and we can find it before the infection takes hold of me," Mildred added, "I may have a chance. It's my only chance."

"Where is this Patient Zero?" Krysty said.

"Louisiana," Ryan answered. "In what our prisoner, there, calls the cannie homeland."

After a moment of shocked silence, the albino teen snarled a blistering curse. "Know people there," he growled, advancing on Junior. "Left friends. Cannies take over?"

The companions had recently left Jak's birthplace after taking down an evil baron. How quickly things changed.

"How the fuck do I know?" Junior replied in defiance.

"Only way to find out for sure is to go back, Jak," Mildred said, putting her hand on his slim shoulder.

"Correct me if I'm wrong, my dear Ryan," Doc said as he leaned heavily on his walking stick, "but are you and Mildred proposing that to save her we six enter the belly of this slouching beast, that we steal its greatest treasure, this life-giving serum, and to forestall any repetition of the threat we currently face, that we hunt down and chill the cannibals' queen?"

"Nothing less," the one-eyed man said. "Any objections?"

Though on its face the task seemed impossible there was none.

One by one, the companions turned toward Mildred and nodded their assent. They had long ago thrown their lots together, to do or die. They valued the lives of their comrades more than their own. A pact signed in sweat and blood. A pact of selflessness and sacrifice that served the survival of all.

"Looks like we're gonna have to backtrack to the Hells Canyon redoubt for another mat-trans jump," J.B. said.

The return trip was a four-day hike. But it was more than just a hard, uphill trek. Their descent along predark Highway 84 had been perilous, to say the least. Cannie snipers had taken potshots at them from the ridgetops all during the day; after dark, the flesheaters had come out in force. In beating back the cannies their third night on the road, the companions had nearly run out of ammo. If they hadn't reached the ville berm by nightfall on the fourth day, they never would have survived.

"We've got no choice," Ryan said. "Walking to Louisiana isn't an option. Check your ammo and food."

"We're full up in that department," J.B. told him. He, Krysty, Doc and Jak had spent their morning searching the ville's rutted lanes, scavenging appropriate caliber centerfire cartridges from the dead, norm and cannie; and gathering unspoiled eats. Their pockets and packs bulged with the booty.

"Then let's get a move on," Cawdor said. "We've already lost most of the day. We've got to find cover we can defend before sundown."

With Jak in the lead, the companions and their bound captive turned their backs on the ruined ville and headed north, along the newly christened stretch of the Red Road, the Highway of Blood.

Chapter Five

A rifle slug whined a foot over Ryan's head, slamming with explosive force into the underside of an uptilted slab of road bed. The one-eyed man instinctively averted his face as he ran on; flying shards of concrete stung the back of his head and smacked his shoulder.

Then came the gun crack.

From the time delay, the cannie shooters were five hundred or more yards away. They were firing from well-concealed, hardsite positions on the slopes above the highway. The snipers had the kill zone zeroed in, but because of the distances involved they couldn't predict exactly where their targets were going to be when the bullets landed downrange.

The companions were doing their best to complicate the problem. They zigged and zagged along the rutted wag tracks on the shoulder of the ruined highway. Their advantage was in speed and in erratic movement, in being someplace else when the slugs hit. Highway 84, itself, was impassable to wags and an obstacle course for foot traffic. The jumble of fractured concrete plates and eroded asphalt was the result of earthquake, flooding and a lack of maintenance or repair for more than a century. To run the highway proper would have been suicide. The companions couldn't move quickly enough over the tangle of rubble.

Ten feet in front of Ryan and five feet behind Krysty, who was running ahead of him, another heavy-caliber rifle slug plowed into the concrete, sparked and whined off into the trees.

It was like being the turkeys in a turkey shoot.

Ryan and his companions handled the danger the only way they could, by blocking out the possibility that the next incoming round had their name on it and by concentrating on giving the snipers the most difficult targets. Seasoned fighters all, they sorely hated holding fire when under attack. But they knew they had to conserve their ammo and use it only when kills were absolutely assured. The only one with the firepower to reach out and touch their harassers was Ryan. And given the cover of the enemy and the distances involved, even he couldn't be certain of a lethal hit with his scoped Steyr SSG-70 rifle.

The cannies' use of snipers was a switch from the tactics and behavior Ryan and the others had come to expect. Flesheater packs usually chilled up close and personal, this so the chillers could battle over and take their respective shares of the spoils. Snipers who scored a hit from half a mile away would lose out to their brethren hiding much closer to the roadway. It was an unworkable situation unless the cannies were sharing the bounty in a more highly organized way, a way not based on brutal dog-eat-dog dominance. A real army instead of a gaggle of loosely knit bands.

Ahead was a testament to the effectiveness of this new strategy. A string of waylaid wags dotted the highway's shoulder. The convoy was made up of crudely armored minivans, pickups, SUVs and RVs. The burned-out, overturned hulks were pocked with bullet impacts. Strewed along the ground were stripped, charred human skeletons, obviously cooked on the spot. No other convoy had passed this way in a while. The wrecked wags hadn't been shoved out of the ruts to clear the path for traffic.

Cannies were picking apart the trade route, and doing a bang-up job of it.

Their cannie prisoner stumbled along near the end of the file. Doc acted as a rear guard and pacesetter, poking and whacking the flesheater with his sheathed swordstick whenever he started to lag behind. From the determined, head-down way Junior Tibideau ran, Ryan got the impression that he wasn't sure his cannie kin would free him if given the chance. He was helpless, already trussed up, prime for spit-roasting.

Ryan had no doubt that cannies hid among the dense stands of fir trees above the highway. They were keeping well back from danger, letting the long-distance chillers do the work. If one of the bullets struck home, and the companions abandoned the unlucky victim, they would sweep in like cockroaches for the feast. Their bottomless appetites were balanced by a healthy fear of destruction. Darkness increased their courage and magnified their hunger pangs. The degenerate humans had largely become nocturnal hunters; that was when their chosen prey was the most vulnerable. Night blind. Sleepy. Easily approached. When cannies committed to an attack, day or night, they were almost impossible to turn back. Like cougars or jaguars, once switched on, once they had a target selected, nothing less than a bullet in the brain would switch them off.

The highway shooting gallery was the fastest and safest route to the Hells Canyon redoubt. It was the best of the bad choices available to them. Ryan could have led the others on a more direct forest route, short-cutting up and over the mountains, but the chances for a close range ambush there were too great. The trees were too tightly packed. Slopes too steep. Progress too slow. And it was perfect terrain for concealing dead-fall and pit traps. Or antipers mines. Cannies weren't fussy about picking their dinners out of the branches.

Besides, Ryan had mentally mapped this road on the descent; he didn't know anything about the mountains. He had already selected the best defensive sites. There was no hope of reaching the spot where they had spent their last night on the highway and successfully turned back the cannies. They had gotten too late a start to make it all the way there. One of the secondary sites was going to have to do. A dead-end side canyon, mebbe. Mebbe a cave. A place with a single opening they could defend until dawn.

Daylight was already starting to fade around them, the sky edging from azure to brilliant turquoise to lavender.

Ryan sensed movement behind the dark trunks and thick branches of the trees on both sides of the road, but saw no targets. They were being tracked by more and more flesheaters; a gathering storm shadowed them. The intermittent rifle fire was the dinner bell ringing.

Fifty yards ahead, an enormous hump transected the ruined roadway from shoulder to shoulder. It looked as though a gargantuan tree root had torn through the pavement. On the way down they had made a detour around the partially heaved-up, ten-foot-diameter culvert.

Jak was within fifteen feet of the hump when heavy slugs slapped the earth; not one at a time, but in an ungodly hail, sending dust, bits of rock and bullet fragments flying. It was a triangulated crossfire from rifles stationed on the ridgetops on either side of them. These weren't bolt guns; these were semiauto longblasters with 30- or 40-round magazines, all working in unison to frame and seal off a predetermined kill zone.

The albino youth ducked through the roiling dust and skidded down into the wide mouth of the culvert. It was the only hard cover close enough for them to reach. Krysty, J.B. and Mildred disappeared inside after him. Ryan followed, striding into the knee-deep, standing water. Doc and the cannie made it safely, as well, although Junior tripped and slid headfirst into the stagnant slop. Doc grabbed him by the collar and jerked him back up, dripping. The bath might have done Junior some good had the surface not been topped with a dense mat of bright green scum and floating human bones.

The clamor continued for a full minute as the cannie snipers poured fire onto the exposed top of the massive, corrugated steel pipe. It was ineffective in terms of penetration, but the roar of bullet impacts was deafening. They shook loose the crusted dirt from the top of the pipe; it fell on the companions' heads and rained down into the water, making it hard to see and hard to breathe without coughing.

Then the shooting stopped.

Gradually the dust settled and the ringing in their ears faded.

"Everyone okay?" Ryan asked, looking from face to face.

There were nods all around.

"Not going to be so lucky for long," J.B. said. "If they can keep us pinned down in here until sundown, we're dead. Cannies can come at us unopposed from three directions."

Krysty stared into the darkness that led under the highway. "This pipe is mebbe a hundred feet long," she said. "Could be open at the other end, or ruptured someplace between here and there with a hole big enough for cannies to slip through."

"Wouldn't have to be that big," J.B. said. "Just big enough to drop in a few grens, and we'd be their next meal."

"Wonder why didn't they spring this trap on us on the way down?" Mildred said.

"Trap not set," Jak said.

"Mebbe they learned something when we slipped past them on foot the last time," Krysty suggested.

"While it's still light, I've got to do a recce up the pipe," Ryan said. "If there's no holes and if other end is blocked off, we might be able to hold out from here—we've got ourselves a ten-foot-wide shooting lane, if we mass our fire we can control the entrance and keep the bastards off us. If there's another way in, we're going to have to make a break for it."

"Come, too," Jak volunteered.

Ryan trudged ahead, sloshing through the vile water. He advanced with his handblaster drawn in case they already had company in the culvert. The deeper they went, the darker it got. The smell of death and corruption couldn't have gotten worse. Again and again, Ryan nudged aside unseen floating objects with his knees.

After fifty feet, it began to get brighter and brighter, until he could make out a wide shaft of light piercing the gloom, illuminating a charred rib cage that bobbed in the slime.

"Bad luck," Jak said as they looked up at the wide rent in the steel cylinder. The split ran from the top of the pipe halfway down its side. It was easily large enough for a man to slip through.

Ryan holstered his SIG-Sauer and passed Jak his longblaster, then he climbed up into the split and pulled himself out on his belly, crawling into the shadows beneath a shelf of uptilted concrete. After scanning the tree lines above them, he retreated back down the hole.

"No point in going all the way to the end of the pipe," Ryan told Jak as he took back his Steyr. "We can't stay the night here. Go back to the entrance. Draw some fire from the snipers so I can pinpoint their hides."

Without a word, the albino teen turned and splashed off into the darkness.

Ryan crawled back out into the softening light. He squirmed into a comfortable prone position under the angled slab and dug in his elbows. Downrange, a wall of trees loomed in front of him. The snipers could have been hidden anywhere. He opened the rifle bolt and snicked it back an inch, making sure a round was chambered. Then he flipped up both of the scope's lens caps. With the setting sun behind him, he wasn't worried about a reflection off his front lens giving away his position.

Ryan didn't sight through the scope. He needed as wide a field of view as possible to locate the targets. But he did drop the Steyr's safety and snug its butt firmly against his shoulder. While he waited for Jak to make his move, Ryan listened to his own heartbeat and consciously relaxed, breathing deeply to slow it. He smelled the forest. Clean. Green. Thud. Thud. Thud. Thud. Ryan stretched out the pause between heartbeats, getting the rhythm right, finding the null, the shooting space.

From far behind him came a clatter of boots as Jak jumped out of the end of the pipe.

The snipers were waiting for just such a move.

Bullets screamed over Ryan's head, then came the flurry of sharp reports. Multiple, tightly spaced shots made the blasters easier to find against the dark curtain of trees. Ryan caught the faint orange wink of a muzzle-blast as Jak continued to draw sustained fire. The hide was a stand sixty feet up a fir tree. Ryan looked through the scope and rested its crosshairs below the erratic flash, adjusting his aimpoint for the distance and the forty-five-degree uphill shot. Then, with his cheek against the stock and his finger curled lightly around the trigger, he concentrated on his heart-beat.

Thud. Pause.

Thud. Pause.

He steadily tightened down on the trigger, taking up the slack, bringing it to breakpoint.

Thud. Pause.

Thud—

With a thunderclap roar the 7.62 mm slug sailed away.

The Steyr punched Ryan hard in the shoulder. Tensing his muscles, he rode the recoil, swinging the scope back on target. In the field of view, fringed tree limbs shivered as a body fell heavily through them. Then they were still.

The other two long blasters continued to rage. Jak's odds of being hit increased with every passing second.

Cycling the Steyr's action, Ryan quickly located the second target up the highway to his left on a high out-crop that jutted like the bow of a vast black ship from amid the tall trees. A more difficult shot because of the solid cover.

Ryan settled into position, adjusting his aimpoint through the scope. As his finger tightened on the trigger, as he was about to ice the crossfire and open the way for the companions' escape, he heard crunching sounds coming toward him.

Footfalls.

Hard, running footfalls from the other side of the highway.

Swinging the rifle barrel down, he looked over the

scope and saw three figures dashing along the hump, straight for him.

He snapfired and hit the lead cannie in the midsection, blowing him off his feet and flat onto his behind.

As Ryan worked the bolt to eject the spent shell, handblasters blazed and bullets chipped the concrete rubble on either side of him. The cannies were trying to reach and control the hole in the pipe.

Ryan fired again and the 173-grain, M-118 slug blew through the flesheater's chest, taking most of his heart with it. The cannie's momentum sent him crashing, spread-armed onto his face.

The third cannie was undaunted by the deaths of his pals. On the run, he dumped an empty mag. As he slapped home a fresh one, he stumbled on a loose bit of rock. It took only a second for the cannie to regain his balance, but by the time he snicked his blaster's action closed, Ryan had cycled another live round into the Steyr's breech and pushed up to his knees.

Before the cannie could bring his blaster to bear, Ryan shot him in the front of the throat, just under the chin, taking out three inches of his spinal column. Instant chill. The body dropped rag-doll limp, its head connected to torso by glistening threads of muscle.

Concrete exploded ten inches from Ryan's nose, peppering the side of his face. As he ducked, he heard the hollow boom. The sniper up in the rocks was now targeting him, trying to pin him down. At the far end of the pipe, he could see more cannies filtering out of the trees. Swarms of them. They knew where he was, too. Their bullets zinged all around him.

Under concentrated fire, Ryan backed down the hole and hit the water running.

He shouted the bad news to his waiting companions. "They're closing in quick. Light's fading. We've got to break out. It's now or never. Move fast, move low. Jak, you take the point."

J.B. rammed his fedora tight onto his head and pushed his spectacles against the bridge of his nose. "Let's do it," he said.

As Jak lunged for the culvert entrance, the distant crash of steel on steel, of breaking glass, and the screech of bending metal stopped him in his tracks. Then from down the highway they heard the rumble and roar of powerful wag engines.

A second later came the unmistakable, full-auto, rolling thunder of an M-60 machine gun.

"It would appear we have company," Doc said.

Chapter Six

Ryan led the others out of the pipe. They peered over the top of the concrete rubble as the chatter of machine-gun fire and the howl of engines got louder. This while cannie return fire dwindled to nothing.

The wag convoy lumbered uphill toward them. Huge, hulking forms bounced over the ruts, headlights off in the gloaming. The M-60 atop the second wag swept the far side of the roadway, streaming white hot tracers over their heads.

"Keep down," Ryan warned the others. "They might mistake us for cannies."

With nothing to distinguish them from the enemy, rescuers could quickly turn into executioners.

It turned out not to be a problem.

The convoy crews had already assessed the situation and singled out the good guys from the bad.

The lead vehicle was a dually tow truck with a high cab and a wedge-shaped steel snowplow attached to its front bumper. Overlapping steel plates protected the cab and windows. The tow truck pulled past the culvert entrance and stopped, giving the companions cover with its broad flank. Then the driver and passenger cracked the armored doors and opened fire over the hinges at fleeing cannies with night sight-equipped, Russian SKS semiauto longblasters.

From the clatter of the sustained gunfire, their rescuers had deduced what was going on up the road. As a rule, cannies didn't wage all-out war on one another. The wag crews knew what an unfolding ambush sounded like.

A gray-primered Suburban 4x4 rolled up behind the tow truck and parked. The Suburban's chassis was jacked up for two feet of additional ground clearance. The windows, grille, hood and wheel wells were covered by crudely welded sections of steel plate; gaps left between the plates served as view and firing ports. A hole had been cut in the roof amidships, providing a gunner access to an M-60 mounted on a circular track. The 7.62 mm machine gun's arc of fire encompassed an unobstructed 360 degrees.

A vehicle for the serious, postnuke entrepreneur.

The back doors of the SUV popped open and a burly giant of a man jumped out. He shouldered the RPG he carried and took aim at the edge of forest on far side of the road.

With a blistering whoosh the rocket launched and seconds later came the whump of explosion. Trees along the opposite shoulder fireballed. In the hard flash of light Ryan saw cannie silhouettes cartwheeling through the air and the survivors scattering like rats low and fast into the forest.

The tow truck crew continued to peck away at cannie wounded and stragglers. The crews from the other wags joined them, raining fire on the enemy caught out in the open. The convoy was the usual jumble of pre-dark makes and models, but they all had horsepower to spare. Serious muscle was required to move the weight of cargo, armor and personnel over the waste-land.

"Look at the bastards run!" the RPG shooter said with pleasure.

He was a mountain of a man, nearly as tall as Ryan, but a hundred pounds heavier, solid muscle covered with a thick layer of jellylike blubber. Most of his weathered face was hidden by a full brown beard. He wore stained, denim bibfronts and a black leather vest with no shirt underneath. He didn't need one. The layers of fat and the mat of hair on his back, shoulders, arms and chest provided plenty of insulation.

"You the convoy master?" Ryan asked, checking out the man's personal armament. The twin, well-worn, bluesteel .357 Magnum Desert Eagles in black ballistic nylon shoulder holsters looked like peashooters tucked under his massive arms. The mountain reeked of joy juice, stale tobacco and gasoline.

"Harlan Sprue's the name," he said. "You look mighty familiar to me. Mr...?"

The one-eyed man hesitated a moment. "Ryan Cawdor."

"Not the same Cawdor what used to run with Trader?"

"Same."

"I locked horns with you and your old crew once, back east," he said. "We had ourselves a little disagree-ment over ownership of some predark knickknacks. You probably don't recognize me now. I was quite a few pounds lighter back then."

"I remember you, Sprue," Ryan said. "You weren't any lighter in those days and as I recall, you lost the argument."

"Memory is a funny thing. I recollect just the opposite." Sprue looked over the other companions. When he got to J.B., he stopped and grinned broadly. "Four-eyes was with you then, too," he said. "One mean, sawed-off little bastard."

"You got that right, fat man," J.B. said, shifting the weight of his pump gun on its shoulder sling. "Only I got even less patience nowadays."

When Sprue took in Junior Tibideau, his hairy smile twisted into a scowl. "You caught yourselves a cannie?" he said incredulously. "Looks like a sick un, too. Are you out of your rad-blasted minds? That's like taking a mutie rattler into bed. For a thank you, he'll bite you in your ass first chance he gets."

"He isn't going to bite anybody," Ryan said.

Then a single sniper round skipped off the Suburban's hood and whined into the trees.

Which drew a volley of answering fire from the wag crews.

When the shooting stopped, Sprue said, "We've got to move a ways up the road before the bastards regroup. You can pile in the 6x6 at the end of the line. All of you but that cannie. My crews won't share a wag with a goddamned, oozie-drippin' flesheater. They'll blow him out of his socks soon as look at him. If you want him to keep on breathing, you'd better tie him to the back bumper and let him hoof it."

To lead a wag convoy through the hellscape, to deal with Nature run amok at every turn, to face coldheart robbers and mutie attacks, a person had to be one hard-headed, pedal-to-the-metal son of a bitch, the kind of leader who never buckled, never bent, who kept on pushing until he or she got where he or she wanted to go.

For Ryan, looking at Harlan Sprue was like seeing himself in a distorted, carny show mirror.

There was only one way to argue with that kind of man, and that was with a well-aimed bullet.

This wasn't the time or place for that kind of an argument.

The companions trotted down to the idling 6x6. J.B., Jak, Krysty and Doc scrambled up onto the armor-sided cargo bed. The Armorer threw Mildred a coil of rope he found inside, and she slipped it around Junior's waist, and, leaving about fifteen feet of slack, tied him to the wag's back bumper.

"You could take this tree limb off my back, Mildred," the cannie said. "Make it easier for me to keep up."

"Yeah, I could, but I won't. Making your life easier isn't way up there on my to-do list."

"How far are we going?"

"We'll both know when we get there."

Doc leaned over the bumper. "Best step lively, cannie," was his sage advice.

As the wags at the head of the file started moving, Ryan climbed up on the 6x6 cab's step. He spoke through the louvres melted through the side window's steel plate. "Take it easy," he warned the driver, "you're towing a prisoner on foot."

"Yeah, I'll be sure and do that," a hoarse-voiced

woman replied. Then she gunned the engine and popped the clutch.

The big wag lurched ahead. Ryan had to hustle to swing up beside Mildred and the others.

No way could the cannie keep up. He fell after a dozen steps and was dragged across the dirt on his belly. Lucky for Junior Tibideau, progress was stop and go as the heavily loaded wags in front maneuvered around the route's deepest ruts. Before Mildred could hop down to help him, before the wag could roll on, Junior jumped back to his feet, grinning fiendishly.

"Piece of crap," was Mildred's terse assessment.

To Ryan, she still seemed normal. On top of her game even. He wanted to make sure.

"You all right?" he asked her.

"No problems as far that I can tell. Got my fingers crossed."

So had Ryan.

Behind him, a propane lantern swinging from a roof strut cast a wildly shifting light over the interior. On either side of the truck bed were battened-down fifty-five-gallon drums of gasoline and joy juice leaking fumes, and smaller drums marked "Drinking Water." Between the barrels were stacks of car batteries, long wooden crates of ammo and unmarked boxes of other trade goods. The enclosed space—windowless except for rifle firing ports—smelled like a bear pit. Wag crews had been camping out in back of the truck for months, perhaps years. Five pairs of eyes stared back at Ryan with suspicion and disdain. The other three crewmembers were so disinterested in the newcomers that they had already curled up and gone back to sleep on their rag pile beds among the crates.

The howl of the 6x6's engine and the groans and shrieks of its springs as it jolted over the track made conversation as well as rest impossible.

For about half an hour, the convoy continued along the shoulder of Highway 84, stop and go. Occasionally a rifle round or two would spang into the truck's side armor, but there was no concerted attack, no enemy regrouping of any consequence.

When a horn up front honked, the wags slowed to a crawl and circled for the night. Virtually bumper to bumper.

Ryan jumped from the truck bed. The convoy had parked on a flat field of hardpacked earth. The stars were out in force.

Junior Tibideau nowhere in sight, but one end of the rope was still tied to the bumper. Cawdor squatted and peered under the wag.

The cannie cowered on his knees behind the rear axle. He knew how much danger he was in. "You gotta protect me, brother," he insisted. "If you let me get chilled, your woman friend is gonna die hard."

Ryan didn't need the reminder.

When he straightened, some of the other wag crews were already closing in on the 6x6 with burning torches in hand. Their faces were hard and scarred by struggle.

The companions jumped from the cargo bed and closed ranks, barring access to the cannie.

"Looks like we got ourselves some entertainment tonight," one of the male drivers said as he peeked under the wag with his torch.

"You don't wanna mess with our fun," his shotgunner advised the companions.

The 6x6 driver put in her two cents. "Let's soak the cannie in gas and light him up," she said. "We can take bets on how many times he makes it around the circle."

"Slice him open and feed him his own guts," was another suggestion.

"Stake him outside the circle," said a skinny crewman in his late teens. "Use him as live bait to draw in his kin. We can nail a bunch of the bastards that way."

Ryan understood the depth of their hatred; he shared every millimeter of it. The crews wanted to exercise their power over this pure evil creature. Not just for vengeance's sake. In a situation of terrible, unknowable threat, there was nothing like a little mindless brutality to take the edge off one's fear.

"You better stand aside quick, One-Eye," the 6x6 driver warned, her hand dropping to her holstered Beretta 92.

"Back off, now!" Sprue shouted, clearing a path for himself by shoving the intervening bodies aside. "Cut this droolie bullshit. That cannie ain't yours to play with. You all got work to do. Set up the defensive perimeter and get dinner a-cooking. Move it! It's gonna be another long night."

The would-be disembowelers drifted away without comment. The fat man didn't have to touch the butts of his Desert Eagles. None of his crew had the guts to try to take him out. Their continued survival depended on his experience and judgment.

A couple of the men set up an iron tripod in the middle of the circle. While one of them built a roaring fire under it, the other began pouring ingredients for supper into a big metal caldron—water, dried beans, root vegetables, wilted tops and all, and unidentifiable chunks of meat and bones. He then dumped handfuls of seasonings into the pot and stirred them in with a long spoon.

Sprue noticed Ryan's interest in the fixings. "Don't worry, it ain't human," he joked.

It took both cooks to swing the fully loaded pot onto the tripod over the flames.

The convoy master set out a couple of shabby folding lawn chairs upwind of the fire. "Come over here, Cawdor," he said. "Have yourself a seat while we wait for dinner to boil. You and me need to parlay."

"Don't worry about the flesheater," J.B. assured Ryan. "We'll hold the fort here."

As Ryan walked over to Sprue, the convoy master picked up a blue plastic antifreeze jug and twisted off the cap.

"Go on, sit," he said. He offered his guest the jug. "Swig?"

Ryan sniffed at the contents and frowned. "About ninety octane, I'd say." He passed the jug back without sampling it.

"How about a nice cee-gar, then?"

Ryan declined, then said, "Your folks look mighty jumpy."

Sprue's crew scurried to complete their assigned tasks. They set out extra weapons and ammo, and manned the perimeter, some crawling to firing positions under the wags.

"They've got good reason for that," Sprue told him. "Over the few last weeks, the situation in these parts has been going downhill fast. Cannies have been hitting us almost every night. Half my crew sleeps during the day so they can fight all night. The other half tries to get some rest at night so they can go all day. We've kept the bastards out so far, but I gotta tell you it's starting to wear us down."

"Where are they coming from?"

"Hard to say for sure," Sprue answered. "But they're following the same trade route we are, between here and Slake City. We've caught them riding around in wags, just like norms—except for the goddamned sides of smoked meat packed in the trunks. These ain't no dumbass muties, for sure. They fight just like us, with blasters. They learn from their mistakes. That's something a stickie can't do. Stickie follows instinct, even if instinct says to jump off a cliff. Cannies use their brains."

The convoy master took a deep swallow from the blue jug, gasped as the alcohol burned its way down his gullet, then shuddered and said, "I want to hear the whole story about your pet flesheater."

The whole story was something Sprue wasn't going to get. Ryan had no intention of mentioning their destination, the Hells Canyon redoubt. The companions kept such things to themselves. It's what gave them a leg up on the competition.

"Have you ever heard of a queen of the cannies?" Ryan asked the bearded fat man. "Down Louisiana way?"

Sprue paused to scratch his chin. His hand disappeared up to the wrist in the tangle of coarse hair.

"Can't say that I have, but it's been a couple years since I run wags there," he admitted. "Louisiana norms are good folk for the most part, but they're shitpoor. Not enough jack thereabouts to make me wanna go back. Don't like the humidity or the gators, neither."

"Incoming!" someone shouted from the perimeter.

Suddenly everyone took up the cry. "Incoming! Incoming!"

Ryan and Sprue vaulted from the lawn chairs as streaks of light arced in from the darkness. Streaks of light that hissed as they fell almost lazily into the convoy's midst.

Crashing to earth, the Molotov cocktails bloomed orange, their explosions sent flaming fuel flying in all directions. It sprayed over wags and a few unlucky crewmembers. Men and women screamed and batted at themselves as they ran and burned. Their comrades immediately caught them and knocked them down. They smothered the flames with blankets and dirt, then dragged the still-smoking, still-screaming victims to cover beneath the wags.

Gunfire roared around the defensive perimeter. Every blaster was cutting loose at once. The din was tremendous; the chill zone a complete circle.

But the gasoline bombs kept falling, turning the center of the ring into a lake of fire.

"It's all flat ground out there," Sprue snarled into Ryan's ear as they crouched beside a van. "There's no cover for 150 yards in all directions. The throwers should be chopped down by now."

He was thinking arm toss; he was thinking short range.

He was thinking wrong.

"Catapults," Ryan told him. "The cannies are using catapults."

Chapter Seven

As the Molotovs rained down, Mildred stuck to Junior Tibideau like grim death, her fingers gripping the back of his trouser waistband.

Krysty, Jak, J.B. and Doc had also taken cover under the 6x6. On either side of them convoy crew was firing longblasters through gunports and gaps in the wheel well armor. The clatter in the narrow space was earsplitting.

J.B. crawled up against the steel skirt and had a look for himself. He immediately turned on the nearest of the two riflemen. "What the hell are you shooting at?" he shouted. "You can't see anything out there!"

The prone crewmembers ignored him. He and his pal continued to rattle off frantic, full-auto bursts from their AKs. They had plenty of ammo to burn. Rows of 30-round mags were laid out beside them.

From their panic, Mildred guessed they hadn't encountered a cannie attack like this before. Up until now Convoy Master Sprue's strategy for surviving the night had been to pick a campsite he knew they could defend. The response to attacks had been to hunker down and fight back until dawn. Unless the present situation changed radically, by dawn the circled defenders would all be dead. The only option was to pull up stakes and make a run for it before the fires took their toll. But there was a big problem with that. Running could put them in an even worse position in a hurry. The road ahead could be mined. Or blocked by an impassable obstacle. In the dark, strung out without room to circle, the wags would be easy pickings for the cannies.

"Flares! Put up some bastard flares!" the convoy master bellowed to his crews as he ran the inside of the perimeter.

The rest of the companions squirmed up to the 6x6's steel skirt so they, too, could see downrange. Still holding on to Junior's pants, Mildred peered under the rear bumper. A few seconds later, 100,000-candlepower illuminating stars burst over the battlefield and slowly floated down on their deployed parachutes.

In the ghastly white light, the companions stared out at a flat expanse. A plain of nothing. No big rocks. No trees. Not so much as a blade of needle grass decorated the pale dirt.

The wild blasterfire around them faltered, then ceased.

Even the hair-trigger crew could see there was nothing for them to shoot at.

The illuminating stars hit the ground, one by one, sputtered and began to wink out. At the edge of the flares' dying light, a tiny yellow dot arced silently up into the black sky. To the right and left, two more dots shot skyward. They climbed higher and higher until the companions lost track of them as they passed, whistling, overhead.

Then gasoline bombs burst in the center of the circle.

J.B. came to the same conclusion Ryan had. "There's no sound, no flash when the fuel grens are launched," he told the others. "They're using some kind of mechanical launcher. They've got them dug in below ground, out of the line of fire. There's no way to hit and break the Molotovs with small arms before they're catapulted. They aren't even visible until the throwing arm swings up, and by then it's too late."

"What about RPGs?" Krysty said. "Couldn't they use those?"

"The cannie targets are only visible at the instant of launch," J.B. said. "And then they're just pinpoints of light. Hell of a trick to lob an RPG into a hole in the ground 150 yards away in the dead of night."

A cluster of Molotovs exploded directly above their heads, making the 6x6 shudder, spilling liquid fire down its metal flanks and onto the dirt around it. Intense heat and the stench of burning fuel engulfed the companions.

"The cannibal bombardment appears to be coming at us from all sides," Doc said.

"There's no telling how many launchers they've got out there," Mildred said.

"Cannies knew this was a favorite overnight spot for convoys," J.B. said. "Probably got their butts kicked here a bunch of times before they figured out a way to attack it. Catapults would be easy to hide in excavated positions. Cover them with mats and dirt during the day. Uncover them after dark with the ranges already zeroed in."

J.B. didn't have to point out that gasoline bombs were a highly effective homemade munition, and they had the double advantage of pinning down the targets and lighting up the kill zone for longblasters. A perfect tactical choice under the circumstances.

As if underscoring that conclusion, the 6x6 was again rocked by overlapping explosions and blasts of heat.

"They've locked in on us," Krysty said.

"Biggest wag, biggest target," J.B. said.

Even as he spoke, a different sort of smoke began to filter under the wag. Blacker. Thicker. Chokingly abrasive.

Jak put his palm against the undercarriage, then immediately jerked it away. "Hot!" he said in surprise.

J.B. touched it, too, and had the same reaction. "Wag's on fire!" he exclaimed "Fuel from the Molotovs must have dripped down inside."

The 6x6 absorbed yet another flurry of blistering direct hits.

Mildred envisioned the piles of rags on the cargo bed above their heads, the cargo bed loaded down with leaky fifty-five-gallon drums of highly flammable liquids and stacked ammo crates.

The smoky air under the wag suddenly became almost too hot to inhale.

"Run!" J.B. shouted to the others. "Run, quick! Before the bastard blows!"

As the companions scrambled out, he helped Mildred drag Junior from under the wag. Then they grabbed the cannie by the armpits and half carried him away from the raging heat at their backs.

Ahead, wide puddles of fuel burned out of control. Dead folks lay facedown in them, their clothes melted away, their flesh charring to ash. Smoke and flame spewed from wags all around the ring. Even as the crew resumed shooting, more Molotovs slammed on target.

Mildred sensed the wheels were about to come off.

And in the next second they did. Literally.

The 6x6 exploded with a horrendous boom as hundreds of gallons of gas and booze detonated almost simultaneously. The fuel ignited in a withering fireball, which expanded to fill the interior of the circle. Before the wall of flame swept over them, J.B., Mildred and their bound captive were flattened by the shock wave, and momentarily knocked unconscious.

The blast saved their lives.

Mildred came to on her stomach, her beaded hair still sizzling as the wags parked on either side of the 6x6 began to explode in a chain reaction, like a string of five-hundred-pound firecrackers.

In a flash, a third of the defensive perimeter was wiped away.

And then it began to rain.

First came the heaviest debris: truck wheels, engine blocks, armor plate, axles, wag frames, transmissions, car seats. All crashing down from the dark. Then came the lighter stuff. Pieces of broken metal, glass, plastic. And finally, mixed in with the dust and smoke, a mist of sulfuric acid from the wag load of ruptured car batteries.

"Keep your head down!" Mildred cried to Junior as she shielded her own eyes with her hand. J.B. was wearing a hat and spectacles, so he was well protected.

Others in the fat trader's band weren't so lucky. Blinded by the falling acid, shrieking in pain, they blundered stiff-armed into the flaming pools of gasoline and the spray of bursting bombs. Wild flurries of bullets crisscrossed the circle as Mildred, Junior and J.B. reached the far side. The blasterfire wasn't incoming; it was homegrown. But the cook-offs from the wags' burning ammo stores had exactly the same effect—they chopped down the helpless crewmembers where they stood.

Then the Molotov barrage abruptly stopped.

The flesheaters had either run through their stockpile of fuel bombs, or somewhere in the dark, cannies were popping out of holes in the ground, sprinting for the breach they had made in the perimeter.

There was no time for a look back.

Bullets kicked up the dirt at their feet and whined past their ears as Mildred and J.B. steered Junior along the inside of the ring to the convoy master's Suburban, where the others had gathered to make a stand.

Doc stepped forward, his Le Mat raised in a one-handed dueling stance. As Mildred, Junior and J.B. ducked under his outstretched arm, Doc cut loose, sending forth a yard-long tongue of flame and a billowing cloud of smoke. Over her shoulder, not ten yards away, Mildred saw two cannies go down hard, their heads hamburgered by bits of steel shrap and shards of broken glass.

The perimeter was leaking cannies like a sieve.

They poured through the breach; they jumped from between the wags and crawled out from under them, darting around the lakes of fire.

Jak, his teeth bared, his ruby eyes flashing with cold fury, dealt death with his .357 Magnum revolver. He punched out careful shots, aiming center body, blowing the running enemy off their feet.

Krysty fired her Smith & Wesson .38 from a kneeling position, two-handed. The left sleeve of her shaggy coat was singed and smoking, her prehensile mutie hair drawn up in tight red curls. About ten feet away, Harlan Sprue touched off both Desert Eagles at once, raining .357 Magnum slugs on cannies as they leaped through the curtains of flame.

J.B. swung his M-4000 up to his hip and joined the fray.

Behind Mildred, Ryan dived through the back doors of the Suburban. A second later he appeared in the hole cut in the roof. He swiveled the M-60, shouldered the stock and opened fire on the perimeter gap, trying to turn back the tide.

It was a hopeless task. The cannies were in their midst, the disintegration of the convoy's defenses nearly complete.

Then another wag exploded, sending a section of steel plate hurtling across the circle like a giant scythe. It slammed into the side of an armored Winnebago, rocking it on its shocks.

"You're done here, Sprue!" Ryan yelled down to the convoy master. "You can't hold out. This is going to be over in minutes."

The bearded man furiously reloaded his pistols with

fresh 9-round mags. His life's work was burning to the ground. He resumed firing, alternating left and right hand shots.

Ryan shouted for the others to get into the SUV.

Mildred shoved Junior ahead of her, through the open double doors. Tying him to the bumper wasn't an option this time. She laid him out flat on his belly, then she and J.B. sat on him to keep him pinned. Krysty, Doc and Jak scrambled in after them, pulling the doors shut. No one complained about the presence of the cannie or his necrotic aroma.

Ryan abandoned the M-60 and crawled forward toward the steering wheel. Before he could reach it, the driver's door opened and Harlan Sprue squeezed in. He tossed his smoking, locked-back-empty handblasters onto the front passenger seat.

"I ordered what was left of my crew to bail," he announced as he turned the key in the ignition and gunned the big engine. "It's every son of a bitch for himself."

For most of the hellscape's traders, that's what passed for a code of honor. Everything boiled down to cost versus benefits. There was nothing to be gained by dying here tonight.

The convoy master switched on the SUV's powerful headlights, cut the steering wheel hard over and, spinning all four wheels, accelerated away from the spreading conflagration.

Almost immediately there came a solid thump of impact.

Sprue bellowed in triumph. Then he swerved left, sending the companions sliding into the wag's opposite wall. Another thump. This time followed by a double bump as front and rear left side wheels bounced over an unseen object.

"Nailed 'em!" the convoy master cried.

Cannies were trying to nail him back. Bullets hammered the Suburban's armored hull. Bullet fragments flew through the wag's view slits.

"By the Three Kennedys!" Doc exclaimed as a shard of rifle slug exploded the right shoulder pad of his frock coat, turning it into a fluffball epaulette.

"Some of your guys made it out," Krysty shouted up to the driver. "We've got two wags following us."

When she turned back to the rearview port, the two sets of headlights were gone; the plain behind them pitch-black. "Gaia, they just vanished!" she exclaimed.

"Mebbe they crashed down into the catapult pits," J.B. said.

"Their bad luck," Sprue snarled out of the corner of his mouth. He had no intention of going back to find out for sure, or to try to rescue any of his surviving crew. Gas pedal flattened, he skidded the SUV back down onto the highway's shoulder, then headed up-valley at tremendous speed.

The companions rode in silence, still tingling head to foot from the adrenaline rush.

After a shuddering, jarring, two-mile sprint, Sprue slowed the wag to a stop. He shut off the headlights, opened the console and took out a pair of bulky Soviet-made night-vision goggles.

"Where are we headed?" he said over his hairy shoulder.

The question hung in the air, unanswered.

Chapter Eight

Ryan climbed over the Suburban's console into the front passenger seat. As he did so, he picked up the pair of Desert Eagles and set them on his lap. "Better reload these," he told the driver.

Sprue pulled a couple of full mags from a bibfront pocket and handed them over. "You didn't answer my question, Cawdor," he said. "Where are we headed?"

"Just stay on this road until I tell you to turn off," Ryan said. "Doesn't get any simpler than that." He slapped the mags in the gun butts, released the slides and uncocked the hammers. Then he put the hand-blasters on the floor between his boots.

"I want my blasters back," Sprue told him. "Feel naked without three pounds of steel tickling my pits."

"Not gonna happen," was Ryan's reply.

"What's with that? I'm your prisoner now?"

Krysty reached around the headrest and pressed the muzzle of her .38 Smith & Wesson behind the convoy master's right ear and thumbed back the hammer.

"So that's the way it's gonna be?" Sprue said, his irritation barely under control. "After what we've been through together? Wasn't for this wag of mine you'd all be dead."

"Do you think we're dimmies?" Krysty said. "We know hardly anything about you."

"And what we do know isn't so rad-blasted wonderful," J.B. added. "For example, you just left your crews hung out to dry."

"If you're a good boy and do what you're told," Krysty told the convoy master, "don't worry, you'll get your blasters back."

She didn't explain what would happen to his blasters if he wasn't a good boy. She didn't have to. It was immaterial. Blasters were useless on the last train west.

"You've got the upper hand on me," the fat man conceded. "I'm outgunned and outnumbered. Even though you don't trust me, I've got no choice but to trust you."

"You're right about that," Ryan said.

"I've got nothing up my sleeve," Sprue assured him. "No tricks. No plan to turn the tables on you. How could I? You saw my crews get wiped out. I'm on my own. Just me. I can be a righteous team player. I'm willing to work to earn your respect. I'll do what I'm told. Like it or not, from here on we're all in this together."

That was true, at least for the moment.

"Don't screw up," Ryan warned him.

"Do you mind, Red?" the convoy master said to Krysty. "It's gonna be hard to concentrate on my driving with a cocked handblaster shoved against my head."

She pulled back her pistol.

Sprue turned to Ryan and said, "My eyes are watering and I'm about to hurl. How about getting that goddamned stinking cannie out of here?"

"We can't tie him to the bumper," Mildred said. "You'll drag him to death."

"Then tie him to the fucking roof."

It wasn't such a bad idea. They had a long way to go.

Junior bleated in complaint as J.B., Jak and Ryan roughly hauled him out the SUV's rear doors. They hoisted him up onto the roof, then lashed him, belly-down, behind the roof's gun port.

"Much better," Sprue said as they climbed back in. He pulled on the night-vision goggles, then shut off the SUV's dash lights. The wag's interior was so dark the companions couldn't see their hands in front of their faces.

Above them, Junior moaned pitifully.

"How about some road music?" Sprue said as the Suburban again picked up speed. A second later a tape machine started up.

A primitive, raucous beat blared from the stereo speakers. An electrified guitar, bass and drums created a wall of sound, above which a thin male voice sang about a woman "with legs" who knew how to "use them."

The insistent repetition of this theme puzzled the time-trawled Victorian. "Is the singer attempting to argue that a woman who can walk is preferable to one who can't?" Doc asked over the loud music.

"It has nothing to do with walking," Mildred said.

"It's about the objectification and sexualization of a female body part."

"As in 'Lips so sweet'?" Doc ventured.

"Uh-huh. Or feet. Or toenails."

"A lengthy paean at the altar of toenails would indeed be a challenge for the poet and for his or her audience," Doc countered. "Its lyrical shortcomings aside, I must admit I find the rhythm of this selection somewhat infectious."

Jak agreed wholeheartedly. "Play again…" he said.

The companions and their prisoner rode north, listening to a pirated audio tape of a band whose name had been lost to history, who had gone the way of culture, religion and politics. Vaporized by nukestrikes. Smothered by skydark's frigid shadow. Rendered irrelevant in a world of new peril.

If not entirely forgotten, entirely misunderstood.

ON THE OUTSKIRTS of Islandcity ville, Sprue eased back on his hell-bent-for-leather pace.

"Why are you slowing down?" Ryan asked him.

"Got a ville berm coming up fast. Old highway runs right through it. Should be seeing the lights of the gate about now."

"When's the last time you were this far up the road?" Ryan asked.

"Been almost two weeks."

"We came through here the day before yesterday. Take my word for it, there aren't gonna be any lights on the gate."

"Cannies?"

"What do you think?"

Sprue pushed the night-vision goggles on top of his head, then turned on the SUV's headlights and hit the high beams. "Shit!" he exclaimed as he slammed on the brakes.

Through the view slits, the headlights lit up the facing wall of a high dirt-and-rock berm, about forty feet in front of them. There was no one manning the gate. There was no gate to man. On either side of the rutted track leading into the ville were fifteen-foot-tall wooden poles, from the tops of which hung gruesome scarecrows. The stripped, blackened human skeletons were held together with remnants of their own sinew and tendon. Their arm bones were stretched out and tied to skinny crossbeams, as if they'd been crucified. Knowing cannies, the crucifixions had come postmortem.

"Did you see any evidence the bastards were still lurking around here?" Sprue asked.

"Nothing for them to eat," Ryan said. "No one left alive. Bastards chilled them all—men, women and children."

"Then mebbe we should get out and stretch our legs for a minute," Sprue said.

Stopping for a stretch was something Ryan was about to suggest anyway. The companions needed to talk in private. "Park the wag closer to the opposite gate," he said.

When Sprue had done so and shut off the engine, Ryan took the keys out of the ignition and yanked the night goggles off Sprue's head. He handed the goggles and the Desert Eagles to Krysty.

The companions climbed out of the back of the

wag and Mildred made sure Junior's lashings hadn't worked loose. It smelled real bad inside the berm. Junior-bad times one thousand. From their previous pass through Islandcity they knew what was causing it.

Corpses.

Lots of corpses, left half eaten and unburied. Like wolves, cannies sometimes chilled for sport.

"Stay here with Junior," Ryan ordered Sprue. "Don't move away from the taillights. Krysty's got the night sight. She'll run you down in a hurry. If you try anything, anything at all, this is the sad shithole where you're going to die."

The companions moved away from the SUV, out of earshot. It was decision time.

"Are we going to take Sprue with us?" Krysty said, laying out the question in front of them. "He claims he's been to Louisiana more recently than us. Mebbe he can help us find La Golondrina. If we take him, we don't have to rely one hundred percent on what the cannie tells us. And he'd be an extra gunhand."

"Know Louisiana, too," Jak said. "Not need deadweight. Take wag, leave fat man here."

"We do that and cannies will get him, for sure," Krysty said.

"And your point is?" J.B. countered.

"Be kinder to just shoot him," the redhead replied.

"If Sprue finds out how to use the mat-trans system," Mildred said, "he's going to exploit it to the max. That's guaranteed."

"Just because we take him along doesn't mean we have to give anything up," Ryan. said.

"I trust you are not proposing that we commit mur-

der after we get what we want?" Doc said with dis-
taste.

"No, I'm not," Cawdor assured him. "All we have
to do is blindfold the fat man nice and tight before we
take him into the Hells Canyon redoubt. Make sure
he never even sees the entrance. We keep the blindfold on while we make the jump, hopefully closer to
Louisiana than we already are. If his blindfold comes
off during the jump, he'll wake up in the mat-trans
chamber but he won't know where he is. We blindfold him again before we take him out of the chamber. When he steps out into Louisiana, he'll know we
pulled off something bastard unreal, but he won't
have a clue how we managed it, or how to find out
what it was."

"We're going to have to blindfold Junior, anyway,"
J.B. added. "We sure as hell don't want cannies using
the system."

"Something could easily go afoul with such a
plan," Doc said. "If we lose control of either of them
in transit..."

"We're talking about Mildred's life here," J.B.
countered. "It's a risk we've got to take."

"I am not suggesting that we should not proceed exactly as you say, John Barrymore," Doc said. "I was
merely pointing out a possibility."

"Possibility noted," Ryan said. "We're going to
make triple sure everything goes right. Now let's find
us some blindfolds."

In the glare of the Suburban's headlight beams the
companions rooted barehanded through the ville's
trash heap. Ryan and J.B. found some discarded plas-

ticized grain sacks. The empty bags were big enough to fit over heads and shoulders with room to spare.

When the companions returned to the rear of the Suburban, Mildred climbed up on the roof. Kneeling, she pulled one of the grain bags over the cannie's head and cinched a cord loosely around his neck, so the hood couldn't slip off. Junior's response was to giggle uncontrollably.

"Put your hands behind your back," Ryan told Sprue.

"Aw, come on, now," the fat man said as Krysty took aim at his hairy chest with one of his own Desert Eagles. He didn't fight as Jak bound his wrists together, but his eyes were narrowed in fury.

"Feel better, now?" he asked Ryan.

J.B. flapped open the other bag, then jerked it over Sprue's head from behind.

"This isn't necessary!" the convoy master protested as J.B. tied the bag in place. "I'm on your side!"

"Now I feel better," Ryan told Sprue.

Chapter Nine

Outside the parked Suburban, Mildred and J.B. stood beside the hooded prisoners. They watched as their companions walked off into the night, their backs lit by the glare of the wag's high beams.

The max-volume strains of ZZ Top had muffled Junior's shrill cries during the journey. The tape wasn't playing now.

"Feed me, feed me," the cannie moaned plaintively from under his grain bag. He couldn't stand still. As he shuffled his feet, he bobbed his head up and down. "It hurts so bad. I think I'm dying. Pleeeeease feed me!"

"If you don't shut that piece of shit up, blindfold or not, I'm going to find him and stomp him to death," Sprue threatened.

"Better zip it right quick, Junior," J.B. hissed, "or we're gonna turn him loose."

The cannie's pleas dwindled to soft whimpers, but he continued to bob and dance in place.

They were very close to the canyon's west rim. Mildred couldn't see it, but she could sense it deep in her bowels—a vast, yawning void, blacker than black, a two-mile dead drop through the cool night air. It had taken four uncomfortable hours to make the hundred mile trip up by wag, much better than four uncomfortable days on foot. Without the caravan's other wags to slow them, they had made good time, despite makeshift roads that had steadily deteriorated as they'd climbed closer to the summit ridge.

At the end of the high beams' tunnel of light, Ryan and Krysty bent and began searching the knee-high outcrops while Jak and Doc stood guard with drawn weapons. The redoubt's entry keypad was well concealed. If they hadn't already marked its general location they never could have found it in the dark.

"Got it," Ryan said as he opened the lid on the door lock's keypad.

A few seconds later came a low, mechanical rumbling sound; Mildred could feel the powerful vibration through the soles of her boots. A wide section of bedrock ahead began to rise up, like the peak of a huge tent. The massive, double-vanadium steel doors of the Hells Canyon redoubt were framed by a basalt slab and angled roughly twenty degrees above the horizontal at their far end; their outer surface was camouflaged by a thin veneer of natural rock.

As the doors locked back with a resounding clank, the redoubt's entry lights switched on, blasting up into the sky from the rectangular hole in the ground.

Mildred and J.B. pushed their prisoners toward the geyser of light. As they walked past the front of the wag, Mildred reached through the open driver's window and turned off the headlights. They abandoned the Suburban with the keys in it. They had no more use for it.

The entrance revealed a wide ramp carved out of stone; it was grooved for added vehicle traction. Electric lights studded the high ceiling, casting a harsh glare over featureless walls. The ramp led down.

Mildred made Junior walk ahead of her. To control him she gripped the end of the rope still tied around his waist.

"Mind your feet," J.B. told Sprue as they stepped over the down-angled threshold.

As the companions descended single-file, the scrape of their footfalls echoed off the smooth but unpolished walls and ceiling. Ryan paused at the keypad mounted on the left wall and tapped in the locking sequence.

Inside the ramp, the rumbling of machinery was much louder, the vibration much stronger. The doors overhead made a hollow clank as they slammed shut and the locking bars slipped closed.

The companions continued the descent in silence. Sensors concealed in the walls or floors triggered the banks of overhead lights, which kept winking on ahead of them, and winking out behind. They followed the ramp's gentle bends, breathing stale air heavy with ancient dust.

Rounding a blind turn, they were confronted by a flashing, whirling, red beacon in the ceiling. Then a Klaxon shrieked a deafening warning. From speakers hidden in the walls came a string of brusque commands. The recording was more than a century old and completely unintelligible. The garbled words and the hisses and scratches cycled over and over for a full minute before they stopped.

"Redoubt, eh?" Sprue said from under his hood.

They had never hoped to fool the convoy master about that, but they could keep him guessing as to where it was and what it contained.

"Keep your legs moving, fat man," J.B. told him.

Two hundred feet farther on, the corridor was blocked by staggered, hardened, concrete barriers. No way could they have threaded the Suburban through the narrow gaps in the ramp's dragon's teeth. And the antitank defenses were too heavy to move aside without the aid of a bulldozer.

Beyond the barriers, the ramp was bracketed by deserted guard posts. The hardened, bunker-like positions had firing ports for small arms and shoulder-fired rockets, which was an unusual feature for a redoubt. Beyond the guard posts, the ramp widened and the floor flattened out, turning into an enormous dead-end room. The doors to a huge elevator dominated one wall.

Krysty pressed a button and after a moment something clunked and whirred. The doors rolled apart, revealing a cavernous elevator car that was big enough to hold two 6x6s parked side by side with room to spare.

The companions entered the car with their blindfolded prisoners. Ryan touched the control panel and the doors rolled shut. With a sudden lurch, the elevator started down. The descent was a precipitous, stomach-dropping dead fall.

"What the fuck!" Sprue exclaimed in shock, bracing his back against the wall, spreading his legs to keep his balance.

The smell of burning oil and arcing electrics filled the air.

"Don't worry, Sprue," J.B. said. "We're all in the same boat, just like you said."

Junior didn't react to the sudden drop or its seemingly endless continuation.

Maybe his oozie-infected brain couldn't process the sensory overload, Mildred thought. Or mebbe his hunger had finally and totally shortcircuited his fear.

Their rapid descent covered the equivalent of one hundred floors, roughly fifteen hundred feet. When the car finally jolted to a stop and the doors opened, they crossed another wide dead-end hallway and entered a mirror-image elevator. The distance between the top of the canyon and the redoubt at its bottom was too great for one shaft to span. The trip had to be made in stages. It took several elevators to reach the canyon floor, and there were two more below ground level.

The strategic advantages of the setup were enormous—nukeblast protection, fallout protection, concealment, inaccessibility. The elevator system was vital in case the mat-trans unit failed. An entrance at the canyon bottom would have meant a nine-mile, vertical climb in or out, with no way to move matériel or wags up from that depth. If the amount of rock that had been excavated was staggering, the deepest canyon in the world was the perfect place to spread it. Mildred couldn't hazard a guess at the cost of such a project. Or how it had been hidden from taxpayers. It was clear that vast sums had been diverted without the public's knowledge or consent.

When they finally entered the redoubt proper, the

hallways were no longer dead ends; they spread later-
ally, branching out into mazes of interconnected corridors. The usual hallmarks of looting were absent.
There was no trashing of the fixtures. No litter. No
residue of cook fires. No graffiti. Yet the place was
stripped of the expected cornucopia of predark goodies. Food. Clothing. Weapons. Ammo. Fuel. Scattered
about were broad, low-ceilinged rooms jammed with
cramped, partitioned-off work stations, each equipped
with a desk and computer monitor. The cubicles had
never been occupied. There were no personal items
hanging from the bulletin boards, no unfinished work
left lying on the desktops.

As the companions walked past the redoubt's control center, Mildred glanced in. On the other side of
double glass walls, tall banks of CPUs erratically chit-
tered and occasionally blinked in a dust- and humidity-
free, temperature-controlled environment. The
computers were on, running minimum upkeep pro-
grams for more than a century, waiting patiently for
their full potential to be fulfilled.

Like ville folks, scratching out a minimalist existence, cowering from a hostile world behind man-
made barriers. They had blind faith that sometime,
somehow things would get better, this despite overwhelming evidence that Providence was at best indifferent, at worst malevolent.

The companions stopped their own roaming only
when they had a desire to explore, or needed to recover
from stints of combat or the stresses of mat-trans
travel, but soon enough, the itch to move on took hold
of one and all. It was a fact that no place in the hell-

scape was safe, not long term. Upheaval was constant. New dangers evolved before their very eyes. The spreading cannie plague was a prime example.

But that didn't fully explain their wanderlust.

Using the floor maps mounted to the walls under Plexiglas shields, the companions retraced their steps of two days ago. They entered a much smaller, human-size elevator and continued down. The lower they went, the hotter it got. The redoubt's cooling system was not operational. They were so deep that the air temperature was driven by the planet's core.

"Where are we going?" Sprue said from under his hood.

"To hell, Sprue," J.B. said. "We're almost halfway there."

As the floor indicator lights winked on and off, the numbers dropping rapidly, they heard a horn from below. A constantly cycling bleat.

A warning.

"I don't like the sound of that," Mildred said.

"It wasn't going off when we left," Krysty said.

"Careful, now," Ryan told the others. "Watch yourselves."

The car abruptly stopped on the selected floor, and the companions raised their weapons, ready to engage whatever danger lay ahead.

The enemy was liquid.

When the elevator doors slid apart, a low wave of brownish water rushed in, surging over their boot tops.

"Dark night!" J.B. said, lowering his pump gun.

The hallway in front of them was awash; the water level almost a foot deep. They exited the car and fanned out, sloshing through it. The corridor's fluorescent lights flickered and snapped.

The Snake River ran through Hells Canyon, but that was nearly half a mile above them, so it wasn't the source of the flooding. It was more likely the water had flowed in from underground aquifers.

"The levels below us are probably submerged," Ryan said. "Pumps down there must've failed."

"Mebbe we screwed something up when we arrived," J.B. suggested. "Mebbe the power drain…?" J.B. caught himself before he said too much.

"We'd better hurry," Mildred said. "It looks like the water level is still rising."

Slogging ahead, the companions pushed their blindfolded prisoners. They followed the strobe-lit corridor for fifty yards, then turned through a security gate that connected to the mat-trans area. The low steady hum of nuke engines was very reassuring. Hopefully they still had power for the jump.

In the mat-trans anteroom they found the water hadn't risen above the bulkhead door's foot-high jamb, but it was close.

One by one they climbed inside, slopping brown water onto the raised metallic plates of the chamber floor. Then Ryan pulled the door shut tight after them.

Mildred felt the sudden increase in pressure on her eardrums. The door was both air and watertight.

"Better have a seat, quick-like," Ryan told Sprue.

As Ryan hurried to sit beside Krysty, the convoy master sagged to the floor. A faint mist began to form around the ceiling and the wall and floor plates began to glow. There was a distinct ozone smell in the air.

"What's happening?" Sprue asked in alarm.

No one answered.

Finally, Ryan spoke up. "You're going to be fine. We're in a safe place. We're all going to take a little nap. Been a long night. Need some rest."

The mist thickened into a dense fog that expanded in volume, swirling down from the ceiling in sinuous coils.

Worried that the starving Junior might wake up before the others, somehow get his hood off and try to eat someone, Mildred forced him to lay belly-down and headfirst in a far corner of the chamber. She quickly tied her wrist to his waist so he couldn't move without dragging her along.

Then the floor fell away and oblivion swallowed her whole.

Chapter Ten

"Dear friends, I'd like to propose a toast," Doc said, pushing back from the rough-hewn table, then raising his tankard to the soot-blackened ceiling beams. "To our beloved Mildred, who by God's grace has safely passed this awful trial…"

The other companions rose to their feet. "To Mildred!" they shouted, hoisting brimming pewter mugs.

Mildred basked in the double glow of the gaudy house's roaring fire and the warmth of treasured friendships.

Cured.

Never was there a sweeter word.

"Speech!" J.B. demanded. "Speech!"

Krysty, Jak, Doc and Ryan merrily took up the cry, thunking their tankards on the tabletop in ragged rhythm. A great array of food had been laid out for the victory celebration, so much that a sideboard had been added to hold the considerable overflow. Roasted meats. Game and fruit pies. Mounds of freshly baked loaves and rows of frosted cakes. Small wooden casks of brandy and a barrel of foaming ale.

Mildred got up, her cup and her gratitude running

over, her dark face flushed from the heat, the alcohol and the amazing surfeit of delicacies. "I could never have gotten through this ordeal without your help and support," she said, her voice thick with emotion as she looked from face to beaming face. "As long as I live I'll never forget what you all have done for me. You saved me from the most horrible fate imaginable. Thank you from the bottom of my heart. Thank you, one and all."

Then they drained their tankards dry.

"But how do you really feel?" J.B. asked, grinning as he wiped his chin with the back of his hand.

"I feel wonderful. Still a little hungry, though."

"Go on, then, get to it," Ryan urged her. "There's plenty of seconds for everyone."

Mildred picked up her emptied plate, but when she turned toward the sideboard, she stopped cold. She blinked several times, as if unwilling or unable to believe her own eyes. Then the ceramic dish clattered to the floor and shattered, followed by her knife and fork.

Upon the sideboard, Krysty Wroth was laid out nude. She rested on the six-foot-long platter like a white trout, sliced open from throat to groin, her body cavity cavernously gutted. Her pale limbs and fiery hair were decorated with green and yellow apples and clusters of fat purple grapes. Mildred stared in horror at her own bright reflection in the tipped-back lid of the enormous silver salver. Blood dripped from her mouth, chin and fingers. Blood not her own. Gray pendulums of snot swayed from her nostrils.

She whirled around, looking to the others for help, for an explanation. They were of no help, and the ex-

planation they had to give was not the least bit com-
forting. Ryan, Doc, J.B. and Jak were dead, too. Half
eaten where they sat, red, raw bones showing through
torn layers of muscle.

Infinitely worse, she could still taste them.

And they tasted delicious.

Mildred doubled over at the waist and a torrent of
vomit erupted from her throat.

The cannibalism was a jump dream; the vomit
was real.

Mildred regained consciousness on her knees, her
head spinning as she puked bitter bile on the mat-trans
chamber's floor.

HARLAN SPRUE STOOD over his captors who lay
sprawled over the floor of the small chamber, still
sleeping soundly. The convoy master had awakened
before them. The bonds around his wrists had loosened slightly, just enough for him to wriggle free. He
bent over the leggy redhead and retrieved his match-
ing Desert Eagles from the pockets of her shaggy coat.
After checking that the magazines were full, he slid
them into their snug shoulder holsters.

Looking around, he recalled that before he'd
blacked out Cawdor had told him they were having a
nap. The small room wasn't a sleeping chamber. There
were no beds or cots or even piles of rags to lay on.

His first impulse upon waking and seeing his adversaries helpless had been to chill them all, but he
hadn't done it. As a trader, he understood the value of
crew. He still needed them. Sprue had no such com-
punctions about the cannie. He would have shot the

bastard, but he didn't want to rouse his new friends just yet. He could have quietly throttled Junior with the discarded rope, but the black woman had tied herself to him, and he couldn't do the job without moving and possibly waking her.

Sprue carefully collected all of the companions' blasters. Then he unlocked and opened the chamber door and carried the armload of weapons outside.

The air was still scorchingly hot; it was time to explore.

The convoy master knew roughly where they were in relation to the predark highway. He reckoned the wag had turned northeast, then south, then northeast again. The steepest and slowest part of the journey had been the last couple of hours. It had taken several descents to reach the ground floor of what had to be one of the largest and deepest-sited redoubts ever built. Only one location close by fit the particulars. And that was somewhere near the bottom of Hells Canyon. By his estimate, they were eight or ten miles down from the summit ridge.

Why in radblazes had they brought him here? he thought. To hunker down and escape the cannies? Cawdor and company didn't seem like the hunkering down and escaping kind, and the one-eyed man had briefly mentioned Louisiana and had asked him about a "queen" of the cannies. Never said why he was so interested. Sprue hadn't gotten the story about their cannie prisoner, either. Mebbe they had their own caravan of wags stashed away here, fully stocked with fuel, ammo and food. Mebbe they were planning on taking a little road trip to the South. For what reason, the fat man had no clue.

Sprue could understand Cawdor's mistrusting him, but the whole hood thing seemed excessive unless…he was sitting on a gold mine. The dream of every free-booting trader and scab-assed scrounger in Death-lands.

An untouched redoubt.

He trudged out into the flooded hall, sending wave-lets of brown water rushing ahead of him. The over-head lights flickered wildly, snapping like blaster caps. He sloshed into the open elevator car and pushed a but-ton on the control panel. As the doors closed and the car lurched upward, the water around his feet quickly drained away.

The car doors opened on the next floor. The extra-wide, extra-tall corridor in front of him was bone-dry. All its lights were on, as bright as day. As he stepped out and scanned the hall, he noticed a set of towering metal doors along one wall. Sprue broke into a trot, his heart pounding with excitement. He leaned into the left-hand door, sliding it back on its rollers. As he did so, the banks of fluorescents came on automatically in-side.

When he looked in, his knees nearly gave way.

He saw bumper-to-bumper vehicles, semi-tractors and what he knew to be Army Bradley Fighting Vehi-cles. Dozens upon dozens of them. All brand-spank-ing-new. And behind them covering the entire rear wall were shelves of spare parts stacked to the ceiling.

For Sprue it was a religious moment, that only got more profound.

On the other side of the vast room was largest wag fuel reservoir he had ever seen. It consisted of immense balloon-like bladders that contained hundreds of thousands of gallons.

With an effort, the convoy master tore himself away.

Farther down the hall, he found the redoubt's armory. Inside were long wooden crates of assault rifles still wrapped in Cosmoline. There were hundreds of cases of centerfire ammo, towable cannons and mortars.

The huge storerooms next door were stocked with boxes of packaged rations and drinking water, enough to keep a small ville alive for twenty years.

And the redoubt's nuke power was still operational.

Harlan Sprue, who had just lost everything, was poised to get it back, with interest.

Cannies were the turd in the pudding.

Because of them, moving this vast treasure to another safer site was going to be impossible. Instead, he had to make the redoubt his stronghold, to branch out from it. To do that, he needed trained personnel, recruits to man the Bradleys and shoulder the M-16s. He figured he could draw them from the hard-hit villes along the Highway 84 corridor. The desperate bastards didn't know it yet, but they were an army waiting for a leader. A leader who could give them hope.

For an instant, Harlan Sprue had a dizzying glimpse of his own future. Everywhere that cannie bands threatened norms, he had more willing soldiers. With this gift of predark technology, he and his army would hunt the cannies down and crush them, and in the process unite the hellscape's scattered peoples under his control. He was poised to become the most powerful baron in the history of Deathlands.

To take the first step, to venture out of the redoubt on a recruiting mission, he needed a crew of fighters. He had to convince Cawdor and the others do his bidding. Three Bradleys would be enough to start with. They could gather volunteers and return them to the redoubt for training. The next time he'd send out six, then twelve, and so on. The crews could then work their way down Highway 84, pacifying it mile by mile with hot lead.

A little farther down the corridor, Sprue found the redoubt's fully equipped medical bay. Operating rooms. Recovery rooms. Insolation rooms. In an unlocked storeroom, he discovered quantities of drugs and cases of joy juice. He broke open a paper box and took out little vials that read Morphine. The do-it-yourself units each had their own built-in hypodermic needle.

Sprue pocketed a handful of vials, then picked up a glass bottle of century-old, amber whiskey. He cracked the cap and took a sniff of the contents.

"Oh, Mama," he groaned in delight. "That is sweet…"

The convoy master tipped back the bottle and took a long, thirsty swallow, expecting mellower than mellow.

What he got was not mellow at all.

It was like ground glass mixed with lava, like a blazing flamethrower thrust down his gullet.

The shock to his system was galvanic, every muscle in his body clenched in rejection.

Had he misread the label? Was it mismarked? There was no way to find out. The bottle shattered in his convulsive grip.

Sprue spewed pink foam from his mouth, shedding his throat lining like a second skin. He screamed, high and shrill as the liquid burned through both cheeks, his palate and tongue, and dissolved his teeth.

The convoy master staggered backward, his beard and chest hair smoking as it melted away. The massive swelling of his throat completely blocked his airway. Unable to breathe, he couldn't yell for help.

Help was too far away, anyway.

Sprue's pulse pounded in his temples. His lungs screamed. Clutching at his throat, he dropped to his knees. As hard as he tried, he could not pull in so much as a sip of air. As blackness tunneled in on him, he knew he was about to die.

In this case, jump dream and reality were one.

Chapter Eleven

"Get up!" Ryan ordered the convoy master as he nudged him with a boot tip.

Harlan Sprue didn't respond.

"Is he breathing?" Krysty said. "Ryan, I don't think he's breathing."

The one-eyed man leaned down, grabbed a handful of Sprue's shoulder and shook him, hard. The obese body quivered, loose and rubbery. There was no muscle tension. And no reaction.

"Fat man's chilled," Jak said matter-of-factly as he leaned against the chamber's dark smoky-blue armaglass wall.

For a moment Mildred just stood there. This third jump sleep had left her with an odd, jittery sensation in the pit of her stomach. The eerie feeling lingered, occasionally, inexplicably, coursing outward, making her hands and feet tingle. It wasn't the aftermath of an adrenaline rush. Adrenaline come-downs never lasted this long. It was more like withdrawal from a powerful stimulant drug. Amphetamine. Methamphetamine. Which of course was impossible, since she hadn't taken anything of the sort. She shook off the sense of unease and shouted, "Turn him over! Turn him over quick!"

Ryan and J.B. strained in unison to roll the limp mountain of flab onto his back.

Mildred unknotted the rope looped around the man's neck and removed the grain sack hood. Beneath it, Sprue's face was purple, his bloodshot eyes bulged from their sockets, frozen with terror. His mouth hung open, but his tongue wasn't protruding from it.

"Did he strangle on the cinch cord this time around?" Doc asked.

"Couldn't have," Jak answered. "Tied loose."

Mildred knelt over the fat man, searching for a pulse at his throat under the tangle of brown beard. There was none. Red-flecked foam ringed his violet lips. She pried his jaws open wider, tipping his head so she could see inside. "Swallowed his tongue during the jump," she said as she plunged two fingers deep into his mouth. "He's suffocated himself."

Adroitly, she pulled loose the fleshy obstacle, unplugging his throat. Mildred immediately began artificial respiration and two-handed chest compressions. She worked furiously on the unconscious man, but gave up after five futile minutes.

"He's a goner," J.B. remarked.

"Just like that?" Krysty said.

"Yeah, just like that," J.B. agreed.

The danger of mat-trans, the incalculable physical and psychological shock of dematerialization and rematerialization, was something Mildred and the companions chose not to dwell on. They weren't in the habit of looking gift horses in the mouth. After years of hard experience, they knew the hazards of crossing Deathlands on foot or by wag. In the hellscape there were a million ways to die, most of them neither clean nor quick. That said, jumping from redoubt to redoubt with hardware and software that was over a hundred years old was by no means risk-free. What had happened to Sprue was tangible evidence of that. Every time the companions jumped, it was a fresh roll of the dice. A new set of variables. An act of faith. Would they all make it through the next time? There was no way of knowing. And they had jumped three times trying to end up in Louisiana.

Her face flushed with exertion, Mildred stared helplessly at the still form laid out in front of her. There was no resuscitation gear on hand. No defibrillator. Cutting open his chest for heart massage would have been both pointless and messy. Out of sheer frustration, Mildred balled her fist and delivered a tremendous blow to his sternum.

The convoy master's body jerked from head to foot, his eyes blinked, then he coughed and gasped, filling his collapsed lungs.

"If the fat man's croaked, let me tear off a hunk…" Junior begged from under his hood.

"I ain't dead yet, you evil bastard," Sprue wheezed.

Ryan and J.B. helped the convoy master sit up. After he had regained his breath, Sprue said, "What happened to me? I had this nasty dream. I was all alone and I was choking."

"It wasn't a dream," Ryan told him. "You were choking." He pointed at Mildred. "She saved your hide."

Sprue squinted up at her. "That true?"

"It's true."

The convoy master soberly absorbed this news as he rubbed his bruised chest.

"Put the hood back on him, Jak," Ryan said.

"Why, for nuke's sake?" Sprue asked. "I owe you folks my life. That's not something I'm gonna ever forget. I always repay my debts."

Jak jammed the bag back over his head and retied the noose around his neck.

The companions hoisted the bound prisoners to their feet and ushered them out of the chamber, through the anteroom and control center. They headed single file down the redoubt's pale cream-colored stone corridor.

As soon as Mildred started moving, the odd, jangled sensation returned with a vengeance. And there was suddenly a bad taste in her mouth, too, as if she had been sucking on iron. It was probably nothing, she assured herself. The effect of all the dry heaving she'd done after her rematerialization. She put the back of her hand to her forehead, testing it. It didn't feel hot.

Ryan saw the gesture and was immediately concerned. "Are you okay?" he asked.

Mildred mentally kicked herself. She was being hypervigilant, inspecting her every sensation under a high-power microscope. It wasn't diagnosis in any detached medical or scientific sense. She had no real symptoms to work from. If she kept it up, she was going to drive herself crazy. She didn't want to worry the others unnecessarily. She didn't want to distract them from the difficult task at hand.

"Yeah, I'm fine," she replied.

The companions led their blindfolded captives out of the small redoubt and sealed the vanadium steel door behind them.

SEVENTEEN HUNDRED MILES southeast of Hells Canyon, day had long since dawned. The dome of sky was a solid mass of sulphurous, low-hanging clouds, the heat and humidity lay over everything in a stifling blanket. Moss-draped trees—cypress, pecan, spreading oak and elm—framed either side of the chemrain-eroded, two-lane blacktop. Strangler vines spiraled around thick trunks, climbing toward the hazy sun. Greasy-looking, redheaded buzzards sat perched in the highest branches of the canopy, their wings spread out to soak up the withering heat. Here and there between the stands of trees, Mildred caught the sullen glint of coffee-and-cream-colored standing water. The air hung thick with the stench of decay, both vegetative and animal. The high-pitched drone of insects sawed from all sides.

When the companions were well beyond the redoubt's sec perimeter they unhooded their prisoners.

"Welcome to Louisiana," Ryan said.

Sprue was rocked back on his heels. "Not possible," he said, shaking his head. "Couldn't be…"

But his eyes, nose, ears and skin told him it was.

"I don't know what you did, or how you did it," he said to Ryan, "but this is amazing."

"Let's get a move on," the one-eyed man said, "we're exposed here."

They were back in Jak's old stomping grounds

again, not far from Interstate 10, which had once connected the southern United States from coast to coast. For much of its length, the predark highway was just a ghostly shadow across the landscape, a ribbon-like imprint only visible from elevation. Unusable for its original intended purpose, it had vanished entirely in some areas.

As they moved through the steamy air, they dripped with sweat.

Half a mile farther on, the pancake-flat roadway was gapped by a wide, brown river. Pink azaleas dotted the muddy banks.

"How deep do you think?" J.B. asked Ryan as he cleaned his spectacles on a scrap of cotton cloth.

"Too deep to wade," Ryan replied.

Then Jak waved at them from downriver.

When they joined him, he showed them a pair of crude dugout canoes tucked under the brush along the bank.

"Figures the locals would have a way to cross it," J.B. said.

"We can't all fit in those canoes," Mildred said. "It's going to take us two trips."

"Three can go in each boat," Ryan said. "Krysty and Doc take Junior, and J.B. and Mildred take Sprue. After you reach the far side, J.B. can paddle back to get me and Jak."

The companions put their prisoners amidships and set off across the sluggishly flowing river. Mildred paddled in the bow of the second canoe. Even on the water, the air was oppressively still.

"Hellfire!" J.B. said from the stern. "Over there…"

Mildred looked where he was pointing his paddle. Upriver, the shallows erupted. Amid splashes and swirls, a pair of gators launched themselves from the shoreline. Big ones, about fifteen feet long. They glided downstream with the current, then swung into the wake twenty-five feet behind Mildred's canoe, lazily following with slow, sinuous sweeps of their tails. They weren't hungry. Just curious.

The alligators lost interest when the companions reached the opposite bank and beached the canoes. While J.B. turned back to pick up the others, Mildred, Doc and Krysty stood lookout and guarded the prisoners seated on the muddy shore.

"You don't look so good, Sweet Cheeks," Junior told Mildred. He was damned pleased with the idea and didn't try to hide it. "It's coming on you, isn't it? You're getting the itch."

"What it is, is damned hot," she said. "And there's too damned many bugs." Mildred smacked a mosquito the size of a quarter, leaving a splatter of red on her sweat-beaded brown forearm.

Junior licked his lips with a gray-coated tongue. "Yeah, sure," he said, unable to take his eyes off the blood smear. "Oozies aren't burrowing into your brain. It's just the humidity."

Mildred wiped her arm on the back of her BDU pants. "Screw you," she said.

When J.B. returned from the other side of the river with Ryan and Jak, they set off again along the predark road bed. Brown water stretched off in all directions, dotted here and there by stubborn, rotting remnants of drowned jungle. Ahead, on the horizon, was what looked like an earthen berm, only it was string-straight and ran for miles.

"Levee." Jak said. "Highway on other side." Although the companions had visited the albino teen's birthplace several weeks earlier, Jak had no desire to revisit West Lowellton. There was nothing left there for him, no loved ones or close friends. Just bad memories.

The companions moved through swampy, knee-deep water, from tree clump to tree clump. They kept their eyes open, watching for snakes among the looping roots and hostile movement along the upraised strip of land. When they reached the levee, they climbed it, fighting their way through a snarl of underbrush.

From the top of the dike, they surveyed the ruined highway. To the east, it was clear for perhaps 150 yards before doglegging to the left. Fifty yards to the west, a concrete overpass had collapsed across the road. The impact had reduced it to a jumble of massive blocks sprouting twisted, rusting spikes of rebar. The blistered metal sign that had once decorated the overpass lay propped up against one of the larger chunks.

White letters on green: Interstate 10.

"Which way to La Golondrina, cannie?" Ryan asked.

"Not gonna say," Junior told him defiantly. "Not until you feed me."

"Don't tell us and you'll starve, I guarantee it."

The cannie considered that promise for about half a minute. He had good reason to believe Ryan wasn't pulling his leg. "We go west aways on this road," he said, "then head south, down to the Gulf of Mex."

Junior was no dimmie. He kept the rest of what he knew to himself. It was the only reason he was still alive.

The companions skidded down onto the roadbed, then trudged toward the fallen overpass. They weren't going have to climb over it; wag convoys had already cleared a wide gap in the dropped slabs.

"Dead 'un over there," Junior said as they neared the break in the rubble barrier.

A body floated facedown in a water-filled ditch at the edge of the disintegrating tarmac. Above it, fat black flies buzzed in an ever-shifting cloud. The red plaid shirt and dark pants were stretched to the splitting point by the gas-bloated flesh beneath.

"A whopper," J.B. said, grimacing at the stench.

With a low moan, Junior broke free from Mildred's grasp and lunged for the ditch. Ryan caught him by the arm before he got there and dragged him back, kicking.

"By the Three Kennedys!" Doc exclaimed. "Look there!"

Doc pointed his ebony sword stick at the road behind them. The companions turned as one. A two-ton flatbed wag rounded the near bend and hurtled toward them along the shoulder of the highway. The cab and the wag bed were crammed to overflowing with dark figures.

Human figures.

But given the circumstances that cannies were flocking to La Golondrina, probably not norm.

Junior confirmed this when he started to cry out for help. Before he could make a sound, Jak stepped up and punched him straight in the face, dropping him hard on his behind.

"Cut Sprue's hands free," Ryan told J.B. "Give him back his blasters, Krysty."

Chapter Twelve

The flatbed wag sent up a swirling cloud of dust as it roared along the ruined highway shoulder. Krysty, Doc, Mildred and Sprue scattered for cover among the jumble of fractured concrete blocks, taking up firing positions on either side of the breach.

Jak grabbed hold of the dazed Junior and dragged him by the collar through the gap to the far side of the barrier. He quickly tossed the sack over the cannie's head and cinched it closed. Then, pinning the cannie facedown with a knee, he tied his ankles together so he couldn't wander off.

As the wag closed on the fallen overpass, Ryan jumped up on a slab of concrete and started waving his arms for it to stop. His hands were empty. His longblaster was slung, his SIG-Sauer tucked in its holster.

The one-eyed man smiled as he waved. He was just another cannie brother, looking for a free ride.

Squeaking and groaning as it bounced over the ruts, the oncoming flatbed didn't slow down. The dented wag had once been light blue, now it was mostly rust-colored. Its headlights were held on with overlapping strips of silver duct tape. Its front bumper and grille were missing; the buckled hood was held shut with loops of baling wire.

The driver saw Ryan waving and honked his horn.

Through the cracked, dirty windshield, Ryan counted six bodies crammed into the cab. The cannies were sitting on one another's laps. One of them half hung out the open passenger side window. In the wag-bed were at least twenty more cannies. A bunch stood clustered behind the cab, looking over the roof at him. They all had blasters, but they weren't taking aim.

Not yet, at least.

The driver slammed on the wag's brakes. Dust thrown up by the locked rear wheels rained on the bed's occupants. The wag came to a stop below and to the left of where Ryan stood.

"We're full up," the driver said as he leaned out the window. He was grizzled, weepy-eyed, with snaggly yellow teeth. "Can't squeeze in another body."

"Then let's make some room," Ryan told him.

J.B. popped up over the top of a concrete slab right beside the wag. He cut loose with his 12-gauge as he broadjumped the distance between slab and wag hood. His first blast spiderwebbed the windshield in front of the driver. A fraction of a second later, his bootsoles landed on the wag's hood. He ejected the spent brass and fired, angled down this time. The spread of the second blast overlapped the first, sawing a ragged hole in the safety glass above the steering wheel. Blood and skull fragments splattered the inside of the windshield. Standing with his feet spread and short legs braced, J.B. pinned the trigger and pumped the slide. Every time the slide locked closed, the firing pin snapped and the 12-gauge bucked and boomed in his grip. Overlaid patterns of double-aught buckshot blew out the windshield from right to left. They also blew out the cab's rear window. The cannies inside died where they sat, heads exploding, torsos ripped by dozens of .31-caliber lead balls.

Before the stunned cannies in the back of the wag could bring weapons to bear, Krysty, Doc, Mildred and Sprue opened fire with their handblasters. The wag's passengers had no cover and no place to run. The companions poured bullets into the packed mass of cannies. As bodies toppled, some where they stood, some falling from the bed and crashing limply to the ground, the survivors jumped down to the road and took off in a full sprint back the way they had come.

Mildred, Krysty and Doc quickly ran out of ammo and had to stop to reload; Sprue continued to blast away with his Desert Eagles, his bullets kicking up puffs of dust all around the fleeing cannies.

Jak rushed through the gap and brought up his Colt Python in a two-handed grip. He squeezed off a single, carefully aimed shot. The magnum slug hit one of the running targets at fifty yards, taking the cannie down in midstride, driving him into the dirt. Jak's next two shots went wide.

"Too far for handblaster," he said over his shoulder.

Ryan had already figured that out. Scrambling higher on the rubble pile, he shouldered his scoped longblaster. One by one, he nailed the madly dashing cannies, punching out seventy-five- to one-hundred-yard, center-torso chill shots. It finally dawned on the last pair of survivors that the road wasn't safe. As

Ryan cycled the Steyr's bolt action, they darted over the levee. Crashing through the brush, they plunged headfirst into the brown water.

Maybe they thought they could dive under the surface and make the sharpshooter miss, but the water only came up to their knees.

When they dived in, their backs still showed.

Ryan fired twice more, 7.62 mm slugs slapping into wet fabric and warm flesh. The cannies thrashed their arms and legs, trying to swim or to stand or to breathe, then they stopped moving. Both floated facedown in spreading films of red.

Transfer of the flatbed's ownership took less than three minutes, start to finish.

Doc and J.B. pulled open the wag cab's doors, dragged the bodies out of the cab and dumped them unceremoniously on the ground. They stripped the coats from two of the chills and used them to sweep out the broken glass and wipe away the gore.

Mildred, Krysty and Jak used their bootsoles to propel the bodies off the rear of the wag bed. That done, Jak went back to retrieve Junior. He untied the cannie's ankles, jerked him to his feet and shoved him forward.

"Hitch him to one of the eyebolts," Krysty said as Sprue and Jak shoved Junior onto the bed, then climbed up after him.

Ryan slipped in behind the idling wag's steering wheel and shut the driver's door. "Take that blindfold off," he told them through the missing rear window. "Junior needs to see so he can tell us where to make the turn."

Sprue pulled off the grain sack hood and pointed at the tangle of corpses laying around the wag. "Who were they?" he asked the cannie.

"Pilgrims," Junior replied. "On their way to La Golondrina to get the cure."

"How do you know that?"

"They were all last gaspers. Otherwise they would've put up a better fight."

"Hard to put up worse," Krysty said.

"Piss poor," Jak agreed. Then he spit.

Mildred and Krysty jumped down from the bed and joined Ryan on the cab's bench seat.

"It's gonna be mighty breezy without a windshield," the redhead said.

"Mebbe it'll blow out some of the stink," Ryan said, screeching the tranny as he hunted around for first gear with the floor shifter. It turned out to be a compound low. The wag crept through the gap in the overpass with its engine howling blue blazes. Ryan shifted after ten yards, again grinding the tranny. Second gear got them going a bit faster, then Ryan popped it into third. The wag's steering was sloppy, its front suspension shot. There was no speedometer, just a round hole in the dash where it had been ripped out. The fuel or oil pressure gauges were missing, too. None of that mattered to Ryan. He planned to drive until the wag ran out of gas or oil, then they would dump it and continue on foot.

Sprue leaned down and spoke through the broken rear window. "Big wags still using this road," he said. "Can tell by all the fresh ruts."

"You mean, wags like this?" Mildred said.

"No, I mean semis and 6x6s. In convoys."

"What traders would be dumb enough to try to do business in cannie country?" Mildred said.

"Not norms, that's for sure," Ryan said.

"Cannies are organizing their own transport?" Krysty asked.

"Got to be."

"Doin' on-the-fly road maintenance, too," Sprue said. "Filling in the deep, axle-busting holes with rock as they go. Digging ditch drains to bleed off standing water."

"Gaia, what are they up to?"

No one had an answer to that. If Junior knew why, he kept mum, despite Sprue's well-placed kicks.

Ryan drove west along Interstate 10, stopping the wag in front of a Holiday Inn. The single-story, white, American-Colonial-style building had been set on fire at some point, but hadn't completely burned. It had lost its roof. The hotel swimming pool, once overgrown with bougainvillea and azalea creepers, had been cleared of vegetation. Now human bones, bleached white by the sun, lined the long rectangle.

"Bones could be from the neutron strike," Krysty suggested.

"There aren't any skulls," Mildred remarked. "I see ribs and long bones, but no skulls."

There were no live folks in sight, either.

But there were animals.

A quartet of scrawny, timid pigs ducked into one of the roofless, doorless rooms. Chickens pecked for bugs along the edge of the bougainvillea. A ram sheep stood watching them from the collapsed portico.

"You bastards never eat livestock?" Sprue asked the cannie. "Not even in a pinch?"

"They give us the triple squirts," Junior said. "Sometimes we chill 'em for fun…"

Ryan drove on, through the wasted landscape. On a low hill, surrounded by water, was a cemetery. All the above-ground crypts had been broken open, the bodies taken. Cannies built nothing, Ryan thought. They grew nothing. They were exclusively human predators. Sooner or later there would be nothing left for them to eat. They would have to move on or truck in their food. Ryan couldn't guess where the supply chain was coming from, but he had no doubt what it was carrying.

"Look up ahead," Krysty said, pointing through the empty windshield at the edge of the road.

A line of shabbily dressed, but well-armed men and women waved and yelled from the right-hand shoulder. There were no children among them. There were never any children. Cannies ate children first, even their own.

"Hitchhikers," Mildred said. "They're looking for a ride to La Golondrina."

"Let's give them a ride to hell, instead," Ryan said.

As he approached the hitchhiking cannies, Ryan reduced speed to minimize the wag's bouncing. Instead of mowing them down, Sprue-fashion, and maybe missing one or two, he let his passengers do the job. The companions opened fire all at once, shooting through the empty windshield frame, the passenger window and from the bed.

Their withering fusillade chopped down the cannies

where they stood. Gutshot. Head shot. Heart shot. They were either blown off their feet or dropped like ragdolls.

Ryan continued on without stopping.

There were ten fewer flesheaters to worry about.

JUNIOR SIGNALLED for Ryan to make the turn before they reached the next town. The narrow cutoff road headed south and doubled-back east. A century or so ago it had been a tidy, two-lane blacktop. Now it was more of a patchwork affair. The potholes and wash-outs in the road bed had been repaired with gravel and rock and sheets of metal. The large, upheaved plates of tarmac had been broken into wide bands of rubble to level out the pavement and to make the road passable.

A hot and dusty ride.

It was early afternoon, the sun still hadn't come out, but the air temperature was well over 100 degrees. Even with the steady breeze through the missing wind-shield, it was sweltering. Ryan, Krysty and Mildred sweated into the bench seat. Perspiration dripped from their chins and rolled down their arms and legs. At Mildred's prompting, they sipped from a water bottle and swallowed a few salt tablets.

Doc, Jak, Dix, Junior and Sprue sat on the wag bed, heads lowered, breathing shallowly.

With the ten-foot-tall walls of briar, mangrove and brambles bordering the sides of the road, it was like driving in a green ditch. There was no way to tell how far the scrub land stretched to the east and west, or whether it was broken by swamp or drowned in sink holes. The road ahead was flat and straight, all the way to the next turn, which was about a mile and a half away.

As Ryan motored along, another wag popped into view around the distant bend and came barreling toward them.

"Swamp buggy," J.B. said through the rear window.

The wag had about four feet of ground clearance, thanks to its huge knobby tires. The roof over the passenger compartment had been cut away, and there were lots of folks packed inside.

The one-eyed man spoke over his shoulder. "Get Junior up, quick," he said. When the cannie's face appeared in his rearview mirror, he demanded, "Who the fuck are they?"

Junior smiled. "Direction they're coming, looks like cured brothers and sisters returning from their pilgrimage."

The distance between the converging wags narrowed rapidly.

"We gonna chill them?" J.B. asked Ryan.

"Have to stop to do that," the one-eyed man replied. "But if we stop, we risk having more cannies roll up on us while we're wiping them out. I think we'd best take another tack."

Ryan honked the horn repeatedly and waved out the side window. "Wave and smile," he told the others. "Just wave and smile."

They all did as he asked.

The Chevy Blazer full of cured flesheaters waved back as they zoomed by. The swamp buggy didn't slow down. It just kept on going.

By that time, the flatbed was almost on top of the

dogleg left. As Ryan braked for the turn, another much bigger wag appeared around the bend, traveling at high speed. He didn't have time to honk a greeting. The wind of its passing nearly whipped the flatbed off the road. Then the companions' wag was into the turn, and the monster wag was out of sight.

"Damnation!" Doc exclaimed, rubbing the grit out of his eyes. "What in God's name was that?"

"Ventilated trailer, for hauling cattle," Sprue said. "Pulled by a honking big tractor. It was running empty. Already dumped its load."

"They're sure as shit not hauling cattle," J.B. said.

"You got that right, Four Eyes," Junior said with glee. "It's long pig for the big luau."

The wag engine suddenly lost power. Ryan tapped the gas pedal as they slowed sickeningly. The wag accelerated with a lurch, but immediately lost power again. It coasted a few yards while Ryan pumped the pedal hard. Once more it lurched to life but much more feebly this time, then the engine stopped. The wag glided along in silence.

"Shit!" Ryan said. "That's it. No more gas." He steered the wag onto the narrow shoulder.

"Guess we've got to walk from here," he told the others as he braked. "Let's get this thing off the road."

Ryan left the tranny in neutral and the emergency brake off. Jak untied Junior from the eyebolt and shoved him off the bed. Working together, the seven noncannies pushed the wag off the shoulder, nose-first into the bordering brush. There was water in there. Or quicksand. The front end of the wag sank down over the windshield; the rear stuck up in the air.

"How far do we have to go?" J.B. asked Junior.

"Mebbe fifteen or twenty miles," was the vague response.

"Not enough daylight left to cover that much ground," J.B. said.

"We'll go as far as we can, then slip into the boonies," Ryan said. "Nasty spot to pitch camp, but we'll make do."

They left the wag and continued down the patched road. The air was blistering hot and dead still. From the dense undergrowth, ten billion insects sang. Mosquitoes and no-see-ums swarmed around their heads; the companions couldn't move fast enough to escape them, and swatting soon became too much of an effort.

In the space of an hour, three more wags drove by, coming up from the south. The drivers and passengers all waved. The companions waved back, each time growing more confident that they weren't going to be attacked by the occupants of passing wags. After all, this was cannie country these days. No norm in his or her right mind would be out in the open, caught on a long, deserted stretch of road. It didn't hurt that they were dragging Junior behind. Seeing him all trussed up around a tree limb, the cannies driving by probably thought he was their dinner.

Ahead, the road rose in a slight incline as it cut across a low dome of higher ground. The dirt under the tightly packed, waist-high scrub looked dry. Again there was no telling where the dry land ended and the surrounding swamp began. In the distance everything was the same monotonous green.

Jak had point. He moved quickly up the road, searching the bracketing stands of vegetation with his blood-red eyes, his ears pricked up to catch the slightest sound.

But it was the lack of sound that froze him dead in his tracks.

The bugs' mind-numbing hum had stopped as if cut off by a switch. Jak handsignaled a halt.

Something was very wrong.

"Fan out!" Ryan cried.

As they turned, blasterfire roared at them from the road ahead and the road behind.

Chapter Thirteen

Caught in a crossfire, bullets freight-training over their heads, the companions dived for the only cover at hand—the wall of low brush beside the road. Junior tried to duck in after J.B., but could only get his head and shoulders into the scrub. The stick thrust through his arms effectively held him out. Like a cork in a bottle, his body kept Mildred from following the others.

She pulled the pole free, then booted him in ahead of her. The waist-high, stunted trees were so thickly intertwined at their tops that she had to fall on hands and knees and crawl for her life.

Volleys of longblaster slugs swept through the vegetation, clipping off leaves and small branches, raining down dust and fine debris. The attackers from the road above and below had joined ranks to finish the job.

Junior Tibideau couldn't crawl for beans with his hands tied behind his back. His halting progress was slowing Mildred down, big time. Fearing she would lose the companions in the stand of brambles, she reached up with the point of a sheath knife and deftly slit his bonds.

Even though she and the cannie were following the path Ryan and the others had made, the going was tough. The low, springy branches that sprouted from the skinny trunks blocked every foot of ground. They were too flexible to break off. And there was no room to swing a panga. It would've taken a chain saw to clear the way. The companions had to twist over or around the branches to advance.

The farther they got from the road, the more the land sloped downward. The ground got wetter and wetter, too. Mud soaked into their elbows, knees and stomachs. Incoming fire gradually dwindled. After they had squirmed about 100 yards into the bush, the shooting stopped altogether.

"Hold it," Ryan ordered from the head of the file.

Mildred turned to look over her shoulder. Behind her, the tree limbs had closed in like a door slamming shut. She could see less than a yard into the scrub. Weak daylight filtered through the mesh of branches overhead. Under the low-hanging canopy it was like a bake oven.

Breathing hard, Mildred wiped away the cobwebs that clung to her face. There was dirt up her nose and in her mouth. Grit crunched between her back teeth.

In front of her, Junior rolled onto his side, gasping. His shirtfront was black with mud, and so were his pants. He had big holes in the soles of his boots. She could see the balls of his dirty feet.

Why would cannies be hunting the road on foot? Mildred asked herself. It made no sense. All the flesh-eaters in wags had driven past without giving the companions a second look. It was their turf. And they knew they'd already picked it clean.

From up the line Krysty whispered, "What now?"

"We make them come in and get us," Ryan said.

"Think they can track us down?" the redhead said.

"For sure," J.B. answered. "But to do that, they've got to crawl on their bellies, and meet us face-to-face."

"We chill enough of them," Ryan said, "and they'll turn tail."

Then they heard a rustle of movement in the brush ahead of them, not behind where they expected it.

A second later, autofire swept through the branches, bullets whistling over their heads, toward the road.

It was a warning, brief and to the point.

"We're boxed in," J.B. said. "The bastards had a trail cut through the boonies parallel to the highway."

At Ryan's command, the companions squirmed into a fighting circle, bootsoles at the center. J.B. rested his pump gun's barrel on a low limb. The others drew their blasters and braced their elbows for rapid fire.

"Breathe through your noses," Ryan reminded them. "Don't waste ammo. Don't start shooting until you see them."

Nothing moved. Not even a leaf.

The long silence was broken by a raspy male voice from deeper in the brush. "Give up, you murdering bastards. Give up right now, and you'll die quick."

His accent was so thick it took a few seconds for the sense of the words to sink in.

"Know that kind of talk," Jak said. "Man is Cajun. Know that voice, too."

"Fair enough," the speaker drawled after about fifteen more seconds had passed. "You had your chance. Now you cannies gonna die triple hard. Got buckets of big ol' black leeches saved up. Gonna shove 'em up your asses with a long wooden pole. Then we gonna smoke some ganja, play some music, watch while you devil dance yourselves to death."

"Who is he, Jak?" Ryan said.

"Triple mean," the albino teen replied. "Stone ass chiller. Quick with blaster and blade. Not miss."

"Perhaps it is an appropriate time for you to get reacquainted with your old chum," Doc suggested.

"Yeah, do that," Ryan said.

"Cheetah Luis, that you?" Jak called out.

"How you know my name, flesheater?"

."From times I kicked your scab ass," Jak told him. "I'll stand up if not shoot."

"Nobody shoot, hear me. Get on up, cannie. Show yourself."

Jak rose from his knees, then struggled to thrust his head and shoulders through the scrub branches.

"My, oh my, lookee what we got here!" the Cajun exclaimed.

"Hot as hell in bush, Cheetah Luis. Friends stand up now, too."

"Come on ahead, then," the Cajun said. "But keep your blasters tucked away."

Mildred holstered her weapon, then pushed up through the crisscrossing branches. Dirty, tattered men and women stood lined up along the trail, well-worn assault rifles shouldered and aimed. They looked grim and impatient, but their leader seemed delighted.

"Snow Wolf, I been away. You, too?" Cheetah Luis said, displaying his even, yellowed teeth. "Shitstorm going on down here now, man."

From Jak's description and the deep baritone voice, Mildred had expected someone more formidable-looking. More menacing. The Cajun was a skinny black man no taller than five-foot-eight. He wore a little snap brim hat on his head and a moth-eaten jaguar cape tied around his stringy neck. A crudely rolled cigarette dangled unlit from the corner of his mouth. Over his right shoulder, a machete hung on his back in a canvas sheath; in the holster under his left armpit was a hogleg .45-caliber Smith & Wesson wheelgun. In one hand he held battle-scarred M-16 with duct-taped back-to-back mags.

"Been traveling some," Jak told him.

Cheetah Luis took the jumbo handrolled cig from between his lips, looked at its extinguished tip, then relit it with a wooden match.

The pungent aroma wasn't tobacco.

"You still smoking that fuddleshit?" the albino said. "Thought you give it up."

"Helps me focus on the chilling," Cheetah Luis replied, blowing smoke out from between his clenched teeth. Then he turned to his firing squad and waved for them to lower their weapons. "This here's the Snow Wolf, for you who never met him," he said. "You all know what he done. How he fought off Baron Tourment with his little army, how he saved us from that crippled butcher. Heard he and his friends here cleaned up a mess a few weeks back. We owe him, if what I heard was true."

He turned to Jak. "Sweet girl told me you lit out after the chillin'."

"Not have reason stay," Jak stated. "Your people safe?"

"Nah," the Cajun said. "I came back from a huntin' trip. Cannies got most of our people. Chased 'em down and ate 'em up. Wiped out man, woman and child. Left the split bones piled up in their firepits. When they were done eating, they burned down the homes out of pure cussed meanness. We chill the bastards every chance we get. They hunt us, but we hunt them harder, we hunt 'em smarter. It's our daily chore. It's what we do. I wasn't foolin' about them buckets of leeches, neither. That's just the beginning when we get hold of a live one. When we catch cannies, we hurt 'em triple bad before we send 'em to hell. Nothing sweeter than seeing the bastards die slow."

As he spoke, Cheetah Luis had the look of a man possessed, his eyes bulged from their sockets and gobs of cottony spittle gathered at the corners of his mouth.

Ryan glanced around. "Where's Junior?" he said.

Mildred quickly counted heads. There were seven instead of eight. She and J.B. ducked under the brush for a look. Not that they could see very far. The cannie wasn't there.

"He's gone, dammit," J.B. told the others. "Sneaked off into the bush when we stood up."

"Who're you talking about?" Cheetah Luis asked.

"We had a cannie captive," Ryan said. "We starved his ass and made him lead us here."

"There he goes," one of the black man's crew announced, pointing at barely rustling treetops farther down the hill.

Even though they turned to look, none of the Cajun fighters bothered to take aim.

"Don't fret about that one," Cheetah Luis told Ryan.

"Nothing but swamp in that direction. He might not come out, neither. Cannie butt smells like fresh baked bread to a gator. If you need him, we can track him in the morning."

Ryan nodded, then the companions busted through the belt-high brush to reach the narrow path.

As Mildred stepped out, Cheetah Luis's eyes lit up. He swept off his snapbrim hat and said, "How de do?"

"Been better, thanks," she replied.

"Boss, we got company…" said one of the Cajuns.

Cheetah Luis tore his gaze from Mildred's stocky figure.

Even before she looked over her shoulder she heard the sound of multiple wag engines and the screech of brakes locking up. A cannie convoy from the north had stopped on the highway behind them and armed folk were jumping out of every wag.

"Too many to fight," Cheetah Luis stated. "Got no surprise working for us."

Slapping his natty hat back on top of his head, he turned to Jak and said, "You all come on this way, Snow Wolf. We'll lose the bastards right quick."

The companions fell in behind the Cajun fighters as they hustled down the winding track. Before the cannies on the road could bracket them with fire, they ducked below the line of sight and squirmed into a tunnel bored into the brush. The entrance was well hidden by branches, invisible if a person didn't know exactly where to look. The path ahead had been cleared of springy branches, but was still so low that they had move ahead on all fours. As they descended the slope, the roof of the tunnel rose overhead. The trees at the base of the hill were taller than those on the summit, but the branches were just as densely intergrown. Looking across the treetops from the road, the difference in height wasn't evident.

Mildred scrambled to her feet. As she ran, her boots made sucking sounds in the mud. This trail had seen heavy use. Foot traffic had exposed the backs of tree roots. Sprue stumbled over one but caught himself before he fell. For a big man, he moved well.

The farther they went, the deeper the mud. They had to jump puddles of sour standing water. The puddles grew wider, joined together, turned into ribbons and pools. Soon there was more water around them than land, and the land was isolated in little, vine-choked islands.

The Cajun called a halt in the middle of a shallow, leaf-littered pool.

"This is where the rubber leaves the road," Cheetah Luis said. His giant cig had gone out again, his saliva stained the cigarette's paper yellow. "Cannies can't follow us through the deep water," he said to the companions. "You best unbuckle your gun belts and hold them over your heads." The Cajun looked at J.B., and made a wry face. "Short stuff, there, he gonna need some water wings."

"I'm taller than Jak, you asshole."

"Just yanking chain," the albino teen said. "Loves doin' that."

Cheetah Luis grinned, sucking on his cold smoke. "How you holding up, Buttercup?" he asked Mildred.

"Bring it on," she said.

The Cajun chuckled at that. Then he told the others, "You all keep a tight sphincter, now. Lots of hungry leeches in this swamp. Don't want none crawling up where the sun don't shine."

Cheetah Luis led the way, heading down a five-foot-wide canal between the stands of tightly packed mangrove. Tepid water slid over their knees, then their waists.

Sunlight streamed in through breaks in the canopy, lighting floating patches of bright green slime. Spanish moss draped the higher branches, trailing down to the water. The air hung heavy with the rotten-egg smell of hydrogen sulphide. They were entering a fetid, malarial swamp. As they waded, insects buzzed in dense clouds around their heads. They couldn't help but inhale the soft, fluttering bodies. Jak wiped a gob of black mud on his face and neck to keep the bugs off. The others followed suit.

They slogged on for an hour without another break. It was too dangerous to stop. Time and again they saw huge gators sunning themselves on mud banks where the canopy gaped. The swamp wasn't quiet. The steady whine of insects was punctuated by loud splashes just out of their sight. Splashes followed by shrill cries and more splashes.

Gators weren't the only danger. Mutie water moccasins prowled among the exposed mangrove roots. Six feet long, with gaping white mouths and long fangs, they swam just out of the travelers' reach, waiting for the chance to turn and strike.

When a snake made a rush for one of the Cajuns, the man waved his arms and splashed to drive it away. This particular cottonmouth wouldn't take no for an answer.

Jak shook a leaf-bladed knife from his sleeve, and in a blur hurled the blade at the snake's triangular head. A razor sharp point slapped into its skull just in front of the ear hole, cutting the critter's pea brain in two. The snake went as rigid as a stick, then weighted by the blade, sank headfirst into the discolored water.

"See you ain't lost your touch, Jak," Cheetah Luis said as the tail disappeared.

After another half hour of trekking, they walked out of the far side of the swamp onto a dry plain. The trees were more widely spaced and mixed in were bursts of color, pink azaleas thriving along the banks of trickling creeks. The going was much easier, even though daylight was starting to fade. Mildred could see the Cajuns' spirits lift. This was their domain.

Another fifteen minutes passed before they reached their destination. From a distance, the rounded hills looked like solid mounds of green. Only when they got close could they see the bone-white of the bedrock peeking out from tangled roots and sprouting vines.

"It's just us!" the Cajun hollered through a cupped hand.

From behind the tumbled-down limestone blocks, people rose, blasters in hand. From bordering stands of tall trees, more armed sentries showed themselves.

Cheetah Luis led the companions past them to an irregular opening in the hillside. "Welcome to our hidey-hole," he said.

They stepped into the torchlit entrance. The original limestone cave had been extensively excavated, the work of many years. Wide galleries for sleeping, cooking, storage and livestock had been hacked out of the living rock on either side of a central passage that stretched deep and straight into the hill.

The Cajun gestured for the companions and Sprue to sit on benches carved into the walls. He took a place beside Mildred, lit up a fresh ganja stick and sucked down a long pull.

"Why you come back here, Snow Wolf?" he said as he exhaled.

"To chill La Golondrina," Jak said.

The Cajun frowned and shook his head. "That's a tall order, even for you."

"How did she come to be here?" Mildred asked.

"No one knows for sure. Rumor is that she slipped in along the Gulf coast a short time ago with a few other cannies. The pack started off raiding small fish camps and farms for meat. People just up and disappeared. Young 'uns at first, then folks of all ages. By the time we figured out what was going on, there were lots more of the bastards hunting these parts. They come down here from the east, west and north to join up with the bitch. When La Golondrina had collected herself a big enough crew, she set up business on Marsh Island, at the mouth of Vermillion Bay. There's a big old freighter wreck on the island's south shore. That's her headquarters."

"The cannie who got away told us about some other bay," Ryan said.

"West Cote Blanche," Krysty said.

"Same thing, really. There's a little spit of land that divides the two. Closest way to Marsh Island is from West Cote Blanche."

"You fought from beginning?" Jak said.

"Hell, yes, we fought 'em. We attacked the island with everything we had. Cannies' firepower was much better than ours. And they had fortified the place. When we got to the freighter, we couldn't make a dent in that steel hull. We lost a lot of good folks that night.

"After that, the cannies started driving deeper into the countryside. We couldn't stop 'em. They come ashore from Vermillion Bay to Atchafalaya Bay in canoes. Stole horses to ride, or wags if they could get 'em. Chill poor folks and take their bodies back to the island to eat."

"You ever see this queen cannie in person?" Ryan said.

"If I had, I wouldn't be breathing, now. I'd be a pile of shit, drying in the sun."

"She hunt with her cannies?" Jak said.

"La Golondrina never goes off that island no more," Cheetah Luis said. "Cannies come to her. Hundreds of them. We try to pick them off both coming and going, but they control most of the territory around here. Chilled and ate just about everybody inside it."

"What do they use for food, then?" Mildred asked.

"We saw the tire marks from heavy wags," Ryan said.

"Them's the meat wags," the Cajun said, his eyes once again radiating pure hate. "Cannies are doing their hunting on predark roads. They round up folks from a long ways off and truck them back here, live on the hoof. The bastards use semi-trailers. When they run out of tractors to haul the trailers, they hitch up teams of horses and cattle."

"Cannie called it the Red Road," J.B. said.

"Now that's the truth. Trailers go out full of cannies, come back full of norms. Norms go to the island, they never leave."

"How many strong are you?" Doc said.

"Sixty-three."

"Have chill queen, friend," Jak said. "Help?"

Cheetah Luis flicked his cigarette away. "You're talking about a suicide mission, Snow Wolf. No way to chill that bitch. She's got herself too well protected."

"You just going to let her whittle you down?" Ryan said.

"Better that than us dying all at once," the Cajun countered. "Don't forget, we're whittling them down, too. Making 'em pay for what they done. Taking our revenge."

"For every cannie you chill, ten more are gonna pop up," Ryan told him.

"How you figure that?"

Ryan had no choice but to lay out the cards. He started with the cannie queen's cryogenesis. "La Golondrina's blood is what's drawing the cannies here," he said. "The power of her blood. It can cure the oozies for a while. Longer cannies live, more cannies there will be. Simple as that."

"All that freezie stuff is bullshit," Cheetah Luis said. "I heard it before and I don't believe it. She got no special powers. What she got is soldiers. Lots of them, and lots of guns."

"You won't help?" Jak repeated.

"Shit, no," Cheetah Luis said. "We ain't fools. We can't hurt 'em no more if we're dead." Then he changed the subject. "I'm hungry. Let's eat."

At his signal, other Cajuns carried in wooden platters heaped with long black sausages, fried okra and stewed mustard greens.

When Doc inquired as to the nature of the sausage, Cheetah Luis said, "That's possum blood. Boudin noir don't get no better than that. Okra and greens come from a garden we got hid out in the meadow."

The companions ate ravenously until they could hold no more. Soon afterward exhaustion kicked in. Conversation ended. Eyelids drooped. Doc actually nodded off sitting up, and began to snore like a hibernating bear.

"Time for you folks to take your rest," the Cajun said. He directed the companions toward one of the cave's communal sleeping chambers. "Plenty of room. Make yourselves comfortable."

As Mildred walked past, Cheetah Luis pulled her aside and whispered huskily in her ear, "I like my women nice and thick in the behind, just like you. Got me a big soft straw pallet way back in the cave. No one hear us going at it, if you're fussy about that. You gonna love playing with my balls. They're big as duck eggs." He reached over and gave her right breast a pinch through her T-shirt.

J.B., who was watching the attempted seduction from the sleeping quarter's entrance, unshouldered his pump gun.

Mildred shook her head at him. This was something she could handle herself.

She took hold of Cheetah Luis's hand and gently lifted it off her breast. With her thumb against his palm, she pressed her fingertips into the back of the hand, pinning nerves against unyielding bone.

As if he were lightning struck, the Cajun dropped to his knees. He let out a piercing yelp.

Mildred kept the pressure on, not letting him break free of the grappling hold, twisting away as he tried to grab her, making him do a little pain dance on his knees. Around and around they went. The doctor hurting, the Cajun knee-dancing.

J.B. looked on uneasily as she reached to her belt for the handle of her sheathed knife. His expression of surprise and dismay snapped her back to reality. Despite the adrenaline coursing through her veins, she stopped herself before drawing the blade.

"What I'm fussy about is getting mauled," Mildred informed Cheetah Luis. "You mess with me again and I'll wear your duck-egg balls for earrings."

She flung his hand aside.

Chapter Fourteen

Curled up in the brush, Junior Tibideau recognized the Cajun talk, too. Few things had the power to frighten the scar-faced cannie. The sound of that accent was one of them.

Cajuns had been waging guerrilla war in the cannie homeland for weeks. When they took cannie prisoners, they didn't just hand out leech enemas. The black bloodsuckers were a warmup act for the live skinnings, the amputation of limbs with ax blows, the water torture smotherings, the slow burning to ash of the tenderest of body parts.

Junior stood no chance if he fell into their hands.

The companions couldn't protect him as they had from the ville folk and Sprue's crew.

The Cajuns would chill them all to get at him.

Junior and his hungry packmates had pillaged southern Louisiana, weeding out the weak Cajuns. They had spread out over predark roadways, tracking down and chilling the ones who had fled the bayous. The Cajuns who managed to remain and survive the genocide were the meanest, the smartest and the most determined of the lot.

When Junior saw the albino stand, he realized his opportunity might be close at hand. As soon as the other norms rose in surrender, he took off on all fours through the bush. Even though he was in mortal danger, Junior found it hard to keep from laughing as he crawled.

It tickled him how easy it was to escape.

Over the sound of his own breathing and the rasp of tree branches against his torso, arms and legs, he couldn't make out any more of the Cajun talk. He slithered over the low limbs, heading downslope as fast as he could. After a minute or two, when no one shot at him, he stopped crawling. He knew even the slightest movement of the upper branches could give away his position. And he wanted to keep his bearings and stay as close to the road as possible. The road was his lifeline.

When Junior heard the rumble of the wag convoy as it stopped on the highway, he knew help was on the way. Cannie help. When he pushed his head up through the canopy for a quick recce, he saw the Cajuns and the companions hauling ass away from him on a dead run. They knew they were in big trouble.

Busting across the swathe of stunted trees, Junior sprinted after them, confident they wouldn't hear him in their haste and that they wouldn't waste time looking back his way. His path intersected the hidden foot trail, which he turned onto, pouring on the speed.

Tibideau wasn't angry about his kidnapping and subsequent rough treatment by the companions. They had done him no permanent harm. He wasn't driven by a need for revenge on his captors, but by much

stronger forces—a bottomless hunger and an in-
satiable bloodlust. The human brain, even one clogged
and shortcircuited by infiltrating patches of oozie
plaque, had the unique ability to rationalize the bas-
est, the most bestial of acts. In Junior's oozie-distorted
reality, the urge to chill and eat his fellow human beings was connected to a sense of entitlement, and a liberation from the few moral and social prohibitions
that had survived the nukecaust. With entitlement and
liberation came a sense of great personal power, of
every mundane burden having been lifted from his
shoulders. Junior Tibideau, the cannibal, believed he
was more than human, not less.

When he reached the concealed entrance to the tunnel in the brambles the Cajuns had disappeared into,
he snapped off some branches to mark the trail for his
fellow cannies to follow. This was their chance to mop
up the last of the guerrillas, to remove a stubborn thorn
from their sides. The famished Junior had another reason for pursuit. The Cajuns and the companions were
the closest hot meal.

He slipped into the bush and crawled down the tunnel. Hunger was like a burning spear thrust into his gut
and twisted. The pain of starvation animated him. He
moved light, quick and as quiet as a spider. Even when
the tunnel grew taller, when he stood and started running, he made no noise. Unburdened by weaponry or
supplies, he rapidly gained ground on his prey.

Before long he was close enough to hear their muffled footfalls down the path ahead. Slowing to a fast
walk, again he stifled the urge to laugh out loud. He
not only caught their lingering aroma in the tunnel of

trees, he picked out the scent of the one he'd infected, the one called Mildred. He thought he could smell the fever building in her blood. It smelled like sour milk.

Junior moved in short spurts from trunk to trunk, keeping to the edge of the clearing. He maintained a safe distance, making sure he didn't blunder into any rear guard the Cajuns might have posted.

Looking around on the forest floor, he found a sharply pointed rock. He used it to scratch a wide X into the bark of a tree, this to keep reinforcements on the trail.

When he heard splashing ahead, he broke into a run. He didn't want to lose his prey in the swamp. By the time he reached the edge of the water, the Cajuns were gone, but the bubbles from their passing were still visible here and there on the murky surface.

As Junior drew an arrow in the mud with the rock, he kicked himself for overlooking something important. His brothers and sister cannies didn't know who was marking the path for them; they might think they were being led into a trap. They had plenty of reason to think that. Cajuns loved constructing ambushes, deadfalls and spiked-lined pits.

The cannie drew the point of the rock across his palm, opening a shallow, superficial wound. He squeezed his hand, letting his blood drip and splatter on the mud beside the arrow. The cannies would recognize who was marking the path by the taste and smell of it. And they would know it was safe for them to follow.

Junior slipped into the water, careful not to splash, but advancing quickly to keep up with the bubble trail before it disappeared. Soon he was lost in a maze of mangrove-lined canals and tiny, marshy islands that were little more than high points on the mudflat. He didn't know where he was, or where he was going, but he knew he was close behind the Cajuns. He marked the twists and turns in their route by dragging the edge of the rock along trailing branches, stripping loose long curlicues of bark.

As he rounded one of the islands, he saw a small animal swimming toward him, its head out of the water. It looked to be about twenty pounds, with densely packed, four-inch whiskers and a long, hairless tail. It was a nutria.

Before the Apocalypse, the aquatic, vegetarian rodent had been hunted and trapped for its pelt to the tune of two million critters a year. Post-Apocalypse, with no limit on their population, the Louisiana nutria had made a big comeback. So had the gators and cottonmouths who preyed on them.

If the gigantic gator hunkered down in a spot of sun on the far bank hadn't shifted its head to follow the overgrown rat as it swam by, Junior might have missed it. The cannie was wading in water over his hips, completely vulnerable to attack.

The nutria looked at the gator. The gator looked at Junior, its nostrils pointing at him.

A little blood was still seeping from Junior's palm.

The gator forgot all about the nutria. It lunged into the water with a monstrous splash.

Junior turned and swam for the nearest high ground. He wasn't alone. Both he and the nutria scrambled onto the same tiny island, over the mangrove roots and up into the limbs as high as they could get.

From its precarious perch, the dripping rodent blinked and sniffed at him. Though it was terrified of Junior, it was more terrified of what lay below.

Unable to reach them, the gator slapped its tail in frustration.

Junior took aim and threw his rock as hard as he could. The stone thudded against the top of the gator's head. The blow didn't dissuade it in the least. The gator opened its yard-long mouth and hissed from deep in its throat.

Having gotten its attention, Junior reared back with his right boot and kicked the nutria out of the branches.

The rodent squealed as it hit the water, it squealed louder as it tried desperately to climb back to safety.

The gator surged forward and snapped its jaws shut. For a moment the nutria's head protruded from between interlocking, dagger-like teeth. The gator flipped the limp body around in its maw, then with its snout straight up in the air, gulped and swallowed it whole.

Junior seized the opportunity to take his leave. He slipped away from the far side of the little island, dog-paddling with grim determination.

Chapter Fifteen

Troubled, ominous dreams haunted Mildred's sleep. She ran down dark, winding hospital corridors, through slicks of congealed blood and piles of soiled, septic bandages, past overturned gurneys and mounds of decaying, white-gowned bodies. All of the dead had been operated upon. Bristling rows of black stitches ringed their shaved heads, or zippered their loins from hip to hip, or divided their torsos, goobers to gullet. From the hall's doorways, wide-eyed, puffy-faced children Mildred couldn't save pleaded for their lives. Even lost in the nightmare, the symbolism was obvious to her. Failed medicine. Failed science. Failed civilization.

The end of all hope.

For the third time in what seemed like seconds, Mildred jerked wide awake, gasping and drenched with sweat. Her head throbbed as if it was going to burst. Her stomach felt queasy and there was an awful, bitter taste in her mouth. When she put the back of her hand to her forehead, it was on fire.

With difficulty Mildred forced herself to sit up on the lumpy, rag-stuffed mattress. A single torch lit the low-ceilinged, Cajun sleeping chamber. On the other side of the dim, smoky room, she could just make out Ryan and Krysty cuddled in each other's arms on a stone bench. Six feet apart, Doc and Sprue lay on their backs on the floor, playing a snore duet. J.B. was curled up on a straw pallet at her feet.

Unwell in the midst of her trusted, oblivious companions, Mildred felt suddenly, utterly alone. The first stirrings of panic tickled deep in the back of her throat.

Was this how the oozies started? she thought. Was it all downhill from here?

Gritting her teeth, she forced her mind to clear. She made herself think like the trained physician she was. She followed that deeply ingrained, scientific regimen. From the data at hand, she drew a set of objective, logical conclusions. That she had a fever was obvious; the cause was not. It could have come from any number of possible sources. A few drops of polluted swamp water could have gotten into her mouth. Some of the food the Cajuns had served could have been spoiled. It could have been an allergic reaction to all the insect bites she'd suffered. It could even have been the effect of head trauma—after all, she had been knocked unconscious twice in the space of a day.

Could have been.

How will I know when it's the oozies and not just a bad case of swamp fever or ptomaine poisoning? she asked herself. How will I know when it's too late?

These were questions she wished could have asked Junior Tibideau. Not that she could have completely trusted his answers. But any information was better than what she had now.

She leaned her forehead on her knees, trying to block out the stabbing pain behind her eyes. The cave walls and ceiling seemed to close in on her, first pressing against her skin, then compressing her rib cage, making it hard to breathe. She had to get some fresh air or she was going to pass out.

Mildred stepped around J.B. without waking him. Her knees felt rubbery and loose, as though they were about to give way under her. She staggered out of the cave entrance into the sweltering night.

She leaned back against the hillside's vine-draped bedrock, inhaling deeply, trying to slow her thudding heart.

A soft crunch came from her left.

Adrenaline flooded Mildred's veins and as she whirled toward the sound, her hand closed on her pistol butt.

A pale, white-haired figure stepped closer.

"Dammit, Jak, you scared me."

The albino didn't apologize, which was not unusual.

"You're not sleeping, either?" Mildred said. "Aren't you tired?"

The albino didn't answer. He either wasn't going to respond or he was collecting his thoughts. Mildred sagged against the bedrock, too exhausted to repeat the question.

"Not want come back after last time," Jak said at last, in that telegraphic, stripped-down patois of his. "Not want see this place again."

"Bad memories fade, sooner or later," Mildred assured him. "Scars heal."

"Not here," the albino told her. "Nothing left here but bad. Good folks chilled or chased off by cannies. Farms burned. Levees busted. Swamp taking over..."

All Mildred could manage was a sympathetic grunt. She was remembering in great detail her full-color nightmare. Her helplessness. The weight of her despair. Suddenly she felt much, much worse. Hotter. Weaker. Jak's mane of white hair shimmered in front of her eyes and she thought she was going to black out. "Water," she said. "You got water?"

Jak passed her a plastic bottle and she drank deep, trying to put out the fire in her chest. Then she splashed it inside her T-shirt and on top of her head. It cooled her and revived her.

Was it her imagination or was Jak looking at her strangely? It was hard to read those eyes of his, even in broad daylight. Perhaps he had noticed something odd in the way she moved or talked. Perhaps he was looking for early signs of the onset of the Gray Death. She couldn't bring herself to tell him how terrible she felt.

"Hot night," she said as she passed the bottle back.

It was also humid and deathly still. She could hear the drops of her own sweat pelting the ground at her feet. From the south, in the direction of the Gulf of Mexico, chain lightning crackled across the night sky. In the wake of the flash, Mildred noticed something odd. The dark belly of cloud was underlit by a subtle flickering. Orange. Erratic. Distant.

She blinked her eyes, and it was still there. Worried that it might be an hallucination, a symptom of her advancing delirium, Mildred pointed it out to Jak.

"What's going on over there?" she said as thunder rumbled on and on.

"Sea on fire."

"What?"

"Leaks gas wells in Gulf. Fifty, hundred miles out. Fireballs all day and…"

Jak stopped himself in midsentence.

Mildred immediately sensed his tension. A chill rippled up her sweaty spine. Those ruby-red eyes of his could penetrate deep into the darkness, just like a cat's. Mildred's pulse began to pound.

"What's wrong?" she said.

Jak didn't answer.

Then she saw the Cajun sentries sprinting back through the trees as if the devil was on their heels.

KRYSTY LAY CURLED UP in her lover's arms. Nuzzling into the side of his neck, she breathed in his familiar, masculine scent. She drifted in and out of sleep, unable to slip off for long because of the intermittent bursts of snoring from the floor beside her. Though she was bone-tired, Krysty didn't mind the disturbance that much. Moments of security and peace for her and the companions were few and far between; recuperation time measured in minutes or hours, rarely days.

As sweet as it was for her to doze warm and protected in the eye of the storm, in the back of her mind she couldn't help but think about the mission at hand. Like all natural-born Deathlanders, the idea of sickness alarmed her. It was something that couldn't be fought with main strength, with blaster or blade. Its threat was invisible and often lethal. It struck down even the strongest, and when struck, they died like dogs.

Post-nukecaust, the whitecoat arsenal of vaccinations and antibiotics that had kept epidemics at bay for three-quarters of a century were no more. Cholera, typhus and small pox had reemerged as cyclic decimators the remnants of humanity. The fall of civilization had reopened what Doc Tanner called a "Pandora's box" of evils. By Mildred's guess, medical science had been turned back to 150 years *before* the Apocalypse. To even before Doc's time. Hard-won facts about sanitation, hygiene and disease vectors had been forgotten or discarded, in part because of the desperation of the survivors.

Resurgent illnesses followed the hellscape's trade routes, wiping out entire villes in a matter of weeks. That was another reason Deathlanders constructed perimeter berms. Newcomers were inspected before they were allowed inside to mingle with ville folk. The obviously sick were kept out. Sometimes they were chilled on sight and their bodies burned downwind.

In Deathlands, weakness of any kind spelled doom. Weakness therefore had to be stamped out. Crushed before it could spread. Hellish beasts and hellish human bands prowled the ruined earth, all waiting for a chance to grab up an easy pound of flesh.

On their travels, the companions had seen the buzzards lined up shoulder-to-shoulder on the berm tops, so overstuffed with carrion that they couldn't fly. Inside, the ville huts and lean-tos were abandoned, bloated bodies left unburied. And the flies. Millions of them buzzing, swirling up from the sprawled corpses like dense black smoke.

In front of the entrances to many of these putrid chill zones, crude plywood signs had been left behind, propped up with piles of rocks. Under childlike renderings of skulls and crossbones was written the dreaded word: PLAIG.

Mildred Wyeth had been exposed to a different sort of sickness. If what she had said was true, the oozies didn't just make a person ill. They made a person into a cannie. Krysty saw flesheaters as the hellscape's most debased humanity. Worse than common droolies, homicidal sec men, and deranged barons. In the pecking order of the despised, cannies were the bottom of the human barrel.

Ryan opened his good right eye and looked at her. "You okay?" he asked huskily.

"Yeah, I guess."

He kissed her lightly on the mouth.

"Better?"

"Mmm-mmm," Krysty said, opening her lips to receive the probing tip of his tongue.

As they kissed, she escaped into the sensation, relishing a moment of forgetfulness locked in her lover's embrace.

Ryan's hands slipped inside her coat, cupping her breasts through her shirt. Rosy heat bloomed in her cheeks as he teased her nipples erect. She put her palm flat against his groin and felt the already straining stiffness.

Ryan unbuckled her belt and turned her over onto her stomach. As she rose onto her hands and knees in front of him, he peeled her trousers from over her buttocks and down around her thighs.

Doc and Sprue were snorting, growling, steam-whistling in their sleep.

"No one's going to hear us over that," Ryan whispered as he undid his fly and nosed his hardness into the wet warmth of her.

"I don't care if they do. Give it to me, now."

Ryan surged inside, completely filling her in a single thrust. Her mutie vagina gripped him in a maddening, fluttering caress. He groaned softly as the powerful, rhythmic contractions pulled him in even deeper. Ryan's hips bucked violently, slamming into her again and again. She braced herself on elbows and knees to keep from being pushed off the bench and onto the floor. Every savage slam shot a tingle to the core of her being, tingles growing stronger and stronger until the dam broke for them both in the same delicious instant. Krysty collapsed onto her stomach, Ryan lay upon her back, panting. He brushed aside the coils of her prehensile, mutie hair and kissed her neck and ears, gently grinding his hips into her bottom. She held him inside until he softened, then reluctantly she let him go.

When Ryan rolled off, Krysty pulled up her trousers and nestled back into his sheltering arms.

As she started to drift off to sleep, the sounds of running footsteps echoed from the cave entrance, followed by shouts of alarm.

At once, Ryan and Krysty jumped to their feet. J.B., Doc and Sprue rose from the floor, reaching for their weapons.

"Where's Mildred?" J.B. asked as he flipped the M-4000's sling over his shoulder.

"Not here, apparently," Doc said.

"Jak's gone, too," Krysty said.

The tramp of running feet grew louder. Torchlights bobbed down the hallway toward them.

"Perhaps that is the absent pair coming…" Doc suggested.

It was not.

Cheetah Luis entered the doorless chamber, flaming torch in hand. Behind him in the hallway, heavily armed men and women ran deeper into the belly of the hillside. "Come with me," the Cajun said. "Cannies are here."

"We've got two people missing," Ryan said as he slipped the scoped Steyr's sling over his shoulder. "We've got to find them first."

"If they're out of the cave," Cheetah Luis said, "they're a whole lot safer than you are. In a minute or two this place's gonna be a shooting gallery. Come on!"

The Cajun waved them on with his torch.

From outside the cavern came the hard clatter of autofire. Dozens of blasters were cutting loose at once. The battle was joined.

There was no time for argument, and nothing really to argue about. The Cajun was right. If Mildred and Jak were fighting cannies in the woods, they had room to maneuver and a damned good chance to survive.

"All right, let's go," Ryan said.

The companions followed Cheetah Luis out of the chamber and across the cave's central corridor. Down the narrow, straight stretch of hall, Cajun men and women were running close to the left side, next to the limestone wall. At its far end, the hall bulged and widened before it doglegged right. In front of the opening, other Cajuns were frantically pulling together a barricade of timber and rocks. From the sounds at the cave mouth, the fighters there were doing the same thing.

Cheetah Luis led them into another wide, doorless chamber. The lack of doors and the large entries allowed air to circulate in the cave. In the flickering torchlight, they hurried to the back of the room and a large, floor-to-ceiling bulge in the rock. The protrusion concealed a man-size, transverse cleft in the wall, impossible to see from the doorway.

The Cajun stepped into the narrow passage and they all moved in behind him. The ceiling was high enough so that Ryan didn't have to duck his head, but the passage was hardly more than two and a half feet wide in places, and in places the walls were curved in an S-shape. Krysty had to advance sideways, scraping her hipbones and knees against the rock. Convoy master Sprue had real trouble getting through the tightest spots. She could hear him grunting behind her as he sucked in his massive gut and pushed himself forward.

Krysty realized at once that the passage was bending back toward the cave entrance, running roughly parallel to the main corridor.

From outside the cave, rocking booms from frag grens interspersed between sawing bursts of full-auto blasterfire, which started to rage inside the cave as Cajuns tried to hold out the cannies.

Cheetah Luis stopped moving, bringing the line behind him to a halt. His torch hissed in the claustrophobically close tunnel.

A cluster of grens exploded much closer at hand, shaking loose bits of rock and dirt from above their heads. As the debris rained down on them, the torch sputtered and nearly went out.

"By the Three Kennedys!" Doc exclaimed.

The explosions were inside the mouth of the cave.

To Krysty it sounded as though the defenders were giving ground, letting the cannies penetrate their stronghold. It wasn't a happy thought.

"Your fighters are pulling back mighty quick," Ryan said. "Something wrong?"

"Cajuns know what to do," Cheetah Luis said.

They listened as foot by foot, the hated enemy drove deeper into the heart of the cave. The sounds of the horrendous firefight continued, but grew more and more muffled.

"Now comes the fun part," Cheetah Luis said, knocking out the torch on the ground. The tunnel was plunged in darkness. "Stay close."

Ryan moved right behind him. Krysty had her hand on her lover's lower back.

They pushed out of the side passage and into a chamber just inside the cave entrance. Light came from a few torches still burning in wall stanchions and the red flares the cannies had dropped. The fight continued out of sight, deep inside the hill; outside the cave, the shooting had stopped. The silence from the woods was eerie.

The Cajun tapped Doc and Sprue on the shoulders with the muzzle of his M-16. "You two cover the entrance while the rest of us take care of business…"

Krysty, J.B. and Ryan followed Cheetah Luis along the cave wall, blasters up and ready. There was no cannie rear guard. Because they could see into the wide-mouthed, doorless chambers, they were confident they had cleared away all opposition, eliminating the possibility of a backside attack.

It was a fatal mistake.

At Cheetah Luis's hand signal, Krysty and J.B. crossed to the opposite side of the hall. She saw the cannie attackers bunched up on either side of the entrance to the narrow section of hall. They were pouring fire on the barricade at the far end. They were disturbingly disciplined. They took turns shooting, emptying their mags, then stepping aside to let a fresh gunner blast away while they reloaded.

Two cannies rushed from a chamber to the right of the shooters. Between them they hauled a limp body by its arms. They were coming the companions' way.

The Cajun held up his closed fist. Wait. Then he shifted his M-16 to his left hand and with his right unsheathed his machete.

As the cannies drew closer, Krysty could see their victim was a woman. She could see they were laughing as they dragged her along.

Cheetah Luis waited until they were practically on top of him before he struck with the machete. As Jak had said, the Cajun was a stone chiller. With a single, two-handed stroke, he beheaded the nearest cannie. The severed head leaped from the man's neck, hitting wall and rolling onto the ground. Dead eyes stared upward, baffled for eternity.

As the other cannie opened his mouth to cry for

help, the one-eyed warrior swung his panga cross-ways. The razor-sharp blade split open the cannie's face, slicing through tongue and cheeks and both jaw hinges all the way back to his gray-dripping ears. Ryan ripped the blade out, then forehand-slashed under the scraggly chin beard, driving the blade through the front of his throat. The cannie's head flopped over, ear resting on shoulder, blood sheeting from the massive neck wound.

While Krysty and J.B. covered them, Ryan and Cheetah Luis dragged all three bodies into the nearest chamber, out of sight.

Meanwhile, the cannies' rain of bullets had beaten the defenders back around the hallway's bend. Seizing the opportunity, the flesheaters leap-frogged down the narrow stretch of corridor, keeping up a one-sided stream of automatic fire.

Cheetah Luis and the companions dashed forward to take up the positions the cannies had just abandoned.

The flesheaters broke and ran the last thirty feet, charging the barricade. Screams replaced gunshots as a wide section of the cave floor gave way under their combined weight. In the blink of an eye, a dozen cannies disappeared down the dust-belching hole.

"Now!" Cheetah Luis cried, stepping out from cover and opening up full-auto with his M-16.

Krysty and Ryan fired their handblasters side by side, pouring lead into the remaining cannies' backs. J.B.'s pump gun boomed over and over. The massed fire scattered bodies the width of the corridor.

As Cheetah Luis and the companions rushed forward, Cajun fighters appeared around the bend, then jumped the barricade.

Krysty looked down over the edge of the pit trap, over the ends of the buckled and splintered cover that stuck up from the hole. Cannie men and women lay fifteen feet down, impaled on multiple rows of two-inch-thick, four-foot-long green wood spikes. The spikes had punched through necks, chests, limbs and bowels. Those still alive wailed, kicking their legs, moving their arms, their mouths gushing blood. Some tried to pull themselves free, raising up on the gore-greased poles, only to lose their grip and fall, skewering themselves even deeper.

Cheetah Luis watched, grinning as the flesheaters struggled in their own mess. He paused to light up another fat ganja stick and sucked down the pungent, potent smoke. In the torchlight, his eyeballs looked pink, his eyelids drooped to slits. The Cajun stripped away his M-16's spent mag, inserted a full one.

They weren't dying fast enough to suit him.

"Chill 'em all!" he shouted to his fighters.

They obeyed, with gusto.

From both sides of the pit, the Cajuns opened fire, streaming hot lead into the defenseless, dying cannies. Heads exploded and bellies burst open from close-range, full-auto hits. Even the bastards who were already dead were bullet-chewed to hamburger. When the Cajuns were done, the floor of the pit was awash in spilled blood and guts.

The companions didn't participate in the grotesque coups de grace. Nor did Sprue. It seemed a waste of time and good ammo, not to mention the splatter factor.

Cheetah Luis led his fighters and the companions back to the cave entrance. The Cajuns were buoyed by their success, not exuberant, but charged. It didn't last. As they filtered out into the Louisiana night, their mood changed in a hurry.

An unnatural quiet hung over the woods. No bug sound. No frog sound. At the edge of the clearing, tree trunks had been blown apart by high explosives. Dropped branches littered the ground. Some were still burning.

There were no bodies, cannie or Cajun.

Mildred and Jak were nowhere in sight.

"How many did we lose?" Cheetah Luis asked one of his female subordinates.

"Could be more than twenty," the hefty woman replied. "We had almost that many sentries set out, and some of our folk ran out of the cave to fight in the woods."

"Cannies tracked us all the way from the road," the Cajun said. "That's where they'll be heading back to."

Something moved behind the screen of trees to their left.

Three dozen assault rifles took aim.

"Hold it!" someone shouted. "It's one of ours!"

A wounded man staggered forward, then fell. The Cajuns and their guests rushed to his side. Krysty grimaced at the bloody bullet hole. It was low in his belly. A gutbuster.

Cheetah Luis knelt over the fallen fighter. "What happened to the others?" he said.

"Cannies took 'em all. The living and the dead. Dragged off into swamp…"

"Did you see the live prisoners?" Ryan asked. "Did you see them get taken away?"

The dying man nodded, but as he did so, his eyes fluttered shut and his chest stopped heaving.

"He's checking out on us," J.B. said.

"Not yet," Ryan said. He leaned down and grabbed hold of the man's chin. When he squeezed hard, digging in his fingertips, the fighter opened his eyes wide.

"Did you see a black woman and a pale-skinned man? Were they taken prisoner?"

"Cannies took 'em both. Man in bad shape."

Chapter Sixteen

Before Mildred and Jak could turn back for the cave, a flurry of rifle shots from the forest whined past them, slamming into the limestone slope at their backs, cutting off their retreat to the cave mouth.

Cannie fire.

Two of the fleeing Cajun sentries were cut down in midstride as they crossed the clearing, their backs riddled with bullets.

Jak grabbed Mildred's arm and pulled her away from the entrance as more well-aimed fire clipped at the bedrock, pelting them with limestone shards. The danger wiped away concerns about fever and weakness. Powered by pure adrenaline surge, she ran hard on the albino's heels along the base of the hillside, sprinting for the cover of the bordering trees. Mildred drew her target pistol and skidded to a stop on the leafy carpet behind a tree trunk.

She could see the winking muzzle-flashes of the cannie weapons. They were concentrated directly opposite the cave entrance. In the dim light, shadowy forms moved quickly through the woods around her. Not cannies. These were Cajuns. No longer in a panicked retreat, they were heading for already-prepared defensive positions.

Some of the fighters immediately shinnied out of sight into the mature elm trees, to what Mildred supposed were shooting stands hidden in the high branches. Others disappeared with their weapons down into the ground, presumably into hardened bunkers. Though she could only see her side of the clearing, and that just barely, she guessed that the same thing was happening on the other side. The sentries were setting up a delaying action to keep the cannies from charging straight into the mouth of the cave, giving their comrades time to prepare their defense.

From positions high in the trees and low around their bases, the Cajuns' crossfire would slow or turn back any cannie advance across the open space. From the bunkers deeper in the trees, they were protecting the snipers' backs and stopping the cannies from encircling the clearing.

As Cajun return fire clattered back through the woods, Jak took Mildred's hand and led her away from the tree. Keeping low, moving from trunk to trunk, they slipped deeper into the forest, to meet the cannie advance head-on.

Suddenly, Jak stopped and dropped into a fighting crouch. Mildred knelt beside him.

She strained to see ahead in the dark. The trees were black, the earth was black, the night sky veiled by leafy branches. Jak raised his Colt Python and prepared to fire. A moment later Mildred saw the faintly reflected starlight tracing the outlines of sweaty human faces and arms moving toward them. A skirmish line of crab-crawling cannies.

To her right, at the base of a tree perhaps fifteen yards in front of them, something flashed silver. A long knife or short sword.

With a loud crack one of the massive trees groaned and toppled over. The precut deadfall came down on the row of creeping cannies with a horrendous crash and raised a cloud of dust and debris. The combined weight of the tree, easily thousands of pounds, flattened the enemy.

A pair of dark forms scurried out from cover to the felled tree. Again and again, single blastershots rang out. The muzzle-flashes illuminated down-pointing handblasters and Cajuns firing point-blank into the heads of the pinned, struggling cannies.

From high in the trees behind them, staccato bursts of autofire rang out. The cannies trying to drive forward into the clearing were meeting solid resistance.

Heavy-caliber slugs clipped and chipped at trunks on all sides. Rounds screamed through the limbs. The cannies were spraying the woods with automatic fire.

Then came a different sort of scream.

Higher pitched.

Much, much louder.

With a stunning flash and gut-rattling boom, fire blossomed high in a tall tree. As steel shrapnel whistled past, Jak and Mildred pressed harder in the dirt. The legless torso of the Cajun sniper thudded to earth, along with a pile of shattered branches. Then came another earsplitting explosion, and another.

The cannies were tree-topping with RPGs, taking

out the sniper hides one by one. The edge of the clearing was lit by burning, shattered pecan and elm. At the same time, the flesheaters put up intense covering fire for their advancing brethren, raining bullets on the cave entrance. More than once Mildred wondered where the cannies got their firepower. More than likely a trader convoy had been overrun.

Fighters from the barricaded opening returned fire. The din of pitched combat became a steady, clattering roar.

From the dark forest, more shadowy figures moved low and fast. Autofire from a hidden position swept over the invaders. Mildred couldn't see well enough to count them, but there were many. A second later the ground shook under her stomach as a gren explosion took out the Cajun bunker. The acrid smoke was still drifting over her when she heard the cannies pulling the bodies out of the hole.

Harvest time.

Mildred and Jak saw the same opportunity in the same instant. They crawled through the leaves until they reached a wide tree trunk. Peering around it, Mildred saw the cannies bathed in weak starlight, bent over the still-smoldering corpses. They were doing something to the feet, trussing them together, she guessed.

When she ducked back to cover, Jak was nose to nose with her. He nodded, then they both rounded the trunk with blasters up. Mildred, the last ever Olympic pistol shooting silver medalist, had, after her cryosleep thawing, quickly picked up the knack of hitting moving flesh and blood targets. It was a matter of anticipation, of seeing a fraction of a second into the future, of seeing where the bull's-eye was going to be. No target could move faster than she could aim and fire. When she and Jak jumped out from behind the tree, the cannies weren't running.

The Czech-made target pistol bucked in her two-handed grip. Her first bullet smacked a kneeling cannie in the side of the head. As he dropped, she swung her sights on the flesheater standing over him and fired again. It was too dark and there were too many enemies for precision work. Her slug hit the cannie under the point of his breastbone, he staggered backward, clutching his chest with both hands. She was aware of Jak's big Colt popping off, but that awareness was compartmentalized, back-brained; her focus was on acquiring fresh targets. The rest of the cannies abandoned their prey and took to their heels. Mildred swung her sights through the running targets, firing at will. She scored torso hit after torso hit, punctuated by cannies crashing to earth. Then her pistol's firing pin snapped on a spent primer.

As she turned back around the cover of the thick trunk, Jak touched off his last shot. The Python's boom echoed through the woods. A fraction of a second later, somewhere off in the humid darkness, a flesheater screamed high and shrill like a baby.

While the cannie survivors poured slugs their way, chipping at the far side of the tree trunk with full-autofire, Mildred and Jak dumped their empties and used speed-loaders to reload. They had taken down six each, but they had no way of knowing how many had gotten away or how many more had moved up to join them. One thing was clear—for Mildred and Jak to jump out again and return fire would be suicide. And it was only a matter of seconds before the attackers flanked their position or one of the cannies chucked a gren their way.

"We go," Jak said in her ear. "Now!"

Again, Mildred followed the albino youth. As they sprinted away from the tree, near misses skimmed above their heads, slapping into the trunks and limbs ahead of them. Jak turned hard left, heading back for the hillside. It was the only solid, defensible cover they had. Mildred ran for all she was worth, but the albino was too quick. He pulled away from her. Ten feet. Fifteen feet.

As he left Mildred in the dust, a cannie slipping out from the woods blundered right into his path. Jak didn't slow a step and he didn't change course. He shoved his revolver into the flesheater's chest. The Python roared in his fist and the contact wound blew the hapless cannie off his feet and sent him crashing onto his back in the leaves.

Between them and the hillside more RPGs detonated in the treetops, the bright flashes lit up the sky, followed by HE thunderclaps. The smoke from burning cordite hung under the tree limbs like caustic fog. Jak continued to move away from her. He couldn't help it. Because he could see better and run faster, he had trouble holding himself in check. As he turned, looking over his shoulder to check on her position, a rocket screamed overhead.

With a tremendous whump and a blinding flash, the tree next to Jak exploded, its forked trunk shattered in two. The two halves crashed to the forest floor, and Jak went down under the fall of heavy branches.

Mildred closed the distance. Lunging into the dropped limbs, she pulled the albino teen out by an arm. "Jak! Jak!" she said as she turned him on his back.

His eyes were closed, and blood oozed from a shallow wound on top of his head. She felt at his throat for a pulse and was relieved to find a strong heartbeat.

From deeper in the woods, more cannies were coming. Mildred could have picked Jak up in a fireman's carry, but she couldn't have made the hillside with him on her back. She couldn't leave him, unconscious and helpless for the cannies, even if it meant her own life. She scooped up the albino's big Colt in her left hand.

As flesheaters burst through the trees, she fired her ZKR 551. The cannies shot back, but they were firing on the run and their slugs went wide. Hers, on the other hand, went exactly where she aimed. She chilled another six in rapid succession, then switched the Python to her strong hand. The Magnum blaster bucked hard in her fist, but she had braced herself for the increased recoil. Like bowling pins, she knocked down five more in rapid succession, sending them sprawling to the leafy carpet. Unlike those hit with the .38, these cannies dropped as if their strings had been cut and didn't stir after they hit the ground.

Then the shooting abruptly stopped.

She had no doubt that the battle for the clearing had been lost.

Through the trees to her right, Mildred saw about

twenty-five cannies rushing for the cave mouth, some carried RPGs. To her left, more cannies charged from cover, heading right at her. With no time to reload, Mildred whipped out her knife, straddling her fallen comrade like a mother wolf protecting its young.

Before she could blink, she and Jak were surrounded by lunging, taunting cannies. She slashed out with her knife, wheeling, keeping them at arm's length. She knew she didn't have a chance, but she was determined to send at least one more of the bastards to hell.

"If we all jump her at once, we can git her," said a lanky, long-haired flesheater.

He should have stepped back before he opened his mouth.

Mildred plunged the point of her blade into his throat, driving it in to the hilt, then ripping it out. As blood spurted from between his grimy fingers and jetted from between his clenched teeth, she was struck in the side of the neck by a club.

The blow wasn't hard enough to knock her out, but it staggered her and she lowered her knife point. The cannies had their opening and jumped her en masse.

She fought back, stabbing, kicking, punching and elbowing. Every time she drove one of the bastards back, or dropped one to his knees, another leaped forward to take his place. There were too many of them. When her strength finally faltered, the sheer weight of their bodies drove her to the ground and pinned her there. Cannies jerked her hands behind her back and tied them tightly, wrist to wrist. They tied her ankles together, too, but left a couple of feet of slack between them, which kept her from running, but not from walking.

After they dragged her off Jak, one of them snatched hold of his white hair and jerked up his head. The albino groaned and opened his ruby eyes.

"White meat's still kicking," the cannie said with glee.

Before Jak could do anything, they rolled him onto his belly, pinned him and trussed him up the same way they had Mildred.

When the cannies stepped away from them, Mildred saw a familiar, scar-faced bastard bend and pick up her ZKR 551 and Jak's Colt Python. Junior Tibideau admired the blasters briefly before tucking them into the waistband of his trousers. So, Mildred thought bitterly, leaving him to run at large in the swamp was a grand error.

The fight inside the cave was still raging. There was no way to tell who was winning.

Mildred and Jak were hoisted to their feet as a tall man in a long duster stepped from the trees. He carried a Galil assault rifle, a folding stock, in decent condition. Hanging around his neck on a lanyard was a single-shot, exposed hammer, centerfire shotgun. The rear stock had been sawed off right behind the pistol grip and the barrel cut even with the foregrip.

When the other cannies stepped aside to let the tall one pass, Mildred looked at him closely. Such deference was usually shown only to a feared commander. A gray stubble covered his jaws and scalp; his high forehead was streaked with sweaty grime. Around his throat, hanging down in dozens of coils like a breastplate, was a necklace made of drilled and strung human teeth. There were hundreds of them.

"Don't just stand there," he snarled at the others, peeling back his lips to display a set of strong teeth. "Get this meat moving."

The cannies shoved Mildred and Jak forward, forcing them deeper into the woods. In a small clearing hidden in the trees, the flesheaters had gathered the living and the dead. Ten battered and wounded Cajun men and women stood to one side, trussed hand and ankle. In a pile on the ground in the middle of the open space were the newly chilled of both sides. Some of the Cajun snipers were in pieces.

A group of cannies labored over the bodies; when they saw their leader emerge from the trees, they doubled their efforts.

Mildred thought she had steeled herself for the worst. She was wrong. She looked on the doings in horror and shock. These debased creatures weren't just well-organized, they had reduced the handling of large numbers of cadavers to industrial, mass production simplicity. They worked in squads of three. One cannie held a corpse's ankles stacked one on top of the other. A second flesheater positioned a foot-long iron spike against the top ankle. A third drove the spike through both sets of bones and into the ground with a single slam of a sledgehammer. Long traces for dragging the body were looped around the protruding ends of the spike. They repeated the process with speed and precision, until all the corpses were ready for transport. The loose body parts were then tossed into net bags, which were likewise rigged for dragging. Nothing edible went to waste.

Mildred looked at Jak. Although she couldn't read his eyes, she could read the tendons jumping like cables in his neck and forearms. The wild child didn't like being tied up, and he purely hated cannies. The blood on his scalp had clotted into a dark mass.

"Hurt?" she asked him softly.

The albino shook his head.

Muffled blasterfire continued to roll from the direction of the cave.

"Ryan's still alive," Mildred told him. "He has to be."

The head cannie waved his Galil in the air. "Let's get out of here," he ordered his packmates.

Some of the flesheaters slipped their arms through the loops of the tow ropes and headed off into the forest at a trot, dragging the bodies by the ankles, face up, heads bouncing on the ground, arms trailing limply behind.

The other cannies shoved the survivors into a single-file line and herded them forward with rifle butts. Walking was difficult with the short traces on their ankles.

It surprised Mildred that the bastards wouldn't help their brethren finish the job in the cave. Perhaps they figured that chilling was in the bag, too. Perhaps they were following an already agreed-on plan to split up. Or perhaps they were skipping out with the goods while they still could, in anticipation of a furious Cajun counterattack?

After they had traveled a hundred yards or so, the cannies doing the towing lighted a dozen lanterns. Rings of white light danced and spun through the trees ahead. The cannies were less worried about being seen than in moving as fast as possible.

Even with the lanterns, finding their way through the woods was problematic. Mildred puzzled over this until she walked past a luminous, pale green glow stick on the ground. When she looked over her shoulder she expected one of the cannies behind to pick up the light stick and erase the trail. When that didn't happen, Mildred felt a faint spark of hope. The trail markers were being left behind for the cave cannies; without the markers, they wouldn't be able to find their way back to the swamp, let alone the road. If the cave cannies lost the fight, those markers would lead the Cajuns and the companions right to them.

When the cannies reached the swamp, the draggers hauled the bodies in behind them. They actually made better time because the corpses floated and there was less resistance. The dozen captives and their captors plunged into the lukewarm, stagnant water, following the bobbing lanterns. Walking was difficult because they couldn't raise their feet very far with just a couple feet of rope between their ankles. The cannies in the lead followed a trail marked by widely spaced light sticks tied to the mangroves.

They hadn't gone very far when Junior Tibideau sloshed up beside Mildred. "Smell that blood in the water, Lambchop?" he asked. "Feeling peckish?"

"Cut my hands free and I'll show you," she said.

"Nah, I don't think so. Not until the oozies come on strong. Then I'm going to turn you loose on your friend White Meat, here. Let you get your hands all messy."

Jak glared in contempt at the scar-faced cannie.

"What are you looking at me like that for?" Junior demanded. "You think you're hot shit because you sucker-punched me? I think it's time for a little payback."

With that, Tibideau jumped on Jak from behind, driving him headfirst into the water. The cannie held him under the surface, easily controlling his bound limbs. Though Jak struggled, he couldn't break free.

Mildred rammed her shoulder into the cannie's ribs, trying to knock him off. She couldn't get any traction in the mud and the ankle bindings prevented her from using the power of her legs.

After a minute or so of three-way struggle, the pack leader rushed forward and broke up the attempted drowning. He grabbed hold of the back of Junior's neck, pulled him off, then hurled him into the mangrove roots.

"You're slowing us down with this bullshit," he told the grinning cannie. "We're still in Cajun territory. They could be coming up on us from behind."

Chapter Seventeen

Cheetah Luis stared down at the dead Cajun fighter as Ryan slowly rose to his feet.

The one-eyed man could sense the headman's sputtering fury; it came off him in almost tangible waves. He was like a frag gren about to blow. Because of all the pain, all the loss he'd witnessed and suffered, Cheetah Luis was a couple hundred miles around the bend of sanity. But the Cajun didn't explode. He'd learned to use the power of his rage, to shape it, to wield it like a splitting maul, which didn't make him any less dangerous, or any less crazy.

"I want a head count," he told Lyla, his chunky female lieutenant. He spoke with the extinguished ganja stick clenched between his teeth. "I want to know exactly who's here and who's gone."

As she moved to do his bidding, Cheetah Luis flicked away his cigarette. His eyes were unfocused, his expression fixed with abject hatred. He was lost in a waking dream of blood and death, sorrow and guilt.

This, Ryan told himself, was the downside to staking a claim in Deathlands, to putting down roots in anticipation of some kind of an unfolding future. Roots by their nature limited action and mobility. Offense automatically became defense. And in the end, if you were committed to die for a piece of dirt, not even a hundred seasoned fighters could ensure success, short or long term. The hellscape was wicked devious, it unleashed wave after wave of constantly shifting attacks until it found or created a soft spot.

Lyla returned a few minutes later, her weathered face pale with shock. "It's worse than we thought," she told Cheetah Luis. "Close to half our folks are missing."

"What?" the head Cajun snarled. "You're sure?"

"I counted twice." Then she began to recite the names of the lost.

The other Cajuns listened to her in dead silence. These were people accustomed to grief, to chilling, but not to a defeat like this. They looked gutshot.

"We have to cut off the head," Ryan told Cheetah Luis after the woman finished listing the missing. "No matter what it costs. None of us stands a chance if we don't chill that cannie queen. Whether the stuff about the power of her blood is true or not, she's the one in charge. She organized all this shit."

"Fucking freezie." The headman spit.

"Face it, Cajun," Ryan said, "this La Golondrina hit the ground running. Who knows who or what she was before the Apocalypse. But she knew what she wanted when she got here, and she knew damn well how to make it happen. No other cannie before her has done what she's done. No other cannie will do it after she's dead. If we take her out, the flesheaters will fall back to their old ways, hunting in small packs, dog-eat-dog, making their living by picking off the weak and the stupid. That's something we can deal with, just like we always have."

Cheetah Luis stared at him for a moment then said, "I've worked hard to keep it together here. To keep the fighters focused. Keep them on the offensive. That's what we Cajuns do best. You push, we push back harder. It's in our nature. What happened tonight is my fault. I should've planned better. I should've seen it coming. I thought we had it covered."

"You can't plan for everything," Ryan told him. "In war, shit always happens."

"Time to get some shit on the other end of the stick," the Cajun said.

Cheetah Luis waved his people closer, then he addressed them in an agitated voice. "You all heard the names read out," he said. "Half of our people have been taken for cannie meat, either chilled or prisoners. Some of our best fighters are gone. Up until now our hit-and-git tactics worked smooth because we had plenty of folks to control our chill zones. When we struck, we overwhelmed the enemy with firepower. We left no survivors. Now our numbers are cut by half. We can't replace any of the people we lost, which means we've got to run smaller, much riskier ops, and to do the same damage to the bastards we have to run a whole lot more of them. If we do that, the odds are stacked against us. It won't be long before the cannie bastards grind us down and shit us out. That's the only future I can see if we don't seize the moment now, if we don't take the fight to the queen bitch. That way, at least if we go out, we go out in a blaze."

His animated rallying speech didn't bring cheers or shouts of enthusiasm from his audience. Sugar-coated suicide was just that. But his logic was irrefutable. Grim-faced, the Cajuns nodded.

"Gather up all the ammo and pipe bombs you can carry," Cheetah Luis told his fighters. "Bring the lanterns, too. The cannies are gonna be hobbled hauling the dead and the prisoners. We'll run 'em down."

The Cajuns really hustled. In a matter of minutes, pursuit was under way through the woods. Ryan, Krysty, J.B., Doc and Sprue ran in the middle of the strung-out pack. Progress stopped when they came across the first light stick tacked to a tree.

"This is how the bastards found their way out," Cheetah Luis said. "How they got in is another story."

"These'll burn out soon," Lyla said, tearing the luminescent stick from the trunk, "but even burned-out, the cannies could use them to find their way back in daylight. Should we pick 'em up as we go? When we get enough gathered, we could send runners to start moving 'em way off to the west, make a false trail deeper into the swamp. Cannies would never find our stronghold again. Find nothing but gators and snakes."

"No point in that," Cheetah Luis told her, "we aren't coming back here, no matter what. Either we take over Marsh Island by daybreak or we're gonna be somebody's bacon."

The question of how the cannies found their way in was answered a short distance farther on.

Lanterns illuminated crude cut marks on tree trunks.

"These are fresh," one of the Cajuns said.

"Somebody tracked us here from the road," Cheetah Luis said. "Left these signs behind for the others to follow. The convoying cannies were too far away to catch up and find our trail."

He turned to Ryan and said, "Mebbe that pet flesheater of yours did the job?"

It was exactly what Ryan was thinking. Junior Tibideau had doubled back on them.

"We should have tracked the bastard when he ran off," the Cajun said.

Again, exactly what Ryan was thinking.

THE SLOG BACK through the swamp was grueling. Even in darkness, the heat and humidity were smothering. Nothing stirred. Not a breath of air. The stagnant water around their legs felt tepid, like lukewarm soup. At one point Ryan thought he heard distant blasterfire ahead of them. The cannies were popping off at something. Then it stopped.

Ryan kept a close watch on the companions. Krysty and J.B. seemed fine. Not happy about the conditions, but fine. Doc was muttering to himself as he walked. Too soft to make out anything but the occasional curse word. The old man's face was flushed, his breathing labored, but he tracked a straight line through the muck. Harlan Sprue was having a much tougher time of it. Because of his weight, his boots sank deeper in the mud. Because of his girth, his body had more resistance through the water. Every step was harder for him. If Doc was breathing hard, Sprue was gasping. He was stubborn, though. Sweating and grunting like a pig, he somehow maintained the pace.   .

As they hurried past a wide mud bank, at the edge of the lanterns' glow a pair of large, wide-set eyes tracked them. Wide-set, low slung eyes that reflected red in the lamp light.

With a tremendous splash, the monster surged into the water.

Everyone turned toward the sound.

Doc raised his hand cannon as a fifteen-foot-long critter swam straight for him. "Not a good choice," he informed the reptile, cocking back the hammer on the Le Mat's barrel.

"No, don't shoot," the Cajun head man said, pushing aside the black-powder blaster's muzzle. "The noise will give us away. Leave it to us."

Four of his fighters moved into position between the alligator and the Cajuns. Two had long wooden poles, and two had substantial clubs with knobbed ends. These were the band's designated gator-getters. While the pair with the poles occupied the monster's fang-lined jaws, the other two stepped in and beat on its head with the clubs. They laid on alternating, sizzling blows with plenty of snap, concentrating on a precise strike point between eyes and back a couple inches.

After a couple of smacks, the gator forgot what he was about. After a couple more smacks the clubs made wet, squishy sounds on impact, which told Ryan the knob ends had to be lead-loaded. The blows crushed the bony skull and scrambled the brains within. As the clubbers quickly retreated, the gator helplessly spun and thrashed. Unable to swim or to even hold its snout out of the water, it slowly drowned.

In the course of the forty-five-minute forced march, this scenario was repeated only two or three times.

"What happened to all your gators?" Krysty asked Cheetah Luis as they waded through the last stagnant pool. "I thought they were as thick as flies in these parts."

"The big ones are already chockfull," he told her. "Off sleeping in the reeds." To make his point, he reached into the mangroves and between two fingers gingerly picked up a bloody shred of clothing. He sniffed at it, made a disgusted face, then tossed it back. "Wildlife put a big-time whupping on them baby-eaters."

They climbed up the slope to the road, along the tunnel hacked into the bush. After crawling on their bellies the last bit, they came out onto the narrow, hidden path. Having fresh air and space above felt good to Ryan. A long convoy roared down the road from the north. They let the wags zoom past, then running low, they advanced single file to the top of the hill.

There was nothing waiting for them when they got there.

The wags were gone.

The prisoners and dead 'uns gone, too.

Ryan examined the crisscrossing tire tracks on the shoulder. They all pointed south, toward Vermillion Bay and La Golondrina.

"The bastards got away," one of the Cajuns said. "Are we still going after them?"

"Hell yes, we're going after them," Cheetah Luis replied. "Got to get us some wheels first. It's twenty miles to the tip of the peninsula, and another ten across the water. Be way past sunup before we get there walking."

"Set up a barricade?" Sprue asked.

"Won't work, they'd just crash through it. Even if we stopped a wag or two that way, they'd be in bad shape. Either wrecked or shot to shit. Don't worry, we've pulled this off a dozen times before. And it's worked perfect every time."

Cheetah Luis led Ryan and the others to the brush on the far side of the road. "Make yourselves to home," he said as they slipped into cover.

Behind them on the road, three Cajuns handed their blasters to their comrades. Then they laid down in the middle of the tarmac. One lay on his side, one on his belly, and one on his back, heads all pointing in different directions, legs tangled up.

They looked like they had just fallen off a speeding meat wag.

Which was the whole idea.

"These cannies coming back from Marsh Island," Cheetah Luis said, "are all heading back out to join the hunt. The bastards are always hungry. And they can't pass up easy pickings."

"If you've run this trick so many times," Ryan said, "how come the cannies never figured out it's a trap?"

"None of them ever lived to tell the tale," the Cajun told him. "We start fresh every time."

It didn't take long for more headlights to appear on the road from the south. A three-wag convoy rumbled their way. As it got closer, Ryan could see a dilapidated SUV in the lead, and two full-size pickups behind.

For a second Cawdor thought they were going to

roll right over the possum-playing Cajuns. Then the SUV hit the brakes, forcing the other wags to do the same. They came to a stop almost directly across from the companions' hiding place, engines idling.

Ryan counted four cannies in the metallic sand-colored SUV, backlit by the high beams from behind. The second wag had that many packed into the front seat; eight more in the pickup's bed were spotlighted by the headlights of the last wag. He couldn't see much of the second pickup.

The SUV's driver and passenger doors swung open. Two scrawny females jumped out with drawn hand-blasters. They walked around the front of their wag and looked down at the bodies caught in the head-lights. The driver said something in a hoarse voice that Ryan couldn't quite hear, but it made the passen-ger laugh. The driver turned to the wags behind and waved.

Somebody back there let out a yee-hah of delight.

The cannies hopped down from the pickup beds and cabs, and the other two passengers climbed from the SUV. As they pulled out long knives to divide the spoils, the Cajuns opened fire, angling their shots due south so as not to hit their comrades on the other side of the road.

Ryan, J.B., Krysty, Sprue and Doc didn't participate in the slaughter. There was no need. Beside them, Cheetah Luis cut loose with his M-16.

Careful to keep from hitting the tires, fuel tanks and engine compartments, the Cajuns stitched autofire through the cannies. The SUV driver and passenger went down first, hit by so many bullets that their torsos were practically cut in two. The torrent of slugs peeled the rest of the flesheaters off the wags and sent them crashing to the road. It was over in fifteen seconds. The cannies hadn't managed to return a single shot.

The Cajuns lying on the road jumped up and those hiding in the brush stepped out from concealment. They quickly turned over the bodies, making sure the cannies were dead. Occasionally a handblaster popped off, making double sure.

"Check the gas tanks," Cheetah Luis shouted to his fighters. He looked into the SUV's driver door for a second. "Got plenty of gas here."

The other wags were full-up, too.

"Get the bodies off the road," Cheetah Luis said, waving his machete. As his fighters began dragging the corpses into the brush, he knelt over one of the dead. He stretched out the arms on the tarmac, then with two deft chops of the machete, severed both hands at the wrist.

"Why did you do that?" Krysty exclaimed. "Are you taking trophies?"

"Nah." He shook the blood off the stumps and laid the hands on the SUV's floorboards in front of the driver's seat. "Meat wags always give out free samples."

When the road was clear of corpses, Cheetah Luis divided his fighters and the companions between the three wags. J.B., Doc and Sprue laid down in the first pickup's bed with five Cajuns and played dead. Ryan and Krysty got in the SUV with Cheetah Luis. Cawdor took the shotgun seat, with the Steyr propped between his knees. Krysty sat behind him in the rear; beside her was Lyla, the Cajun's chubby lieutenant.

The Cajun K-turned the SUV, then headed south. The other wags followed him.

Ryan stuck his head out the window and let the wind whip over his face. The rush of air felt cool through his sweaty hair. Overhead, the stars were disappearing behind a blanket of cottony clouds. The road was deserted. They traveled down a narrow tunnel created by the SUV's high beams. Ryan actually drifted off to sleep despite the jolting of the wag. He awoke every time a convoy heading north whooshed past. It didn't happen often, and he managed to sneak some much-needed rest.

Half an hour later, Cheetah Luis tapped the brakes. Ahead of them was a string of red taillights. Ten other wags were stopped on the road. No doubt the convoy they'd seen barreling over the hilltop. Beyond the wags was the foot of a bridge that spanned a wide strip of dark water. A mile or more, was Ryan's guess.

"We've got to go over that bridge," Cheetah Luis said.

"Looks like somebody's directing traffic," Ryan said.

"First one way, then the other," the Cajun said.

"What about the people in the back of the trucks?" Krysty asked.

"They'll be just fine," Cheetah Luis told her, "as long as they stay down and don't move. The cannies won't look at them that close. They've been the top dogs around here so long they don't expect this kind of trouble coming in their front door."

As they crept toward the bridge, Ryan saw a battered signpost beside the road that read Intercoastal Waterway. When they were three wags from the cannie directing traffic with an AK-47, he got a good look at the looming structure. There was no guard rail on the right lane. No right lane, either. That side of the predark bridge had fallen off into the water.

As they waited their turn to cross, Ryan took in the cannie traffic cop. He was bug-eyed, with long, greasy hair, a fat, pale face and wispy, dirty-blond beard. He wore a long, cream-colored duster and knee-high rubber boots. The cannie shifted the assault rifle from sling to hand and swaggered toward them.

"Shit," Ryan said, easing his SIG-Sauer from its holster and dropping the safety.

"Leave this to me," the Cajun said. "Don't do anything. Don't say a word."

Cheetah Luis waved out his open window and smiled as the cannie stepped up.

"Nice night for a luau," the traffic director said, pointing the muzzle of his AK toward the sky.

"Brought along the appetizers," the Cajun said, jerking a thumb at the truck lined up behind him.

"Damn, I love finger food," the cannie said.

"Lots of toes back there, too."

The traffic director reached under his coat and pulled out a pair of long-handled side-cutters. "Mind if I snip off a couple? Been a long time since I had my dinner. Don't know when I'm going to get my next meal."

"Why don't I just give you a hand?" Cheetah Luis said, reaching down to the floorboards for one of the pair he had removed. He passed it out the window. "That's fresh as they come."

"Thanks."

"No problem, we got plenty."

"You can go on ahead, now. Take it slow. Keep well to the left. That bridge ain't what it used to be."

"See you later."

The cannie mock-saluted Cheetah Luis with the severed hand. "Y'all drive safe, now," he said, grinning.

The SUV started to roll.

"Flesheatin' asshole," Ryan said as he reholstered his handblaster.

Cheetah Luis shifted into second gear and left it there. The bridge didn't start to shake until all three wags were on it. Ryan could hear the structure groaning and shrieking over the sound of the engines. And he could hear stuff falling off, chunks of concrete and asphalt splashing into the water below.

When they reached the other side, the Cajun shifted to third, then fourth. The SUV rapidly picked up speed. Beyond the traffic waiting its turn at the foot of the bridge, the road ahead was empty. The three-wag convoy traveled without incident for seven more miles, then they came up over a rise that revealed the end of the road. And more.

Across a wide, black bay, Ryan could see orange lights dancing on the far horizon. Bonfires, he thought. And they had to be huge to be visible this far away.

"That it?" Ryan said.

"That's it," Cheetah Luis replied.

"Long swim," Ryan said.

Chapter Eighteen

Rows of headlights swept past on the two-lane highway, lighting up the abandoned meat wags parked on the shoulder. One of the drivers honked long and loud. The wail trailed away as the convoy barreled north.

Ahead of Mildred, the cannies were dragging the bodies and parts bags down the side of the road. Circumstances dictated that they had to do their own dirty work. They hadn't tried to force the Cajun prisoners to haul the dead. With the extra weight and their bound ankles, they would have moved even more slowly, allowing any pursuit the chance to catch up. And if the cannies had cut the ankle ties, their captives would have scattered for the brush in all directions, and many would have gotten away.

Even though the ropes on Mildred's feet were soaked, the knots hadn't loosened a bit. She had rope burns on the outside of her ankles from the friction of the long march.

En route, alligators had taken down cannies in spectacular fashion. If, as Cheetah Luis had said, live Cannie butt smelled like fresh-baked bread to gators, dead Cajuns had to have smelled like raspberry jam. The reptiles ignored the bound prisoners and ripped away corpses, tow ropes and corpse pullers. These were huge animals, possibly mutated, well over twenty-feet-long, easily eight hundred pounders. And they were hell-bent on dinner. Streams of bullets only angered them; the cannies who stood their ground and kept shooting got their heads crushed to pulp by the monsters' back teeth. That tactic was abandoned after the first disastrous try. All they could do was flee while the beasts were otherwise occupied with the unlucky.

At the head of the line of parked wags were three full-size pickups. The cannies hoisted the corpses by their hands and feet and swung them into the beds.

Beyond the pickups were three small semi-tractor-trailers. The trailers were vented with thousands of holes. In predark times they had been used to haul cattle to slaughter. The cannies shoved and booted their shellshocked, bitten and bleeding captives up the rear ramps and into the trailers.

There were already people inside the first trailer. Waiting. They got shoved to the front as the cannies packed in the newcomers. It was either stand up or be stepped on.

Mildred looked into the dirty faces. Some were frightened. Some were blank, dead-eyed—the ones who had already given up. It smelled bad, not just from fear sweat. The wags had been sitting on the side of the road while the cannies went hunting for more victims to top off their load. The trailer's grated floor could have served as a toilet if the people inside hadn't been bound hand and foot. As it happened, the only toilet was in their pants.

With a roar the meat wag engines started up. A dozen headlights blasted deep into the night.

Apparently the cannies weren't going to wait around for the cave crew to join them. Not in this neighborhood. If the companions were coming to rescue them, they were too late, Mildred thought. She and Jak were on their own, to the bitter end.

The cattle wag lurched forward onto the road. The bodies crammed inside swayed into one another. With hands tied behind them, the prisoners couldn't avoid the contact. The steady vibration of the wheels on pavement rattled up through the metal floor and walls.

The glare of headlights from behind poured through the trailer's holes. The captive Cajuns had banded together, shoulder to shoulder, them against the world.

Even though Jak stood beside Mildred, she couldn't see his pupils. She didn't know if he had suffered a serious head injury. The bleeding from his scalp had stopped, leaving a crusty scab in his snow-white scalp.

"How's your head?" she asked him.

"Hurts some," he said.

"Seeing double? Feeling weak?"

"Nope."

Mildred felt better upon hearing that. It meant he probably didn't have a concussion.

"They gonna pay," the albino said flatly.

Jak's forehead was smooth. He wasn't frightened. He wasn't angry. He was determined. Many times Mildred had seen him dance the dance, slipping like a shadow between attacking adversaries, chilling with his leaf-bladed knives and that big Colt of his. She also knew Jak could get down to business with much less.

A piece of sharp metal. A chunk of concrete. A length of power cord. If he had his hands free...

Standing there, packed in like a sardine, with the breeze blocked by hot bodies, Mildred started feeling sick again. Hot. Jangly. Weak. Maybe even a little scared. She had to get her mind on something else.

"Where are you from?" she asked the skinny young woman leaning against her right side.

"Does it matter?"

In the glare of headlights, Mildred saw matted hair, thick makeup and garish lipstick, mascara smeared into raccoon eyes. The woman wore a short skirt that barely covered her bottom and a flimsy blouse; her hightop black sneakers were laced with electrical wire. There were fresh and old bruises on her thighs and knees, and on her bare arms.

"Cannies do that to you?"

"No, paying customers riled up on jolt did that. Like to pound with their fists while they're pounding you with the other thing. Working in a gaudy house is a shitty life." Then to Mildred's surprise and dismay, she giggled dementedly. "I made a funny."

"Yeah."

The slut tilted her head around Mildred to look at Jak. "He a mutie?" she asked. "How come he's so white?"

"Got hit hard in the head," Mildred told her. "Made him go pale."

"Made his eyes all bloody like that, too?"

"Uh-huh."

"Can he still see?"

"Sure."

"He's not a stupe, is he?"

The slut leaned toward Jak and bellowed in his face, "You're not a stupe, are you?"

"He understands what you're saying. You don't have to shout."

"Can talk, too," Jak told her, smiling a crooked smile. Then his face went as blank as an empty page.

"I come from Texas," the slut said. "That's where the cannies got me. Shot all hell out of the gaudy I was working in. Walked in the door and started blasting away. I was under a customer at the time, big old boy. He got hit in the back, died right on top of me. Cannies pulled him off and loaded him in a wag with the rest of the dead. Put me in this trailer."

"Everybody here come from Texas?" Mildred asked those around them.

"We're from Arkansas," some folks answered.

"Louisiana."

"Sippi."

"We been on the road for two weeks," said a short man who was pressed against the trailer wall. "Rained on. Shit on. Pissed on. Starved."

Mildred looked up at the trailer roof. It, too, was ventilated.

"Bastards pour the crap food they feed us through them holes," the little man told her. "Make us fight for it like animals."

"Hard to fight with your hands tied," Mildred said.

"Hard to eat, too. Most of it falls through the floor."

Mildred gathered what information she could from the prisoners willing to talk. They were young and old, early teens to late seventies. Dirt farmers. Gaudy sluts and pimps. Swineherds. Sec men. Merchants. Scroungers. All caught up in the cannie net. All had doom in their eyes.

"We only got one thing going in our favor," said the old man from Arkansas.

"What's that?"

"Damned cannies got to eat all the dead 'uns before they eat us. We won't spoil, but the dead 'uns will."

Wedged in behind her was a fat merchant. Beside him was a little parakeet of a woman. Her stare was fixed, like a doll's. "Michelle's been like that ever since we got taken," he told Mildred. The concentric rolls of his lower face shivered as he spoke; they had a greasy sheen. "She don't eat. Don't sleep. Just stares like that. She hardly ever blinks. I keep telling myself mebbe it's all for the best. Mebbe she won't feel it when they start to chill her. Then I get scared and think mebbe she'll come out of it right when the pain starts."

The woman was textbook catatonic. Trauma and terror had caused her mind to crash in on itself. The prognosis was grim. To change the subject Mildred said, "What did you do in Sippi?"

"We sold this and that from our shack in Poplarville. Scavenged predark items mostly. Farm tools, weapons, ammo, black powder. Also did a good trade in tobaccy and joy juice." The fat man was talking fast, the words spilling out of his small, nearly lipless mouth. "Me and Michelle worked the shack inside Poplarville for ten years. Had lots of friends thereabouts. No complaints about my fairness. I'm not a hard dealer, too easy was what Michelle always said. But I figured life's too short to do people harsh…"

He shuddered, then said, "Not that it mattered in the end. Cannies came and took it all away. Rammed the gate with a 6x6 wag. Jumped out of the back and started chilling. They shot down the folks with blasters right away, then used their knives on anyone still fighting.

"I seen firsthand what they done to my friends and neighbors after they were dead. Cut 'em like hogs around the neck and let the blood drain out. Strung 'em up by their feet and let it drip on the ground. Cannies aren't like us. They aren't human. They look at someone hurting, mebbe screaming, and it gives 'em joy. When they smell blood and guts, it don't make 'em sick, it makes 'em hungry."

"Try to relax, breathe deep and slow," Mildred told him. "You can't help Michelle if you give yourself a heart attack."

She turned away. She couldn't help him. She couldn't help herself. Dust thrown up by the wags in front filtered through the trailer's ventilated roof and walls in a steady stream. The constant vibration and the noise numbed the captives. Some of them actually slept on their feet, held up by the bodies around them.

Mildred knew they were heading south, so when the convoy stopped at the foot of the bridge, she could guess what it spanned. The Intercoastal Waterway. A highway for boat traffic, commercial and recreational, before the Apocalypse. After a few minutes, the cattle wag pulled onto the ruined bridge and crossed the wide channel at a crawl. Because of the low speed, there was little dust to eat. The air smelled of salt and sea. The Gulf of Mexico was close at hand.

They drove for another quarter of an hour, then stopped again. This time, with wag engines idling and headlights blazing, the rear doors of Mildred's trailer opened and cannies climbed in, pulling, shoving, forcing their prisoners to hobble down the ramp.

In headlights, Mildred could see the black water of the Gulf, the shoreline, and a makeshift dock. Tied to the dock was a motorized barge, the kind used to haul gravel or sand. While the prisoners were lined up single file, one by one, the pickups backed up to the bow of the barge, then the cannies rolled the dead 'uns off tailgates onto the deck.

Next to one of the pickups, Mildred saw Junior Tibideau. The scar-faced cannie was evidently back in his master's good graces. He stood beside the cannie commander, grinning.

When the dead were loaded, the living were marched down to the water and onto the boat. The troughlike foredeck was heaped with corpses. The captives were herded toward the tiny wheelhouse at the opposite end. They stood there, sweating.

On the horizon, Mildred could sees the fires burning on Marsh Island. She had never been there, but she had read something about it in a magazine, some controversy about the drilling of a natural gas well on the edge of a state wildlife refuge. It wasn't the kind of place tourists went. There were no hotels. No residences. It had no scenic charm unless you liked bugs, gators and snakes. It was just a lump of marshy land sticking up out of the Gulf.

When the cargo was safely onboard, the cannies cast off the lines and the barge backed away from the dock. For a second, caustic diesel smoke billowed over the deck, then the barge turned and motored forward, heading for the distant firelights.

The water was as smooth as a black mirror. The barge made good time. The wind rushing over the open deck cooled down the huddled captives. When they were about two miles off the island, Mildred heard the sound of drumming. Insistent. Repetitive. And she smelled something wafting from the shore.

Wood smoke and roasting meat.

The instant she was hit by that odor, stark, grainy images flooded her mind. Images of Auschwitz and Rwanda, her only frames of reference. But this was worse than the genocides of a century ago. Worse because the mass chilling wasn't the end of it. The chilling was just the beginning of the evil. The smell engulfed the barge; there was no escape from it. When she breathed through her mouth, she could taste it in the back of her throat. To her horror, out of the blue, she began to salivate.

Fight it, fight it, fight it, Mildred commanded herself, digging her nails into her palms until tears came to her eyes. She focused on the sharp pain until her head stopped spinning.

The barge ducked into a cove on the island's northeast corner, the entrance bracketed by bonfires. Dense plumes of smoke rose straight up into the still night air.

The captives were ushered out onto the narrow beach. Above the sloping shelf of white sand the land was as flat as a tabletop. The drumming was louder and more distinct. Mildred could pick out the rhythmic pattern. Boom-boom-chank. Boom-boom-chank. It reminded her of a rock-song-turned-spectator-sport anthem that had been played countless times at every stadium in the United States. Only there was no singing or chanting now, just the drumming.

After the bodies had been dumped on the sand, the cannies moved among the captives, using knives to cut through the ankle ropes that hobbled them. It wasn't an act of kindness because there was nowhere to run. It was so they could tow the dead.

Junior Tibideau put the loops of rope in Jak's and Mildred's hands. He seemed quite pleased with himself. "Giddy up!" he said, kicking the albino in the butt to urge him on.

As they climbed the slope to the flatland, they didn't look back at who they were dragging. They could see what the slut and the short man ahead of them pulled by the heels. A rubbery, human-shaped bag of bones.

Atop the table of land, there wasn't a single tree in sight. There was no cover above ground. She and Jak followed a dirt path polished slick by dredges of human skin and bone. In the leaping light of the fires, Mildred observed the terrain on either side of the track. It was irregular, potholed with standing water and probably quicksand. Drainage cuts brimming with brine crisscrossed the plain. And there were large ponds. In the daytime Marsh Island would be swarming with mosquitoes, deer flies and no-see-ums. It was the kind of place where alligators happily bred and grew fat. Mixed with the smell of meat cooking was the stench of rotting fish and rotting vegetation. Far ahead, Mildred could see dots of elevated light that marked a structure. The light was too dim to see the exact outlines, but given the distance, it had to be enormous.

With their cannie minders following, the prisoners trudged on, over the winding path. It took a long time to get close enough to the structure to clearly make it out. Mildred figured they had walked about five miles towing a deadweight when she recognized the immense, hulking shape of a grounded oceangoing freighter. Torches burning along the rails and bonfires on the marsh below illuminated it.

A jumble of steel cargo containers had spilled from its deck onto the marsh. They were the source of vile, sweetish aroma. The cannies had converted them into smoke houses. This was where the flesheaters cured their road food.

About a hundred yards from the ship, the dirt path turned gleaming white. It looked like it was paved with alabaster cobblestones. Only when Mildred was actually standing on it did she realize she was walking on the tops of human skulls. Thousands upon thousands of them. Too many for this operation to have produced. They had to have been collected from the neutron-bombed coast, from the emptied, intact buildings.

As the captives passed the cargo containers, Mildred looked inside one of the open doorways. Glistening red corpses hung on crosspoles by their heels, arms trussed behind their backs. The bodies had been shaved of all hair. The eyeballs were cooked white. A cannie standing in the doorway dipped a short-handled rag mop in a bucket of reddish liquid, then basted the corpses with it.

Around and between the containers, other cannies danced to the beat of drummers aboard the freighter, whirling, staggering as if drunk. Their faces, hair and beards were shiny with grease, their eyes wild with delight. Piles of stripped clean rib and thigh bones lay scattered at their feet.

"I'm scared," the skinny slut moaned at top volume. "I don't wanna end up like that."

"A little late to start worrying," said the little man at her side. "You won't know what they done to you after you're gone."

"I can't help but think about it," the slut said. "About them touching me, and pulling my meat from the bones…"

"Shut the hell up!" Mildred snarled.

The slut looked back, sulky and hurt, but she stopped whining.

Mildred had no more sympathy to give. A bonfire raged behind her eyes. Every time she breathed in, it felt like she was inhaling molten lava into her lungs. Her mind raced in looping, alarming circles of rationalization and depravity. She was losing her grip on every moral value she had ever claimed. She could feel herself dissolving into something unspeakable. That idea hammered inside the walls of her head. She couldn't push it aside or throttle it. She couldn't deny it.

Mildred would have fallen on her knees and begged Jak to chill her then and there, but there was no way he could comply with his hands tied behind his back.

She flung aside the tow rope, jumped from the trail and took off across the marsh. She could have run faster, but she wasn't trying to get away. She was hoping to catch a mercy bullet in the back.

The cannies did open fire, but only to send a couple of warning shots over her head. When she didn't stop, they chased her down and tackled her, driving her into a shallow pond. They jerked her to her feet and while one bastard held her arms, the other started slapping her in the face. Using the cannie at her back for leverage, she kicked him in the stomach.

As he crumpled, she spit on him.

Reaching behind her back, she got her hands on the other cannie's privates and squeezed as hard as she could. He let out a shrill yelp, then doubled over, gasping for air. When he straightened, she headbutted him a solid blow. By which time the first cannie had recovered. Grabbing her shoulder, he again flung her down into the pond. He put his boot sole on her chest, pinning her on her back.

"That all you got, you big, brave baby-eaters?" she roared up at them, the water lapping in her ears. "You're nothing but droolies, the lot of you. Brain-damaged pieces of shit."

Suicide by proxy was what she was after.

The cannies had no intention of giving it to her. Meat on the hoof was worth a lot more to them than meat on a rope. They hauled her up by her armpits, dragged her to the path and shoved her back in line next to Jak.

"Dropped something," Junior said. He picked up the end of the tow rope and put it in her hand.

The beating had cleared Mildred's head. There was a stinging cut inside her mouth; she tasted her own blood. She felt almost herself again. "I'm glad you didn't try to help," she told Jak.

"Couldn't," the albino said. "Scar-face cannie had Python against head. You wanna die?"

"Better to die than turn into one of them."

"Better chill some first. Pick time, place."

Mildred didn't know how much time she had. That was the problem. At least Jak was offering hope, even if it was just for some token retribution. "Okay," she said. "Chill some first."

The line of corpse haulers moved on, creeping toward the flank of the grounded freighter. Mildred speculated that the terrible tsunamis that followed the Apocalypse had lifted the great ship over the sandy strip of beach and deposited it, high and dry, on top of the marsh land, where it had sat for more than a hundred years. Its main deck and superstructure faced them, canted at about thirty degrees from vertical. The cannies, or more likely their prisoners, had constructed a crude ramp of hard-packed dirt that led from the ground to the freighter's midship gangway.

The drumming from the ship was so loud that Mildred could feel it in her bowels.

On the edge of the bridge wing, lit by torches, she saw a female figure. She could make out long dark hair, white skin, black clothing. The woman was waving her slender arms at the dancing, weaving throng six stories below her.

On the freighter's main deck, cannies cavorted in long lines up and down the gunwhales. They beat in

unison on the rails and hatches with pipes and rods.
Boom-boom-chank! Boom-boom-chank!

It was a celebration.

A lovefest.

Boom-boom-chank!

Under the circumstances, the predark anthem's
threatening lyrics would have been overkill.

Mildred was already rocked.

Chapter Nineteen

Ten wagloads of cannie victims either shuffled under their own power or were dragged by their dead heels onto the waiting barge. With all the prisoners and bodies and the attending cannies, things were chaotic at the water's edge, which made it easy for the Cajuns and companions to slip on board. There was no longer a reason for any of them to play dead. No reason for the cannies to think they were anything but their own dear brethren.

Cannies not in terminal-stage oozies looked exactly like norms. It was a natural camouflage that allowed them to slip into villes unnoticed and do their worst. The hellscape was crawling with filthy, mean and ruthless sons of bitches. For norms to accurately pick cannies out of a crowd they had to see the bastards in action, taking an unholy delight in the chilling, and of course in the eating that came afterward. The difference between norm and cannie was internal, not external. It was behavior.

In this case, the requisite cannie-mimicking wasn't the chilling of the innocent or feeding on human flesh, but in doing nothing to free the ranks of poor, doomed prisoners.

Doing nothing under the circumstances was hard.

Ryan stood next to the tightly packed, trussed human cargo. Men and women, but no children. Cannies ate the children first. The captives were battered, bruised, bitten. Their clothing hung in shreds. The prisoners either looked at their own bound feet or stared off into the black distance. They wouldn't meet a cannie's gaze for fear of being chilled on the spot. They understood they were caught in the grip of pure evil.

Ryan couldn't look at the poor folk without thinking about Jak and Mildred. About what they might be suffering, or if they were already beyond suffering. It was possible that even in the unlikely event that he and the Cajuns won the battle, his two friends would never be found. Not if they were already dead and their stripped bones were tossed on a pile to bleach in the sun. But he would face that when it came to pass.

There was another possibility, of course. One that was even worse. It was possible that Mildred had succumbed to the oozies, that the good doctor had turned cannie.

Ryan pushed the thought out of his head. Again, he would face that when and if the time came. There were other, more pressing priorities. He had been in the belly of the beast hundreds of times before, places where death loomed on all sides, where survival was measured in split seconds. But he had never encountered anything quite like this. He had never seen organized chilling on this large a scale, like a vast meat grinder into which the population of Deathlands was being slowly poured. That the manifest evil was the product of a disease couldn't excuse it, and it didn't buy those infected a free pass. The disease had to be stamped out. Its victims had to be stamped out, too.

It appeared that the easy part was going to be getting in. All around him, Cajuns with loaded assault rifles sat on heavy packs crammed full of ammo and explosives. No one in charge bothered to check them or the contents of their luggage. Finding out what they had under their butts wouldn't have produced an alarm, anyway. Cannies carried blasters, ammo and explosives all the time. It was how they made their daily bread.

"Where's your meat?" said a raspy voice behind him.

Ryan turned to face a big, rawboned woman. She wore her coarse, white-streaked hair in a braid as thick as a mooring line. Her chisel-edged front teeth were the color of sulfur, she had a bulbous nose and there was a spray of whiskers on her chin. She wore her blaster—a 20-gauge Ithaca Stakeout pump gun—on a lanyard around her neck. The muzzle dangled between her trouser-clad legs, suggestive of another distinctive male feature. The front of her duster was decorated with black blotches of dried blood.

"In a pile at the other end of the barge," Ryan said.

"Got any near-goners in your pack?"

"No, nobody's that bad off."

"You're lucky. Three of mine are laying over there, half dead. Haven't taken the cure yet."

Ryan glanced over at the sick cannies. They were

sitting on the deck with their backs leaning against the low gunwhale, barely able to hold up their heads. Gray spindles of mucous connected their noses to their chins and their chins to their chests.

"Not a pretty sight," the woman said. "They're too weak to hunt. Have to hand-feed 'em. Go on, Luther, give 'em some more…"

The cannie standing next to the terminal cases reached into a parts bag and pulled out a handful of something slimy and tubular. He pressed down on a gray-smeared chin to open the mouth and packed in the goodies.

Gobble gobble.

"Used to be we'd chill 'em when they got like that," the woman said. "We'd crack their heads and eat the brains for pudding."

"Yeah," Ryan agreed.

The fully loaded barge backed away from the dock, then reversed course and headed for the firelights on the horizon.

"Know why?" the cannie asked.

"Sure. They were checking out, anyway. Might as well put the meat to good use."

"Nah. We'd do it even when we weren't hungry, even when we had some fresh chilled hanging close by. We did it because looking at them poor, weak, sick fucks we was seeing ourselves, how we'd end up, and we was scared shitless. And purely hating every minute of it. We was like a dog biting off its own tail out of pure cussedness. La Golondrina changed all that. She freed us from the Gray Death. She pulled us together and made us a people. Made us a cannie nation."

The cannie hag's eyes suddenly got all misty. It wasn't a pleasant sight. "La Golondrina is our life," she said. "Our hope."

It confirmed one of Ryan's long-standing beliefs: one person's hope was somebody else's hell on wheels.

"None of my crew has taken the cure," Ryan told her, "but we're all about to. We never been here before. Come a long ways to get the job done."

"She'll do more than stop your nose from dripping, One Eye," the woman said. "She'll get inside you and wind up your spring, I guarantee it. The sound of her voice is something you will never forget as long as you live. It thrills the soul. It makes you want to march to her call."

"She's the one who planned all this, right?" Ryan said. "Took some doing. Some brains. Does she ever hunt the road?"

"Not anymore," the woman said. "She don't come out during the day much. I've never seen her up close, myself. She stays on the bridge of her ship. It's like a tower. When the medicine's ready, it's brought down to the deck and passed around to the pilgrims."

"You ever been up in that tower?"

"Nobody's allowed up there except her special guards. The same ones she took up with when she first got here. Her original pack. Angels of Death, she calls them. They aren't folks to mess with. Got no sense of humor, believe me. They carry these big old swords with curved blades. Razor-sharp from tip to basket."

"Cutlasses?"

"Yeah, that's it. One swipe and your head's off clean, or split in two, crown to chin, still sitting on your neck."

"Thanks, I'll keep a lookout for them."

Ryan heard the steady rumble from across the water. "What is that noise?" he asked.

"It's cannies drumming. La Golondrina likes it when we swarm the deck of her ship and drum in her honor. That ship is the only shelter on the island. It's where we all stay during the pilgrimage. We store the live and dead meat inside the cargo holds. Dead meat stays fresh about a week after gutting and bleeding."

"Ship don't float, from what I hear."

"Ain't going anywhere, that's for sure. It's sitting on mostly dry land. Except for the bottom, which is buckled some, the ship came through the skydark in good shape. It's rusting in places because we got no paint, but the hull's so thick it'd take another hundred years to wear through. There's plenty of fuel oil left in its bunkers. And gasoline, too. It was part of the pre-dark cargo. We use it to fuel the convoys."

Ryan was suddenly all too aware of the doomed ones standing behind him, heads down, eyes closed, listening as the hag merrily jabbered away. He could imagine how sick at heart they were, knowing she would be jabbering on tomorrow and they and those they loved would be humble pie.

The cannie with the parts bag wandered over to them.

"You want some?" the stumpy bastard said, holding up a handful of wet, gray intestine.

Ryan didn't flinch. He didn't blink his good eye.

"No, thanks," he said. "I just ate. Gotta go check on my crew."

"See you later," the woman said.

"Count on it."

Krysty, J.B. and Sprue were up in the barge's bow, bent over, tinkering with their gear and trying their best not to pay attention to what was going on behind them. Doc was clearly having trouble ignoring the situation. Head lowered, he paced up and down the length of the starboard side deck in long, impatient strides. As he did so, he kept shifting his ebony sword stick from one hand to the other. Ryan could read the body language and the facial expression as Doc took in the lounging, carefree cannies. He wanted to draw his rapier blade and do some well-placed stabbing.

Ryan stopped the time traveler with a hand and pulled him aside.

"You've got to get a hold of yourself, Doc," he said, leaning close, "or you're going to get us all chilled."

"We are crossing the River Styx," Doc rasped back at him, his eyes alight with fury, and perhaps even a touch of madness. "On the far side, the gates of hell await."

"Doc, you're—"

"Listen to that drum beat," Doc interrupted. "Do you know what it presages? Do you have any idea? Ryan, this goes beyond the pale of mere recreational savagery, of the diversionary barbarism to which we have become hardened. This horror is biblical in its scope. What we face is irrefutable evidence that Satan not only exists, that he walks our cursed earth in human form."

"You know I don't believe in those predark tales, Doc," Ryan said. "I can't believe in something I can't see. Look around, for nuke's sake. This is exactly what people do to each other. What they have always done to each other."

"Not so, my boy."

"Any evil that humankind can imagine will come to pass," Ryan said with conviction. "The slaughter of defenseless millions. The flameout of two thousand years of civilization. The destruction of the planet. All products of the hand of man. No devil required."

"In that case I am afraid we are utterly lost. There is no hope of victory or salvation. If this evil resides inside us all, we can never escape it. That you could think such a thing sorely grieves me, my dear friend."

"In your time and in Mildred's," Ryan told him, "people still believed that something could stand between them and their black deeds. A buffer. An explanation. A robed ritual. A way to lift the weight of their guilt for actions or inactions. An illusion to give them comfort so they could keep on doing what they were doing in good conscience. This is my time, Doc, and I don't need that kind of comfort. I bear no guilt for the blood I've shed in the past and the blood I'll shed tonight. I have the right to survive because I breathe."

He patted the butt of his holstered SIG. "My only salvation lies here."

"Then tell me," Doc countered, "why are we crossing this water to do battle if in the end the entire enterprise is pointless, if humanity is already doomed by its own corrupt nature?"

"You know the answer to that. Because our friends have a right to survive, too."

At that, Doc seemed to gather himself. "Yes, of course," he said. "Mildred and Jak. Mildred and Jak. We must recover them." He was silent for a moment, then said, "Ryan, daily I am reminded that I have lived far too long for my own good, that what I am being forced to witness and take part in is something I was never meant to see, let alone comprehend."

"Accept it, and move on. It's the hand you have been dealt. You can't change it."

"Yes, yes, that is the only way to proceed."

Krysty stepped up beside Ryan as Doc drifted slowly away, apparently lost in sober reflection.

"Is he going to be all right?" she asked with concern.

"I don't know. It might not matter."

Before she could ask for more details, Cheetah Luis joined them. "Stay together after we land," he said. "Let the captives go ahead of us."

"What's the terrain going to be like?" Cawdor said.

"It's as flat as the bottom of a washtub. Mostly salt marsh. Soft muck covered with seagrass. You don't want to step off the path, take my word for it. We lost some brave fighters that way."

Ahead, bonfires framed the entrance to the landing cove.

When the bow of the barge crunched up against the bank, the cannie crew jumped out and made the bowlines fast, tying them to clustered wooden posts driven deep into the sand. Standing on the deck, Ryan could see over the level of the beach. He stared at a featureless plain dotted by towering blazes. In the distance far to the south, a string of orange points of light winked at him. Elevated points of light, defining a vague hulking shape.

The queen's freighter.

"Why didn't they put us ashore over there?" he asked the Cajun.

"There's no place to land a boat on the southeast tip of the island," Cheetah Luis said. "If they tried, they'd run aground a mile or two offshore, have to wade in from there, and deal with all the gators and sharks. That's why we walk."

In groups of three and four, the prisoners were shoved off the bow and onto the sand. Some tripped and fell when they hit, knocking others down. Cannies with machetes moved through their ranks, chopping through their ankle restraints.

Under any other circumstances, that would have been a positive development.

The cannies put tow ropes in the prisoners' hands and forced them at blasterpoint to drag corpses up the sand to the path. They weren't concerned about the captives running away. They wanted them to be able to take longer steps, thereby hauling the bodies faster.

When Ryan and the others mounted the path at the end of the line, they glimpsed a grim, sodden landscape. A marsh pocked with pools of water, fingers of it crept trickling downhill into the sea. There was not only nowhere to run, there was nowhere to hide.

"Gators out there in the marsh," Cheetah Luis told them. "That's where the real monsters come to breed. The thirty-footers. They don't like it one bit when you come near their nests. And there's quicksand and plenty of poison snakes, too. During the day the biting bugs come down on your head like a sack and suck you dry."

"Why didn't La Golondrina move off this stinking pile of shit after she got control of part of the mainland?" Sprue said.

"Who knows what she's thinking or planning?" the Cajun said. "I'll tell you one thing—it's a rad-blasted place to attack. We learned that the hard way. Have to come by water. It's the only route. Have to carry everything you need on your back, and when you run out, you're shit out of luck. There's no cover to fight behind on the way in. And she's got that steel ship to pull back and hide in. No reason for the bitch to budge an inch."

"Mebbe she's waiting until cannies control the whole hellscape to make her move," Krysty suggested. "Then she can sail across the Gulf on that barge and step ashore the queen of Deathlands."

A cannie nation, Ryan thought, but didn't say. He didn't have to. They were all thinking the same thing.

"Sooner or later there won't be any more humans left," Sprue said, putting the shared thought into words. "What are the stinking bastards going to eat when that happens?"

"Mebbe they're not thinking that far ahead," J.B. said.

"Mebbe they are," Ryan said. "And we just don't know what they've got in mind."

"Mebbe then they'll start eating each other," the convoy master said. "That'd be sweet. Too bad none of us will be around to see it."

"By the Three Kennedys!" Doc exclaimed from the rear of the file. "What is that awful, polluted stench? It made my eyes water on the voyage over, but it is a thousand times worse on this blasted island. I can hardly breathe for the stink of it."

"Cannies got the coals from their slow fires banked up and burning night and day," the Cajun told him. "They've converted most of the ship's steel cargo containers into giant smokehouses for processing their meat for travel. It's a long way between villes when they're on the hunt, sometimes they get their butts kicked by the norms and come up empty on body count. The bastards are fussy about their vittles. Only thing they're fussy about. They won't eat anything but people."

"An army moves on its stomach, even a cannibal army," Doc said in disgust.

"Do you think the prisoners will help us fight?" Ryan said. "There seems to be lots more of them than cannies."

"They look in real bad shape to me," Krysty said. "Beaten down physically and mentally. They know they're gonna die hard. Mebbe they don't have the strength left to be of any use to us. Especially after dragging those corpses across the island."

"If we can get their hands loose, they'll fight, all right," Cheetah Luis said with confidence. "They'll fight with everything they've got. They know it's their last chance."

"Will that be enough?" Sprue said.

"If we're triple lucky," the Cajun replied.

"We might well win the battle," Ryan said, "but if

we don't get our hands on La Golondrina, we can't win the war. We've got to find her, chill her, burn the body and scatter the ashes. Make sure there's not a single drop of her blood left to make more cure."

Chapter Twenty

To the jarring beat of steel hammering steel, Mildred and Jak hauled their corpse up the ship's earthen ramp. When they reached the canted main deck, the cannie overseers made them deposit the body beside the others that were already lined up like trophies of the hunt. They let go of the tow rope and, following a cannie's impatient gesture, joined their fellow captives near the gangway in the starboard rail.

The ship was a truly colossal craft—five hundred feet long, two hundred feet wide. It had a pair of kingposts aft of midships and a series of motor-driven, gallows-like cranes to lift cargo in and out of the holds. There were six huge hatches in rows of two on the forward deck. There were four more hatches aft of the kingposts. The bridge tower had once been painted brilliant white, now it bled rust top to bottom, in six-story, vertical stripes. Atop it sat the squat wheelhouse. The tower's windows were either missing or boarded up. Behind it, the ship's immense, seventy-foot-high smokestack had caved in on itself.

The deck was certainly pitched, but it wasn't so steep that it couldn't be easily climbed, side to side. It had also once been painted a high-gloss white. Now the surface was pitted, stained, leprous with flaking patches of orange. Torches burned at intervals along the rails. Fires burned in empty oil drums along the deck's low side. Easily a couple of hundred cannies were lined up, pounding in unison, celebrating their queen. Those without pipes used the steel-shod butts of their assault rifles. Their excitement disturbed Mildred more than their sheer numbers. It was *that* frenzied. Flesheaters dervished to their own mind-numbing beat.

All in the name of spilled blood.

In exaltation of murder.

Cannies pressed forward with gun muzzles lowered, packing the captives into an even tighter formation.

The drumming suddenly stopped, and a rousing cheer went up.

From this angle, in the leaping firelight, Mildred could see the female figure atop the bridge more clearly. She was definitely raven-haired and tall. She wore a long black dress that exposed thin, pale arms. When she raised her arms over her head, the undersides were red. La Golondrina had opened her veins. Blood dripped off her elbows into vessels held by figures who kneeled in front of her.

An even louder cheer went up from the deck. Loud enough to cause pain, if not to raise the dead.

Mildred looked around. Cannies hopped and jigged in wild abandon, drunk with promise, with the perceived, unstoppable momentum of their cause. Oh yes, they were in a merry, merry mood. What they anticipated was not the Big Enchilada, not the gift of eternal life, but a pardon from the grisly, tormented death they so richly deserved.

While the revelers reveled, they were joined on the deck by birds of a much different feather. These men and women wore fluorescent orange vests, the same kind used by predark road crews, and walked in perfect step, arms swinging, heads held high. Their faces were masks of joy. Smiling. Cheerful. Yet vacant. The vested crew marched straight for the lined-up corpses.

They handled the bodies without a shred of respect or dignity. They jerked them around like sides of beef, then started dragging them toward the ship's bow.

"Who are they?" Mildred asked Tibideau.

"Those are happy meals," Junior said.

"What?" Mildred said, jarred by the reference. More memories of her previous life flooded back, memories filtered through a screen of present-day horror.

"That's what we call them," Junior explained. "They're still norms. They try to infect themselves with oozies on purpose, hoping to turn cannie. Got no real zest for the gore, yet, but they force themselves to drink tablespoons of oozie-tainted blood or the gray pus from the goners. They're not the triple stupes you might think. They can see the handwriting on the wall, and they want to join the winning team. They're devoted to our cause, even though they aren't part of it. They're eager to please, too. They'll do anything we tell them with great big smiles on their faces. If they don't manage to get sick after week or so, we chill them and eat them. Lots more where they came from."

"Where they taking the bodies?" Mildred asked.

"To the cooler belowdecks," Junior said.

Jak was staring fixedly at his prized Colt stuck in the bastard's waistband. Mildred could see the albino's hands twisting and straining at the ropes behind his back, trying to stretch them. His wrists were bloodied by the effort, to no avail.

"Got too many bodies on the island to smoke all at once," Tibideau told Mildred. "Not enough smoker houses by half. Takes three, four days to do the job right. Besides, the dead 'uns have to be shaved, gutted and bled out. The happy meals do all that shit work for us—that's why we keep 'em alive. We like to age the bodies awhile in the cooler, too. Tenderizes the oldies."

On deck, the cannies had begun passing along tin cups of what looked like pure water. Mildred knew it wasn't. It was water tainted with the queen's blood. The flesheaters sipped daintily and then handed the cup on to the next in line.

"Do you want some of that?" Junior asked her. "It's the real deal. It's the cure. If you drink a big old swig, mebbe you'll nip the oozies in the bud. Mebbe you'll never get them. But on the other hand, one taste of La Golondrina's blood might just push you over the edge. Instant cannie. Do you want to take that chance?"

Mildred wasn't sure, one way or the other. The idea of drinking even highly diluted human blood made her stomach rebel.

"You're not going to give it to me no matter what I say," she told him, "so go fuck yourself."

Junior firmly pushed Mildred and Jak to the rim of the nearest open deck hatch. "Have a look," he said.

They peered down into the deep, steel-walled hold. It was where the cannies stored their prisoners. People were running around like ants. And just as helpless.

"You can feel the fever coming on strong, can't you?" Junior said into Mildred's ear. "Your pulse is pounding in your head. You know you've got to do something, but you're not quite sure what it is. You'll know real soon. Putting you down there with the norms is like dropping a wolf in among the sheep. Of course, with your hands tied behind your back you won't be able to do them any harm. Ain't that too bad."

"What do you want from me?"

"I want to hear you howl for it."

"'It?'"

"Meat."

"That'll be a cold day in hell, Junior."

"Just you wait and see."

A crane lowered a cargo net onto the deck in front of them.

"Get in the net," Junior said, drawing the Python from his waistband.

Mildred and Jak joined about thirty other captives in the first load. After they stepped into the center of the mesh, the crane lifted up the net, swung it over the open hatch and lowered it down into the live hold.

Except for the people and rows of torches along the walls, the vast enclosure was empty. Its steel sides were at least a hundred feet high. They were braced with massive, riveted I-beam girders, as was the underside of the main deck. There were a couple of access

doors but they had no knobs or hinges on the inside.
About 150 people were sitting or laying on the metal
floor. Another fifty or so were milling about aimlessly
or pacing like trapped animals. There was no water in
sight. The latrine was marked by piles and puddles in
the far corner of the hold.

It smelled like a human zoo.

The Cajuns who had stuck together on the trip
down were again gathered in a tight group, this time
back-to-back.

Mildred quickly realized that not all the hold's prisoners had their hands tied. Those who had managed
to get loose were busy abusing those who hadn't.
Mixed in with the docile, scooped up with the honor-
able and the hardworking were a handful of coldhearts. The scum of Deathlands. And with their end in
sight, they were hell-bent on taking a few last liber-
ties with the innocent and the defenseless.

Last beatings.

Last robbings.

Last sex, taken by force.

Hooting and making kissing sounds, they ganged
up on the fat Sippi merchant and the Texan whore.
Then they started booting them around. One for the
sheer fun of it, the other to bully favors.

All the females in the hold were fair game to them,
even Michelle, the parakeet woman. She was jerked
away from her horrified husband while he tried in vain
to defend her. The parakeet didn't react to the kidnapping, or the threat of gang rape—no screams, no struggle, no tears, as if she weren't even aware of what was
going on around her. From the female bodies already

lying on the deck, clothes torn away, faces purple from strangulation, women didn't survive the coldhearts' attentions for long.

"Don't hurt her, please," the merchant said.

The coldhearts closed ranks around their tiny victim, laughing at him. There was nothing he could do but beg.

"Have mercy. Don't do this."

"There ain't no mercy here, fat man," one of them said. "We gonna make this little bird sing."

Mildred recognized their type. The ornate facial brandings. The gruesome gridwork of battle scars. The ground-in, black dirt and grease on their clothes and skin. The duct tape and plastic bag repair jobs on their pants and boots. They were the lowest form of road trash, highway robbers, ville looters, kidnappers. They were as much human predators as the cannies, only up until now they had left their victims to rot by the side of the road. Back in the day, before the end of civilization, Mildred would have expected to find men like them locked up for life in some state penitentiary's violent offender block, or buried in its potter's field. There were no more penitentiaries, of course, and the entire world had become a potter's field. That the coldhearts had had the gumption to keep from going over to the cannie side surprised Mildred. Maybe the cannies already had enough happy meals.

"That one there looks prime to me," one of the road trash said, leering at Mildred. He smacked his stubble-rimmed lips and showed her an alarmingly long, red tongue. "Let's do her, too."

For the second time in twenty-four hours, Mildred

was the focus of unwelcome male attention. This time she paid it back with interest.

When the chiller reached out for her with grimy hands, tongue lewdly extended, she snap-kicked him in the chin, driving down with her planted foot, putting everything she had into the upward blow. His eyes rolled in their sockets as the steel-capped toe of her combat boot made solid contact, splitting his lower jaw in two, shattering his front teeth like glass, but not before he bit off the end of his own tongue. His knees bucked. Blood drooled from his lips in long, swaying strands as he dropped unconscious to the deck.

A second coldheart, a man with a shaved head who was missing both ears, lunged at her, but she easily stepped aside and let him fly past.

Jak roundhouse-kicked the oncoming target in the kneecap. There was an audible crunch as bone and cartilage crushed, and the earless man went down screaming, clutching at his leg with both hands.

The coldhearts weren't done, yet. Not by a long shot. Chilling Mildred and Jak had become a matter of pride.

The biggest of the bunch let out a roar and charged her. He stood about six-three and weighed at least 250 pounds. Greasy coils of brown hair fell past his wide shoulders. His nose had a carved white bone thrust through it. His eyes were small, dark and full of hate.

This time she pivoted away at the last second, and as the chiller swept by, she dropped and leg-whipped him. He landed on his back on the deck. The sudden, unexpected impact knocked the wind out of him. Before he could recover his breath, Mildred's heel stomped his face, turning nose and decorative ornament to bloody pulp.

The coldheart rolled away and staggered up to his feet, clutching his nose as gore spilled out from between his fingers.

Which left his sternum exposed.

Mildred knew better than to give someone that big a second chance to throttle her.

She front kicked him straight in the heart, grunting from the effort, putting all of her weight into it. She felt his rib cage buckle and then snap like a dry branch under her sole.

The man's final breath gusted out in a red mist. He crashed to the deck, his legs kicking and trembling in the throes of death.

"Snow Wolf, over here! Quick!" someone shouted.

Mildred turned and was stunned to see the Cajuns waving excitedly at Jak. All of them had their hands free. Working back-to-back, they had managed to untie each other.

One of the Cajuns expertly picked out the knot that held Jak's wrists bound together.

The albino quickly shook the circulation back into his fingers.

"Let's put an end to this crap," a stocky coldheart snarled at his grim-faced comrades. "We got a lot of screwing to do. The mutie's mine."

As the barrel-chested man closed in on Jak, he addressed the albino directly. "I'm gonna pop out those red eyeballs and stuff 'em up your pasty white butt."

"Shit, he's nothing but a skinny kid," one of the

other chillers called. "Wring his fucking neck and get it over with."

The stocky coldheart tried. He really tried. When his hands closed, Jak's neck was someplace else.

"What?" the coldheart said.

In a blur, Jak had moved behind him. The albino straight-punched his adversary in the right kidney, the youth's mane of white hair flying. The heavy muscles of the chiller's back dulled the shock wave of that first blow, but his face registered sharp, stabbing pain.

Jak didn't stop. He didn't step away. He hit coldheart again and again with consecutive right-hand punches, laying the full-power blows on exactly the same spot.

"The mutie's mine!" one of the coldhearts shouted in glee, mocking his brutalized comrade.

Mildred felt a light touch behind her. When she looked over her shoulder, a female Cajun was working at her bonds.

The coldheart tried to whirl to face Jak and bring his hands into the fight, but the albino circled as he turned, shadowing his every move, continuing to pound on that kidney. Mildred knew that after a certain point even densely layered muscle was no protection from body blows like that. The man couldn't keep his muscle tensed. Under the relentless beating, it would go numb, then slack.

And Jak kept hitting him.

"Ah, shit. Shit," the man wheezed, gasping for air. Piss ran down his leg onto the deck.

The spiraling dance of pain turned closer and closer to the hold's steel wall. Jak was leading. The coldheart was bent double, unable to straighten, unable to lift his right arm.

The other road scum didn't step in to help their pal. Some were busy tearing the clothes off the indifferent, unblinking parakeet. Maybe the rest were too amused to intervene. Or maybe they wanted to watch him die.

Jak grabbed the man by the arm and waist, jerked him off balance, spun him on one foot and slammed the top of his head into the wall. It was heavy-gauge metal. It didn't dent.

The coldheart dropped to his knees, blood leaking from both ears. When Jak leaned over his adversary's wide back, he looked small, way too small to have done all that damage. The albino gripped the man's chin with one hand and his opposite shoulder with the other.

The movement that came next was too fast for the eye to follow.

The snap of the breaking neck was unmistakable.

Jak let the body slump to its side on the deck.

Cannies looked down from the rim of the hatch, cheering and jeering the hand-to-hand combat. They didn't give a damn what happened down in the hold. The prisoners were unarmed and they couldn't get out. If the aggressive ones chilled each other, it would save them the effort.

"That's just poor," remarked a rangy coldheart as Jak stepped away from the corpse. "Come on, let's waste this little shit."

Only one of the road scum deigned to join him, a wiry man with deep creases in his forehead and down his cheeks. The rest were content to remain spectators.

Freed herself, Mildred took Jak's back.

The coldhearts circled, looking for openings. When they found none, they tried to create them with brute force. Mildred blocked a flurry of punches and kicks from the taller man, using her hands, arms and feet. When he couldn't make a dent in her defense, the scum's face turned red with frustration. The doctor smiled at him because she knew it would piss him off even more.

Howling with rage, the chiller tried again. This time she let him in, and when he struck for her face, she struck back with a vengeance. The edge of her stiffened forearm slammed into his larynx, crushing it. Stunned, his airway cut off, the coldheart backed away, holding his throat.

Behind her, Jak ducked under a haymaker swing and backhanded a rabbit chop to the base of the wiry guy's neck. The blow momentarily disconnected brain from spinal cord. Head from legs. The man fell to his knees.

The albino teen kicked him in the head, and when the man dropped to his back on the deck, he kicked him some more. Jak kicked him so hard that one of his eyes popped from its socket.

Turning away, the albino looked around for more.

None of the scum wanted any part of either of them.

The other attacker had collapsed in final spasm, his face purple, eyes bulging and shot with blood, his tongue black and protruding.

"Let the woman go or you're gonna get the same," Mildred told the chillers.

To her delight, the Cajuns stepped up and joined ranks with them, maximizing the threat.

The coldhearts knew they couldn't win. They grudgingly moved away from Michelle, leaving her standing there naked, her torn clothes down around her ankles.

Mildred pulled the poor woman's dress back up. "Get everybody freed," she told the Cajuns. "Untie their hands."

It took only a couple of minutes. The freed prisoners helped release those still bound.

The cannies didn't try to stop them. The only way they could have done that would have been to open fire. And that wasn't called for. Tied or not, the captives weren't going anywhere.

A fact that was obvious to everyone in the hold, as well.

"We've got to find a way out of this pit," said the apparent leader of the Cajuns. He had a blue-dark shadow of beard, a long nose and close-set black eyes. A hunk of his left bicep was missing; there were bite marks around the angry wound. "Got to get hold of some blasters. Got to do some damage, soften up the bastards for Cheetah Luis."

"You think he's really coming for us?" Mildred said.

"You can bet jack on it."

Mildred craned her head, looking at the edge of the hatch a hundred feet up. It might as well have been a mile. There were no foot- or handholds for climbing.

"How are we going to get out?" the Cajun said.

"I might know of a way," Mildred told him, "but there's no guarantee it'll work."

Chapter Twenty-One

The grounded freighter loomed before them, taller from keel to wheelhouse than a twenty-story building. Ryan took in the rusting hull and superstructure, and at the stern, its enormous propeller, high and dry. The deck was tilted toward them, revealing hundreds of cannies drumming and dancing. Pillars of black smoke rose from oil drum fires, and torches burning along the rails.

Ryan saw the vessel as a military objective, perhaps unattainable, but tangible.

At his side, Doc viewed the freighter and the road of skulls leading to it as symbols of something much larger, something more profound, something incarnate.

"It is nothing less than Satan's ark," the old man remarked with venom. "Having ridden out the unholy storm of the Apocalypse, that hellship has safely brought ashore, two by two, every evil known to man. So that as the black, polluted waters receded and drained from the land, they might multiply and spread…"

Ryan couldn't walk in the old man's cracked knee

boots, nor could he see through his ancient eyes. But he understood that Doc was desperately seeking to make sense of something that was at its core senseless, this by tying together bits of this and that from dusty decades of half-remembered study and reflection.

From his private conversations with Mildred, Ryan had learned a little about the mind-set of the Victorian Age into which Doc Tanner had been born. It was an age of global conquest and subjugation, all in the name of ending savagery and ignorance, and spreading the benefits of civilization to the primitive corners of the Earth. In their arrogance, the Victorians defended their crimes against the weak and vulnerable as being not only noble, but ordained by and in the service of their God.

Confronted in the present by the unspeakable and the unthinkable, Doc had reverted to the unknowable.

"Doc, don't go there," Ryan warned.

The old man turned to him and said, "There is a limit to what even I can stomach, dear friend, and we passed that highwater mark hours ago."

With that, Doc strode purposefully away from him, walking past the Cajuns to take the point at the head of the line of fighters.

"What's wrong with him?" Krysty asked. "Is he having another one of his spells?"

It wasn't unusual for Doc's brain to slip the odd cog now and again. The double jump forward in time had done him damage. Whether it was his inconsolable grief over the loss of his family, his beloved wife Emily, his treasured children, Rachel and Jolyon, or whether some trauma related to time travel had injured the tissue of his brain, there was no way of determining. At times Doc rejected lock, stock and barrel the new reality that surrounded him. He faded away from the present into memories and fantasies of the world he had been torn from.

"Mildred might know what's going on, but she's not here to straighten him out," Ryan said. "Cannies have really gotten under his skin. He's been ranting on about how what they are goes against the rules of his old-time religion…"

"I might be remembering it wrong," the redhead told him, "but I don't think the Ten Commandments said anything about not eating your neighbor."

"Bad joke," Ryan said, even though he cracked a smile. "We take this world at face value because we don't know any different. For you and me and J.B. and Jak, there have always been cannies. They are the boogeymen we've had to watch out for since we were little. There weren't any cannies running wild in Doc's day. If they existed anywhere, they were someplace far, far away from his home."

"I get it, lover. Mebbe we should keep closer tabs on him?"

"Yeah, but not too close. Mood he's in, he won't stand for us looking over his shoulder."

As they approached the side of the ship, they passed within ten yards of the jumble of tumbled-down cargo containers. Doc made an abrupt right turn, stepped off the path and walked over to the nearest container. Alarm bells ringing, Ryan followed a few discreet paces behind him. Every one of the corrugated steel boxes was tended by an leather-aproned cook; every box spewed coils of sickly sweet smoke from the holes hacked in its roof. Piles of cordwood and hickory chips stood at one end or the other, in front of the jury-rigged oil drum fireboxes.

A squat lump of a man, sweaty, bare chested and hairy, looked up from his work as Doc neared. Ignoring the rag of a T-shirt hanging on a hook outside the crude doorway, he wiped the sweat from his brow with the back of his hand. It was stained crimson to the wrist from the basting sauce in the plastic bucket at his boots.

As Ryan hurried forward to close the cap, he heard the cook tell Doc, "If you're looking for the best smoked peeps, you're in the right place. I got a secret recipe. It's all in the sauce."

Then he held out the rag mop basting brush for Doc to try a sample.

"I've got a secret, as well," Doc said, releasing the ebony sheath on his swordstick and drawing out the blade.

The cannie cook blinked at him, puzzled by the show and tell, but unafraid. What happened next was something he didn't expect.

Ryan knew exactly what was coming. He lunged forward, reaching out to deflect Doc's arm.

Too late.

Without another word, Doc lowered his point and ran the cannie through with a single thrust, half the length of the rapier blade piercing the bib front of the leather apron. A deft, figure-eight twist of the wrist followed, using the leverage of the sword and its keen double edge to neatly sever the major arteries of the cook's heart.

The cannie's mouth opened, but no sound came out. He dropped his baster into the dirt, a look of astonishment on his face.

Doc reared back and booted the dying cannie off his sword. The cook staggered three steps in reverse, stumbled over the doorway sill and fell into the smoker box.

Ryan darted around Doc, bent and flipped the legs inside the jamb. Then he closed the makeshift door. He looked around, prepared for all hell to break loose. But none of the other cooks had seen what happened. It was over too quickly, and there were no screams to attract their attention.

Pure dumb luck.

"For nuke's sake Doc, get a grip," Ryan said as Krysty, J.B. and Sprue joined them.

Doc shook the blood off his blade and wiped it clean on the dead cook's T-shirt rag. His eyes flashed. "Is that not what we're here for?" he said "To chill them all?"

"Yeah, but not one at a time, if we can help it," Ryan said. "If I can't trust you to keep it together until the right moment, I'm going to take your weapons and tie you up until it's all over."

"You would do that to me? You would leave me defenseless against these godless devils?"

"Damn right, I would. To protect your life and ours, I'd triple hogtie you. And I'd have plenty of help doing it."

Doc looked from face to face and saw that they were all of one mind. And it was against him.

"I'm going to give you another chance," Ryan said.

"No more targets of opportunity. I want your word. I want it now."

"This is one battle I will not sit out," Doc told him. Then he sheathed the rapier with a flourish. "I defer to your wishes and stay my hand," he said. "You have my solemn word."

While the wagloads of captives slowly climbed the earthen ramp towing their awful burdens, the Cajuns and companions had to wait on the path below. The line leading to the ship advanced in fits and spurts. When the drumming suddenly stopped and the cheering started, the companions were standing too close to the hull to see what was going on above.

A few minutes later, at the top of the ramp, it sank home to all of them just how outnumbered they were. Without the help of freed prisoners, they had no chance.

"At least we've got them all in one place," Krysty said.

"And the downside is," Sprue added, "they're all in one place."

Ryan scanned the milling bodies in dismay. "We've got our work cut out finding Mildred and Jak," he said. "Don't see La Golondrina up in the tower, either."

"If she's up there, she isn't showing herself," Krysty agreed.

"She's up there," Cheetah Luis said. "I guarantee it."

Ryan walked to the edge of the open hatch and looked down into the hold. The others did the same.

"Guess we found out where they keep all their prisoners," Sprue said.

A few faces looked up at them, radiating fear and hate. Most of the captives were hunched, sitting with their heads on knees.

"No sign of Jak or Mildred," Krysty said.

"Can't see into the corners from here," J.B. said. "They could be down there."

"You missed the medicine," said a familiar voice at their backs.

Ryan turned to face the cannie hag from the barge. She had been partying hearty. Her hank of white-streaked horse hair had come half unbraided, it stuck out on one side like a busted bale of straw. There were ruddy spots in the centers of her cheeks and a crust of dried blood in her fan of chin whiskers.

"All the cure's gone," she said. "There won't be any more until tomorrow."

"Is this all of the cannie nation?" Ryan asked her, waving his arm to take in the revelers.

"No, some are down in the crew quarters on B Deck, resting up between dinner courses and dancing. The near-goners are there, too. Too sick to celebrate until the cure kicks in. Better go get yourselves something to eat. You're gonna need your strength for the all-nighter."

The hag slapped Ryan hard on the shoulder, then wandered away into the crowd.

"You Cajuns never got this far," he said to Cheetah Luis, "so we don't have any idea what's belowdecks. We're going to have to recce the ship."

The Cajun nodded in agreement.

"On the barge that cannie bitch told me there was fuel oil and gasoline stored aboard," Ryan said.

"Got to be bunkers of ammo and blasters, too," J.B. stated.

"We free the prisoners, get them weapons, take control, then blow the ship," Cheetah Luis said.

"We can't blow the ship until we have the queen in hand," Ryan said. "We can't risk her getting away in the confusion."

Doc was staring into the flames of a burn barrel at the knob ends of human long bones glowing in the intense heat. As Ryan steered him away, a piercing scream split the air.

The companions looked up in time to catch the last thirty feet of free fall. A dark figure plummeted from the tower, arms and legs flailing. It vanished behind the heads of the crowd, landing with a wet thud on the steel deck.

The cannies didn't let a little warm splatter spoil their mood. They applauded like it was a carny act, then resumed their gyrations.

At that point, a crew in orange vests exited a doorway near the bow. They marched like little tin soldiers over to the row of corpses, hitched them up by their heels and started dragging them back the way they had come.

"That's the way down," Cheetah Luis said.

The companions and Cajuns followed the draggers along the deck to the doorway. As they waited at the entrance, they could hear the bodies thunking heavily on the metal steps below. The draggers couldn't be bothered carrying them down the stairwell.

They descended the stairs in a solid mass. The reek of slaughterhouse was like a billowing toxic cloud. On the second landing they found a door marked with a stenciled sign. A Deck. The door opened onto a central, torchlit corridor that ran the length of the ship. It offered access to the immense holds on either side. A few cannies walked the metal hallway. When they passed by, they didn't challenge the newcomers. They smiled and nodded at what had to have been a familiar sight—brethren heading for the ship's armory to replenish their supplies.

There was no guard on the armory half door. And it wasn't even closed. The companions and Cajuns walked right in.

The cannie cache was most impressive, assembled no doubt from the villes they had looted and the convoys they had ambushed. One wall of the room was lined with long, flat wooden boxes, weapons' crates clearly marked as AK 47s of Egyptian and Polish manufacture. There were open fifty-five-gallon drums of loose 7.62 mm ComBloc ammunition and bins of 30-round AK magazines still wrapped in Cosmoline. In a far corner were a few more drums, however these were still hermetically sealed. If their labeling was accurate, they contained enough RDX high explosive to turn the freighter into a mile-wide circle of smoking scrap.

The last Cajun through the door pulled it closed behind him.

J.B. walked straight over to a long rack of RPG-16s. Beside it were crates of individually bubble-wrapped HEAT rockets.

A pair of cannie armorers rose from a cluttered worktable in the center of the room.

"What can we do for you folks?" said the larger of the two. He seemed eager to please, until he got his answer.

"You can die," Cheetah Luis said, pointing his assault rifle at the man's chest.

Cajuns swept in behind the pair and slipped wire nooses over their heads. After that, there was no more talking, just kicking.

"J.B., better start prepping the blasters," Ryan said. "As many as you can."

"I'm on it," the Armorer replied. "Need some help loading the mags, though."

"Stay here and help him," Cheetah Luis told three of his fighters.

As the rest of the companions and Cajuns turned to leave, J.B. began checking the brand-new blasters, making sure actions and barrels were clear, and dry-firing them before loading them up with fresh mags.

The next hold contained the stores of gasoline. Wooden pallets were stacked with full fifty-five-gallon steel drums.

"This will make a pretty boom," Cheetah Luis said.

"Need to make triple sure it ignites," Ryan said. "Give me a hand."

With the help of Doc and Sprue he pried the lids off a half dozen drums, then dumped the contents onto the deck under the rows of pallets. The Cajuns followed suit, emptying a dozen more.

The fumes were dizzying.

They hurried back out into the hall, shutting the hold's door after them, sealing in the explosive vapor.

At the far end of the corridor was the door that led

to the captive hold. There were no cannies standing guard. The lock was a simple but massive steel cross-bar arrangement.

Doc immediately began to lift it up.

"Don't open it," Cawdor told him. "We can't free them yet. We've got to wait. If Mildred and Jak are in-side, they're safe for the moment. We can't afford to show our hand too soon."

They retraced their steps down the corridor, past the armory, to the stairway door. They descended the stairs to B Deck, where the cannie hag had told them the crew quarters were. The freighter's second level was even danker and moldier that the first. The floors were slick with a thin film of slime. The metal walls and ceiling sweated orange drops of corrosion.

They found the crew quarters in the bow end of the hall. Again, the door was wide open, perhaps in faint hope of snagging a fresh breeze. Unlike the rooms in the deck above, the riveted ceiling was low. It, too, was lit by smoky torches, which only added to the caustic bear pit smell. String hammocks hung like insect co-coons from the girders overhead. About half were oc-cupied by sleeping cannies, some in stained underwear, some fully clothed. Below the hammocks, their weapons were neatly stowed.

"What do you think?" Krysty said.

"At least another fifty," Ryan replied as he surveyed the dim expanse.

"Too many to chill without using blasters and rais-ing a ruckus," Cheetah Luis said.

Nobody woke up; nobody noticed when they slipped back out into the corridor.

"The door is solid steel," Ryan said. "We can jam it shut from the outside. There aren't any windows for them to crawl through. They don't know it, yet, but that room is going to be their coffin."

On the bottom deck, they found the ship's engine room, which was deserted and dark. They had to take down torches from the hall to see inside. The engine's immense, elephant-like back stuck up from a sump of black oil surrounded by a catwalk. Its cylinders were as tall as a man.

At the other end of the hall there were signs of life, and the overpowering stench of mass death. They pushed through double-swing metal doors into the meat hold.

Inside, men and women in orange vests labored over the fruits of the cannie harvest. At workstations around the room, they barbered, disemboweled and drained hanging carcasses.

Even Ryan, the seasoned warrior, was taken aback at the sight. His blood ran cold and he tasted acrid bile in the back of his throat. This was the subbasement of Hell. As if to underscore that point, the savage drumming from the main deck started up again, echoing through the cavernous hull.

Ryan looked at Doc, worried that he wouldn't be able to control himself. But Doc seemed just fine.

The Cajuns were the ones who lost it when they recognized their own kin being butchered.

Cheetah Luis walked over to a steel-topped table and picked up a large wooden mallet used for hammering a blade through bone. He tested its weight in his hand.

The worker behind the table beamed at him, his face and vest spattered with blood and bits of fat.

With an overhead swing of the mallet, Cheetah Luis crushed the top of the worker's skull like a raw egg, from crown to temple, dropping him like a stone.

The other Cajuns took that as a signal for the mayhem to begin. They rushed through the room, grabbing up cleavers and boning knives from the tabletops. They hurled the butchers onto their own chopping blocks and pinned them down while they hacked and stabbed their vengeance.

A few of the vest-clad workers managed to break loose and run for the back of the room. There was no way out, of course. Their panicked screams for help were muffled by the insistent pounding from above. The Cajuns trapped the escapees in a corner, caught them and dragged them over to a row of double sinks full of bloody water. Pinning their arms behind their backs, the fighters forced their heads under the surface and held them there until they stopping kicking.

Cheetah Luis then moved through his fighters, some of whom were already weeping, roughly shoving them toward the swing doors. "Go on, get out! Get out!"

This wasn't the time for mourning the dead.

At the aft end of C Deck they located the fuel oil bunker. From the indicator gauges, it looked like ten thousand gallons remained in the double-walled tanks.

"Fuel oil is nowhere near as flammable as gas," Ryan said. "But under the right conditions of high temperature and pressure...ka-boom."

At Cheetah Luis's command his fighters delved

into their packs for some of the pipe bombs they had brought along. He showed them where he wanted them positioned, near the ceiling, their six-inch-long fuses pointing up. They used strips of duct tape to secure the bombs in place.

"What do you think?" the Cajun asked Ryan.

"I think we'd better be a hell of a long way off when this shit hits the fan."

Chapter Twenty-Two

Mildred pulled Jak away from the captive Cajuns. "I'm the only one who can get out of here," she told him. "All I have to do is yell up to Junior that I'm ready to give in."

"You give in?"

"No, but he won't find that out until it's too late."

"What you do alone?"

"More than I can do down here. Maybe I can get close enough to the queen to take her out. Maybe I can find a way to open that door and let the prisoners loose."

Like most native-born Deathlanders, the albino was a pragmatist and a fatalist. If he had warm and fuzzy feelings about anyone or anything, he kept them well hidden behind a stoic exterior. "Luck," was all he said, but he meant it.

Mildred stood directly under the open hatch, looked up and yelled for Junior as loud as she could. It wasn't strictly speaking a howl, but it worked. After a minute, the scar-faced bastard peered down at her.

"You got something to say to me?" he hollered through cupped hands.

"I'm ready for some dinner," she shouted back.

Tibideau gestured to someone on the main deck. As the net came down, Mildred felt a wave of relief course over her. She hadn't told Jak the whole truth. She hadn't dared speak her fears out loud. Mildred had another reason for wanting out of the hold. What Junior had predicted was coming to pass. There was a terrible pounding in her head and a building tension at her core. Her body throbbed, crying out for action, release from the pressure that gripped it. She wasn't hungry for flesh. She knew that. The aching need inside her hadn't solidified into compulsion. Not yet, anyway. That was the last turn of the oozie screw. If she waited for it to come, Jak Lauren wasn't safe from her, nor were any of the other innocent people in the hold.

Mildred stepped onto the net and rode up and out of the pit.

Up on the main deck, Junior had a charred joint waiting for her. "Chow down," he said as he waved it under her nose. "This is a choice cut. You're going to love it."

"I want to see La Golondrina first," she told him.

"Yeah, sure," Junior said.

"I'm not kidding."

"Everybody who comes on this ship wants an audience with her. Nobody gets one. Understand?"

"Listen, Junior," Mildred said, "I'm a freezie, just like her. I need to talk to La Golondrina."

Junior was immediately skeptical. "Don't look like a fucking freezie to me," he said.

"How many freezies have you seen?"

"Just the one…" He gestured up at the tower with his thumb.

"Congratulations," Mildred said, "now you've seen two."

"How do I know you're telling me the truth?"

"You don't. But she will."

"Why should La Golondrina care if you're a freezie?"

"Because I was a research whitecoat before the nukecaust. With what's in my head, I can help her, bigtime. I can turn the cannie groundswell into a tidal wave."

Tibideau scowled, weighing the personal cost-benefit.

"It'll be a feather in your cap, too," she assured him. "La Golondrina is going to be mighty happy you had the smarts to introduce us. I'm talking a major reward, maybe even a command of your own." She paused, then added, "Or if you're too scared to help me out, I can ask one of these other fine flesheaters for a hand…"

"All right, all right. I'll give it a try," he said, relenting. "You're probably not going to get past the Angels, anyway."

Mildred followed him down the deck to the bridge tower. As they got closer, she could see two huge, bare-chested men guarding the entrance at its base. She recalled what Junior had told her, that the Angels of Death were part of La Golondrina's original hunting pack. The first partakers of the cure. What passed for cannie royalty.

So as not to be mistaken for lesser beings, this pair

of bruisers sported some unique skin art. Life-size human skulls had been branded into the middle of their chests. Ropy, red scar tissue made the elaborate designs stick out from their flesh. They looked as if they had been sculpted from blood. More angry branding scars licked like flames over their thick wrists and forearms. Their full beards and long hair had been woven into tight pigtail braids and tied at the ends with leather traces.

There was no sign of wings on these Angels. All that sprouted from the tops of their shoulders were tufts of coarse, dark hair.

The cure was evidently still working, though. Not a gray drop leaked from either trauma-flattened nose.

"What do you want?" said the guard looming on the right of the entryway.

"Need to see La Golondrina," Junior said.

"You know better than that, Scarface," the other Angel told him.

Mildred could smell his cadaver breath from five feet away.

"Back off or you're gonna lose an arm," the first one warned Tibideau. He unsheathed the cutlass at his belt and measured the distance for a strike. The long blade was nicked along its length, but the single, upcurving edge looked razor-sharp, with more than enough thickness and heft along the backbone to do the job right.

"This one," Junior said as he retreated a step. "She's the one who wants to see La Golondrina. Go on, tell them…"

Mildred explained the nature of her request to the Angels, that she was also a freezie, and that she had specialized knowledge their queen could use to advance the cannie cause.

No dice.

"She's nothing but meat. Why are you bringing her here?" the Angel on the right said to Junior. "Live meat don't go upstairs, that's the rule."

"I infected her," Tibideau protested. "She's about to turn cannie any minute. I know it."

"Why don't we just wait and see, then?" the other guard said.

Mildred was slammed by a wave of desperation. If her symptoms were a measure of the time she had left, her window of opportunity was rapidly closing. "Okay, listen to me," she told the guards, "if you take La Golondrina a message for me, and she doesn't want to see me after she hears it, you can chill me."

"We can do that, anyway."

"La Golondrina doesn't like being bothered."

"This is important to her," Mildred said. "She's going to be mighty angry when she finds out you screwed this up. Maybe she'll withhold the cure next time you need it."

The Angels of Death looked at each other dubiously. Then the one on the right shrugged. "If she turns you down," he said, "we're not gonna let you die quick."

He turned on Junior, leaning over the much smaller man. "You, neither."

Tibideau's face fell. "I knew it," he said to Mildred. "Damn you, I knew it."

"What's the message?" the Angel on the left asked.

"I'm a freezie whitecoat and I can stop her bleeding."

"That's it?"

"That's it."

"If that's all you got, you'd better kiss your ass goodbye," the guard said, then he disappeared through the doorway.

As Mildred stood waiting, she tried not to question the strategy she had chosen. In for a penny, in for a pound. The fastest way to soften up the cannies for Ryan and the Cajuns was to chill the woman who was their leader. Under the circumstances, it was the only effective action an army of one could take. If Mildred survived the attack, releasing the prisoners came next.

When the Angel returned, his face and chest were covered with sweat and he was panting hard. He had run down the twelve flights of stairs.

And not for the privilege of hacking them to bits.

"Come on, both of you," he said, "get a move on." He gestured at the door.

"Me, too?" Junior whined.

The Angel grabbed him by the shoulder and shoved him through the entrance.

On the other side of the bulkhead door was a stairwell lit by torches. The rusting metal treads led up into the dark. Mildred guessed the bridge tower had to have had an elevator once. It was either no longer operational, or it was reserved for cannie royalty.

With a torch-bearing Angel in front and one behind, she and Tibideau mounted the steps.

A century ago, the ship's stairwell had been enclosed from the weather by riveted steel plate. The Apocalypse, the tsunamis, nuke winter and chem rains had turned the exterior walls into a cheese grater. Some of the stair treads had corroded away from their mountings. The assent was much more precarious than Mildred had imagined.

After they had climbed eight flights, they took a detour around a collapsed section of stairs above. The Angels led them down a gritty tower hallway. All the window glass was missing. Mildred looked out of the empty frames, down onto the tilted deck, at the cannies cavorting below. The ship's tower was like a mountaintop pyramid or castle, a symbol of authority. Elevation and separation bred respect and awe in the weak-minded.

They crossed the width of the bridge and entered the stairwell on the other side. Below the fourth floor, the steps had fallen away completely. They mounted four more rickety flights, coming out on the unrailed bridge roof. The single-story wheelhouse stood in its center, overlooking the vast main deck. Some of its long, narrow windows were intact. The structure was guarded by four more Angels, each wearing a cutlass in addition to slung, folding-stock AK 47s.

As Mildred approached the wheelhouse, she could see through the windows. Inside, the control room was lit by torches and lamps. Cozy, but for the sweltering heat. Mildred's chin dripped with sweat and her underarms felt like they had been buttered. Gauzy brown fabric hung down in billowing channels from the low ceiling, giving it a Bedouin caravan sort of atmosphere. There were no chairs or couches in evidence, just scattered plush cushions, replete with tassels and embroidery. Through one of the empty window frames, Mildred smelled sandalwood incense.

Definitely a feminine choice, perhaps to cover the putrefying stench rising from the decks below.

"Stand here," one of their escorts said. He left them and ducked into the wheelhouse.

Mildred took a look over the edge of the roof. Below, more bound captives were dragging more bodies up the ramp onto the main deck. The happy meals would soon be hauling them away.

After a moment, the Angel called out to them from the side doorway. "Enter," he said.

Inside the wheelhouse it was a good fifteen degrees hotter. The air was smothering, like breathing steam. At the far end of the room, behind a ceiling-to-floor veil of drooping gauze, faintly side lit by rows of oil lamps, a figure reclined on a mound of cushions.

"Step closer," said a woman's voice.

Mildred and Junior obeyed. It was impossible to make out the speaker through the folds of brown muslin.

As they neared the canopy, Angels stepped forward on either side. Their cutlasses drawn, they were ready to chop down the visitors if they made a hostile move for the queen.

"You know I am La Golondrina," the woman behind the curtain said. "Tell me who you are."

"I am Dr. Mildred Wyeth. I was cryopreserved in December of 1999. I emerged from freezie sleep a hundred years later."

"Doctor?"

"Yes, in research biochemistry and medicine."

"A real live scientist?"

"Yes."

"Why should I believe you? You could have memorized a couple of big words to try to fool me."

"You shouldn't believe me. You should make me prove who I am and what I can do."

"And pray tell what might that be?"

"I can eliminate the need for you to open your veins," Mildred said. "I can cure the oozies without your blood."

La Golondrina was silent. Behind the brown muslin, she didn't move a muscle.

"The endless donations of blood must be a terrible drain on your strength," Mildred went on. "And on your psyche. It must make you a prisoner here, in your own kingdom."

"If you have something to offer me, let's hear it."

"I can isolate the active agent in your blood, the antibodies that weaken and suppress the oozie virus," Mildred told her. "I can synthesize quantities of concentrated pure antivirus through biochemical means. You would have plenty of medicine for your flock, and you would be free to leave this place."

"How are you going to do something like that without access to a research lab?"

"The technology is relatively simple. I can easily scrounge up or jury-rig the hardware I need. The basic methodology is already here." She tapped her right temple with a fingertip.

La Golondrina suddenly reached up and swept aside the gauzy curtain.

Mildred was jolted by the sight of her.

Something had gone very wrong with La Golondrina's cryopreservation, either in the initial freezing or the subsequent thawing.

Parchment-white flaking skin was stretched over nearly fleshless bone. Her eyes were such a pale blue that they hardly had any color at all; her lips were so bloodless that they were nearly invisible; her skin hung down in thin, drooping folds from the backs of her arms and the line of her jaw; her hair was dyed a lusterless black, its white roots showing in the central part; her wrists were heavily bandaged, the bandages spotting with red. La Golondrina was a scrawny, blue-veined hag in a slinky, spaghetti-strapped black cocktail dress, three sizes too big for her.

Her appearance couldn't have been the result of blood-letting, no matter how frequent.

It occurred to Mildred that when the cannie queen had gone into the liquid nitrogen tank she might have already been old. A geezer seeking a cure for aging, and the diseases thereof wasn't unheard of in her day.

"I do know what you are," Mildred told her, "but not how you got that way."

When La Golondrina smiled, displaying black-rimmed, yellow stumps of teeth, Junior retreated three or four giant steps.

"You think you deserve that information?"

"I guess that's up to you."

La Golondrina wetly smacked her pale lips. "It pleases me that you weren't afraid to ask me a question," she said. "Thousands would have shit themselves at the very idea. We who have come through cryo are different than the others. We are changed in many ways."

"That's so."

"Would you believe me if I told you that I have no

idea how I came to be infected? And that I only have a rough idea of when?"

Mildred shrugged. "Without more of the details I really couldn't say."

"As you can imagine, over the years I've given a lot of thought to the source of my infection, trying to pinpoint why this happened to me. Before the nukecaust I was interrogated extensively by military intelligence. They asked me about my daily habits, and my personal and business contacts over and over again, sometimes using drugs to boost my recall. Nothing added up. I got the feeling from my watchers that they thought what I had wasn't a naturally occurring disease, that it had been tailor-made in a laboratory. Perhaps by the Soviet Union. Or even by some covert arm of the U. S. government. Containment was what they talked about most, in front of me and behind my back. They were afraid that whatever it was had already gotten out into the population."

"You mean, a bioweapon?"

"That's what they thought."

"That would have been in violation of the Geneva Accords."

"But think of the payoff. A disease that makes your enemies chill and eat their own people."

"How did your symptoms appear?"

"Out of the blue," La Golondrina said. "One day I was fine, the next I was sick as a dog. The day after that I was on the hunt. Until I was caught, predark law enforcement thought I was a male serial killer on a murder rampage through the South."

After all the years that had passed, that idea still seemed to tickle her.

"Before skydark there was no room for an oozie-infected person like me to come to full flower. You remember what it was like back then. A world cluttered with laws and lawmen. Even so, I couldn't help myself. After a while I didn't even try. Of course, I didn't look like this, then. I was in my late twenties, a Baton Rouge housewife, and I was a babe. I drove around Louisiana in a big old white convertible with the top down, my tanned breasts popping out of my yellow checked sundress, and a big, welcoming smile on my face. I had no trouble getting what I wanted. Dumb, young and tender."

Mildred did the math in her head. La Golondrina was about thirty-one years old, measured in the time she'd spent outside a cryo tank. In other words, she had prematurely aged. As though she had been in an extreme high-altitude/low-oxygen environment for too long, in what predark mountain climbers had called the Death Zone. The top of Mount Everest. A place where every organ of the body slowly suffocated.

"How did you get caught?" Mildred asked.

"I guess you could say I got lazy. I hunted the same territory once too often. The FBI caught me in a dragnet with bloody clothes in my trunk. They didn't know I was the chiller until after they put me in the parish's holding cell with two other women. By then I was too long without food. The cops got it all on videotape.

"As soon as psychological testing showed law enforcement and the state prosecutor that what I had was a disease and not a mental illness, they spirited me off to the Centers for Disease Control. After those folks studied me a bit, they realized what I had could be transmitted by blood and bodily fluids. Then I really fell off the end of the world. Level Four containment on an army base in Maryland. The military scientists there tried to evaluate my weaponization."

"Weaponize cannibalism?"

"Back then I was an oozies-producing factory. Only they never called it that. They used initials. CJCD. Creutzfeld something something disease. I didn't come down with terminal symptoms for another year. That's when the whitecoats finally realized what they had stumbled on. If they could introduce the lethal virus to the opposing side of a battlefield, they could create self-terminating, indiscriminate engines of destruction out of enemy forces. The hypothesis that the disease had come from the Soviets sent them scrambling to find a vaccine. That never happened.

"Rumors about what was going on leaked to the Net. The legitimate press followed up on the story. The scientists had to cover their tracks. That's when they put me in cryostasis, in October 1999."

"How did they keep you alive before that?"

"Finding food for me wasn't hard. These were military black ops. They had unlimited, secret discretionary funding. They opened a funeral home in Baltimore. The remains meant for cremation came to me on a plate. The grieving families got kitty litter."

"How did you get out of cryo?"

"An accident. A computer malfunction shut down the facility after a century of operation. I didn't thaw right. As you can see, I had cellular damage. However, I came out of cryogenesis oozie-symptom free."

"But you're still a cannie."

"Cure is relative term, I suppose. The terminal part of the disease is no longer a factor. Residual cannibalism is a minor inconvenience compared to being dead."

Mildred couldn't draw any conclusions as to what brought on the reversal of symptoms and left the behavior in place. There were too many unknowns—the effect of long-term freezing, the nature of the viral disease and the brain changes attributable to it, prior trauma and predilections to psychosis and violent antisocial behavior. It was also possible that once a cannie, always a cannie, that the infection produced an irreversible effect, a permanent scarring of the personality.

Mildred had to consider the prospect that the cure might stop her from dying of the oozies, but not from turning into a cannie.

"How did you know your blood could cure oozies?" she asked.

"I didn't, at first. But I knew enough about biology from high school and from listening to my captors to figure out I had somehow developed powerful antibodies to the disease. Otherwise I'd still have been dripping gray pus. I didn't know it would work on anybody else until I tried it on a couple of my packmates. They were goners, so I figured it couldn't hurt them. A few drops of my blood made them rise from the dead."

"I always thought the hardships of the nuke winter produced the first cannies, and that the oozies was something transmitted through their lifestyle, like AIDS."

"Cannies and oozies were already out in the world before skydark. I'm living proof of that. Cannies were thriving in the hellscape when I stepped out of the tank. I'd like to think I had something to do with that, but there's no way of knowing."

"What do you mean?"

"I could have infected other people before the FBI caught me. I might have been contagious in the disease's early stages. It's also possible that the original source of the cannie plague, the lab or bunker or whatever that was responsible for my infection, got breached on nukeday or sometime after, and the virus was released into the atmosphere."

"I take it you didn't have a plan when you arrived?"

"A plan? I never thought I'd need one. Never thought I'd end up here, that's for sure. When the scientists prepped me for the cryo with needles and IV lines in my arms, I thought they were going to execute me by lethal injection.

"I started working out a plan when I saw how my blood cured my sick crew. Deathlanders are really stupid, ignorant fucks, as you must've noticed. They walk in the same shallow, muddy rut until the day they die. They don't know anything about the past and they don't care to know anything. Me, I got a hundred blueprints for conquest from my good old middle-school history classes."

Junior Tibideau qualified as one of the aforementioned "really stupid, ignorant fucks." He understood about a third of the words in their conversation, and got none of the references to science, and few pertaining to history. As the two women chattered on, he continued a slow, inexorable retreat. He positioned himself next to one of the wheelhouse windows where he could sneak an eagle's-eye view of the main deck.

"Well, lookee there...." he suddenly remarked, pointing at something interesting below.

Mildred took the glee in his voice for a very bad sign. She stepped up behind him and looked over his shoulder. Down on the deck, at the top of the ramp, stood her four longtime companions. Cheetah Luis and his Cajuns were gathered around them. All were fully armed.

"We got some..." Junior began.

Before he could finish the warning, Mildred reached around his rib cage with both hands and yanked the captured pistols from his trouser waistband.

"Whoa!" the cannie cried, instinctively clutching at his pants as they came unbuttoned and began to fall down over his hips.

While he was thus occupied, Mildred reared back with her right foot and booted him in the base of the spine, hurling him headfirst through the open window and off the bridge.

Flailing his arms and legs, his pants around his ankles, Tibideau dropped the first three stories screaming at the top of his lungs. Then he began somersaulting head over heels. He hit the steel deck with a resounding splat, narrowly missing a crowd of his brethren.

Before Mildred could recover her balance, turn and

open fire, the guardian Angels were on top of her. One jerked her away from the window and the other ripped the blasters out of her hands.

With an arm securely pinned behind her back, Mildred was walked up to face the cannie queen.

"Why did you do that?" La Golondrina demanded.

"He had it coming," Mildred said. "He infected me with oozies two days ago."

La Golondrina didn't seem to care about Junior's fate one way or another. "You're definitely a spicy lady," she said, showing off her stumpy yellow incisors.

In that instant, Mildred saw the vile, frail woman as the helpless victim of her own success, trapped by the miraculous power of her blood. Not a reigning monarch, or a conquering general, but a prize cow who was drained of precious fluids at regular intervals. The Angels of Death appeared to be the ones in control of the situation. They had the blasters and swords. They kept her a prisoner in the tower. They supervised the blood-letting and the distribution of the cure to the needy. Mildred expected La Golondrina to embrace the chance at freedom she was offering, and thereby give her an opening for attack.

As it turned out, Mildred couldn't have been more wrong.

In mentality, the queen of the cannies was as alien as a cockroach. She had no interest in leaving the grounded, rotting ship. She adored her life on the godforsaken island, at the center of the stinking hive.

"Boil some water and throw her head in it," La Golondrina ordered the Angels. "I feel like soup."

Chapter Twenty-Three

Ryan and the others climbed the stairway to the B Deck landing, where Cheetah Luis dispatched two of his men to stand guard on the crew quarters' door. "I want you to do nothing until you hear all hell break loose up top," he told them. "When you hear that, lock the bastards in nice and tight and then join us in the bow on the main deck."

"Why do we have to wait for the shooting to start?" one of the fighters asked. "Why can't we just lock 'em in now?"

"We don't want to arouse any suspicion before we get things rolling," Cheetah Luis said. "Some cannie might come along, see the door jammed, and put two and two together. At the very least, the cannies in the crew quarters would get let out before we're done up top. That's why you got to wait until the last minute."

The explanation seemed to satisfy the Cajun and his partner. They slipped through the doorway and took off at a trot down the wide, torchlit hall.

When the ragtag band reached the A Deck landing, they paused again, preparing to split into two groups, one predominantly Cajun, the other made up entirely of companions. The former was tasked with releasing and arming the prisoners; the latter with the chilling of La Golondrina.

"How are we going to know when to start the attack on the main deck?" Cheetah Luis asked Ryan. "Should we hold off until the firefight breaks out up there?"

"No, that won't tell you whether we've won or not," the one-eyed warrior replied. "You just watch the wheelhouse. We'll let you know when we've taken it."

"What if you can't take it?" the Cajun said "I don't feature waiting around with my thumb up my butt. How long should we wait before we do the job ourselves?"

"If we don't signal you five minutes after the shooting stops up there, you can figure that we're all dead. And the ball's in your court. Don't worry about us. We'll find our own way out."

"I wasn't worrying."

"Suck it up," Ryan advised him.

"You, too."

The Cajun led his fighters through the doorway onto A Deck to pick up J.B. and the others in the armory.

Ryan and the companions continued up the stairs to the exit on the main deck. Looking back from the bow, he gazed down the length of the great, dead ship. The tower was a long way off, and there were dozens and dozens of very excited cannies between them and it.

"Spread out once we're on the deck," Cawdor told the others over his shoulder. "It's okay to hurry along, but don't move in sync like a combat team. We don't want the Angels in the tower to pick us out and know what's coming. Blend in with the action. Dance if you have to. Take different routes. We'll meet up at the far end."

Ryan took the point and began weaving his way through the milling flesheaters, cutting right and left, even turning sideways as he advanced. Again and again, he was slapped hard on the back. Congratulated for being something that he wasn't.

As he passed the first hatch, he saw the horse-faced woman leaning over the rim with her hands on her knees. "I'm going to eat *you!*" she shouted, pointing down into the captive hold. Then she threw back her triple ugly head and laughed. "Yeah, sweetheart, I'm talking to *you!*"

Ryan looked away, repressing a grimace. His face was placid, without a readable expression. But in his mind's eye he was visualizing all that lay in front of him destroyed, burning, the capering cannies left in chunks for the buzzards and the flies.

As he passed midships, a pair of male cannies crossed his path. They were hauling a corpse by its heels, facedown. From the way the top of the head was pancaked like a squeezebox, Ryan guessed it was the body of the person who'd fallen from the tower. Whether it had been a man or woman was impossible to tell. As the cannies dragged the corpse away, the hamburgered face left a glistening red stripe on the deck.

When he was beyond the kingposts, the crowd suddenly thinned out. For a second, he got a better look at the men standing guard on the tower's main deck entrance.

Cheetah Luis had told them that the Angels of Death were the biggest, baddest bastards of all.

Ryan had begun to seriously wonder about that assessment. The Angels' only mission was to protect their queen, who, as he understood the setup, wasn't under any threat on this isolated shithole of an island. After their previous unsuccessful attack, her major adversaries, the Cajun fighters, had been reduced to conducting roadside ambushes on the mainland. The only visitors allowed were other cannies, and she was much too valuable for them to ever think about chilling her. The Angels of Death had retired from the stresses and excitement, the skill-sharpening of hunt, and been turned into palace guards.

Glorified sec men.

Warriors in name only.

No doubt they still did plenty of murder, for their own pleasure and the pleasure of their queen, but chilling defenseless captives wasn't the same as fighting an enemy that shot back. They had no competition, so they had no reason to stay on top of their game. Terror and fear kept them in power. It also kept them safe.

And made them weak.

Cawdor moved closer, halving the distance to the target, then paused at the rail behind a blazing oil drum and adjusted the Steyr's ride on his shoulder. Blocking the tower doorway, their brawny arms folded across their bare chests, were two Angels of Death. They were bigger than Ryan had expected, and they seemed in excellent physical shape, their arms and chest muscles bulged with mass and power. They weren't dozing on the job as he had figured, either. They were alertly scanning the crowd for early signs of trouble.

Ryan doubted that they would actually intervene if a riot broke out on the main deck. There were too many cannies on tap with too many full-auto blasters. It was more likely that they would retreat behind the bulkhead doors until the matter sorted itself out.

"Interesting look," Krysty said as she joined her lover. "Think they take turns braiding each other's hair?"

"I believe there's an excellent possibility," Doc said, stepping up behind them. "Practitioners of the tonsorial arts must be in short supply in these parts."

Harlan Sprue showed up last. He took in the guards, then said, "We can't shoot them down without having an unhappy mob on our asses."

"We shall just have to resort to cold steel, then," Doc said. He unsheathed his rapier blade and held it behind his back, hidden by the long tails of his frayed frockcoat. He carried the ebony sheath in his left hand as a counterbalance. "Shall we proceed?"

Long before the four of them got within Doc's stabbing range of the guards, they were challenged. "Where the hell do you think you're going?" said the Angel on the right. To emphasize his authority, he puffed out his chest and flexed his arm muscles.

Ryan admired the skull branding the cannie was thrusting in his face. He nodded in appreciation. "We need to see La Golondrina, right away," the one-eyed man told him.

"She never sees uninvited visitors, so back off."

His fellow Angel chimed in, "Yeah, why don't you go beat on a railing, or something?"

"You do not understand the situation, my good fellow," Doc said to the first cannie as he closed the last two yards of distance. "This is a matter of some considerable urgency. We cannot possibly take no for an answer."

Looking at the tall scarecrow in front of him, the Angel let out a snort of contempt.

It was his last snort of any kind.

Doc used both hands and the power of his legs to drive the rapier's razor point up under the tip of the cannie's sternum and deep into his chest. The slim blade made a wet scraping sound as it sank in to the hilt.

The skewered cannie stared down at the rapier's crossguard in horror, his eyes slitted in pain. His massive chest heaved; the cords in his neck stood out like steel cables. Blood seeped like red tears from the corners of the two-inch-wide wound.

When the big cannie didn't drop dead instantaneously, Doc followed through with a full-power shoulder strike that knocked the Angel over backward, through the doorway. Together they crashed to the deck inside the stairwell with Doc on top, still holding on to his sword.

Ryan, Krysty and Sprue launched themselves at the other Angel, overwhelming him with their sheer combined weight. As he gave ground, he stumbled over his dying comrade and the kneeling Doc Tanner. For a moment, it was a free-for-all punch-out. The companions rolled around on the deck with the huge cannie, landing blows to his face, doing their best to control his powerful arms, or failing that, to block his hands from reaching his weapons. As hard as they fought, even though they were all hanging on to him, they couldn't keep him from standing again.

Ryan let go of his grip on the flesheater's wrist. As he slipped around behind the cannie's wide back, the one-eyed man drew his panga from its sheath. He short-thrust the long knife under the Angel's left shoulder blade, finding the space between ribs with its point, then with all his weight, rammed the length of the blade through the back of his heart.

The panga's point popped out of the front of the Angel's chest. A red steel tongue waggled from the branded skull's mouth.

The tongue disappeared as Ryan ripped the blade out of the wound track. As the cannie slipped to the deck, the skull mouth vomited a geyser of bright blood onto his boot tops.

To pry free the buried rapier, Doc had to stand on the other cannie's chest and use the strength of his legs.

Sprue immediately started dragging the other body around the stairwell's corner.

"No, leave 'em where they lie," Ryan told him as he grabbed a torch from the wall. The staircase leading up was an all-metal affair, including the tiny grated landings. It was bolted to the well's inner and outer walls.

When Ryan hit the steps running, they shifted sickeningly under his weight, pulling away from the outside wall with a low moan. He paused, arms spread for balance, and they sagged back in place.

"Take it easy on these rad-blasted stairs," he warned the others. "They've seen better days."

With weapons drawn, they began carefully working their way up the stairwell. All the while, rusted steel creaked and groaned in complaint. In some places the treads had come loose from the steel risers and were only held down by the force of gravity.

Ryan alerted those below him of the coming dangers. The slow going was frustrating, especially when an entire flight of steps started swaying under them and they had to stop altogether.

When they reached the fourth-story landing, progress came to an abrupt halt. Above them, the staircase was missing a number of consecutive treads. If they had fallen off, there was nothing to stop them from dropping all the way to the main deck.

"We might be able to jump it," Krysty said, pointing at the gap with her wheelgun.

"There's no telling from here what kind of shape the surviving steps are in," Ryan told her. "They might be loose, too. They'd come off when we landed."

"There's got to be another way up," Sprue said. The last thing he wanted to do was to try to make that jump.

"There are a jumble of footprints in the dust on this landing," Doc said. "They seem to be leading in and out of the door. Perhaps that is the alternate route to the top."

Ryan opened the door and looked inside, his SIG-Sauer up and ready. The deserted hallway ran in a straight line across the width of the bridge tower. On the right wall, spaced at regular intervals, was a series of metal doors presumably leading to rooms deeper in the building. The left-hand wall was divided by a row of large windows, most of which had no glass. The floor was tracked with more footprints.

"Looks like this is our detour," Ryan said, waving the others in after him. "Watch those doors. We don't want any surprises."

As he passed the empty window frames, Ryan looked down on the deck. There was no sign of Cheetah Luis and his Cajuns in the bow, which was a good thing. The drumming had started up again, this time with a vengeance. It shook through the ship's hull and superstructure. He could feel the vibration through the soles of his boots. In their overexcitement, a few of the cannies cut loose with bursts of blasterfire, aimed toward the sky. Which made Ryan glad they hadn't made shooting the attack signal. Cheetah Luis was holding his fighters in check, just like he was supposed to.

Through the door at the far end of the hallway was a mirror-image landing and stairwell. The difference was, this one had all its treads.

"I'll go first," Sprue volunteered.

As he mounted the first step, they heard sounds of fighting from somewhere above.

Not gunshots.

Steel-on-steel clashing.

The fat man stopped climbing and listened.

"That doesn't sound very welcoming," he said, steadying himself as the staircase swayed a bit and groaned a lot.

"What the hell is that?" Krysty said.

They strained to make it out.

"It has the ring of swordplay," Doc announced. "And a rather heated contest, I'd say."

The crashing abruptly stopped, followed a few seconds later by the muffled but unmistakable report of a blaster. What with the din the cannies were making, it was too faint to be heard outside the bridge tower.

"Something's going on," Ryan said. "Could be Jak and Mildred are getting busy."

As the convoy master turned and started up again, the stairs let out a squeal and collapsed under his weight. Lagbolts ripped out of corroded wall plates, slamming into the wall opposite. The staircase pulled away from its moorings. As he dropped between the risers, the fat man somehow managed to get his arms up and his fingers gripped on the edge of the tread above him.

"Don't look down!" Krysty warned him.

"Oh, fuck," he said, looking down. Beneath his stout legs was a straight, sixty-foot fall.

Ryan cast aside the torch as Krysty and Doc knelt and grabbed on to Sprue's wrists. The one-eyed man leaned way over Sprue's back and snatched a big handful of the seat of his pants. Grunting from the effort, working in unison, they hauled the fat man back to the relative safety of the landing.

Sprue's face was beet-red under his beard. He seemed more embarrassed than scared.

"Shit, that was a close one," he said, wiping his palms on his bibfront. "Mebbe someone smaller should go first."

Ryan took the lead. Moments later they emerged from the stairwell on top of the bridge.

"Keep away from the edge," he reminded them. "We don't want the cannies down on the deck to see what's going on."

Ahead, the broad unrailed deck led to the side of the wheelhouse. There was no sign of Mildred or the queen. And no sign of the fierce fighting they had heard from below.

"Who the hell are you?" an Angel demanded as he emerged from the side door of the wheelhouse. He was a gray-bearded version, but still plenty solid through the chest and arms. He had the same decoration on his chest, and the same pigtail hairdo as the others. He stepped forward and spread his tree-trunk legs, standing between them and the entrance to the wheelhouse. Over his shoulder on a sling, he carried a folding-stock AK. His hand on the pistol grip made the blaster looked very small, indeed. He wasn't aiming it at them, yet. Things were definitely tense, but not in the realm of deadly. The Angel still had questions.

"How'd you get up here?" he said.

"Took the stairs," Ryan said.

"No, who let you up here."

"Nobody let us do anything. We just walked up."

"That's crap, and you know it, asshole. There were two guards stationed on the entrance."

"Never saw them. Mebbe they were on a break."

"We don't take breaks," said another voice from the corner of the wheelhouse.

Four more Angels stepped into view. All of them carried folding-stock Kalashnikovs. They were uniformly large, well-developed, well-nourished specimens. One of them had thinning blond hair, but he still sported the pineapple-head braids.

"Okay," the gray-bearded Angel said, "it's time for you idiots to go back where you came from. If you don't move it right now, we're going to blow your fucking asses off this tower."

The other Angels took up firing stances behind him and brought their AKs to bear from the hip.

These sec men were accustomed to seeing trouble run the other way. They still had their safeties on.

The companions didn't need an engraved invitation. They scattered like a school of baitfish evading a predator, for an instant leaving the cannies struggling, flat-footed, caught between dropping their selector switches and choosing a moving target.

Only in this case, the little fishies opened fire as they broke ranks.

The gray-bearded Angel was hit in the same instant by Ryan, Krysty, Doc and Sprue. The volley of lead blew apart his chest and head, and slammed his lifeless body to the bridge wing's deck.

The other four cut loose with their AKs, relying on intimidating firepower, not accuracy, to turn back an enemy. It might have worked before, but it didn't work this time.

The companions weren't intimidated. They knew how to lower their heads and fight.

Krysty dropped to one knee and fired, arms braced, while high-powered bullets whizzed past her ears. She put five quick slugs into the belly of the balding Angel. The first hit hardly staggered him, but as the next four followed in rapid succession, and in the same ten-ring, he started jerking backward, jolted by the bullets' impacts.

As he fell against the wheelhouse wall, the other cannies realized that they were bunched up and vulnerable. They darted apart, which put off their aim.

As they moved sideways, Ryan saw an advantage and he took it. He charged right at one of the Angels, firing on the run. The cannie returned the favor, but his muzzle came around too slowly to track the oncoming target. When Ryan's slugs smacked into the Angel's shoulder, the cannie's AK lost its horizontal momentum; when they stitched up his chest, the front sight took aim at the deck. From a distance of about three feet, Ryan fired the SIG-Sauer three times straight into his throat. The flesheater convulsed and toppled onto his face, dead.

When the next Angel in line tried to shoot Ryan, his AK jammed. He frantically worked the actuator to clear the defective round.

Doc calmly walked forward, sheathed swordstick in his left hand, Le Mat in his right. Assuming a dueling stance, he thumbed back the pistol's hammer and put a .44-caliber lead ball through the cannie's left eye. Billowing black powder smoke engulfed the man's head as the flattened ball burst out of the back of his skull.

The fourth and last Angel stopped firing and bolted for the wheelhouse door.

Sprue unleashed death with both hands, the slides of his Desert Eagles cycling alternately, spitting spent brass. He hit the running cannie five or six times, and just as many near misses spanked into the wall's peeling white paint. The flesheater fell under the hail of lead, well short of his goal.

It was all over in thirty seconds flat.

During that span, roughly seventy-five rounds had been exchanged at close range. The four Angels were down and out. The companions didn't have a scratch on them. Krysty and Doc checked the bodies.

"Are they all dead?" Ryan said.

"On their way to hell," Doc assured him.

As the companions hurriedly reloaded, massed autofire roared up from the main deck.

"Get down!" Ryan shouted, shoving Krysty away from the edge of the bridge.

The others crouched well out of the line of fire.

The clatter continued unabated, but no slugs whizzed overhead or whacked into the front of the wheelhouse.

"What the hell are they shooting at?" the convoy master asked.

Cautiously, they returned to the edge and looked over to see what was going on.

Dozens of cannies fired their AKs wildly in the air as they wheeled and danced.

They were shooting at absolutely nothing.

"Madness," Doc said, "pure and simple."

"Bastards got ammo to burn," Sprue said.

"They think the shooting up here was part of the party," Krysty said. "Look they're waving at us!"

"Let's wave back," Ryan said. He picked up a Kalashnikov and, standing on the edge of the roof, touched off a 20-round, full-auto airburst.

The crowd sent up a rousing cheer.
Confidence could be a good thing in battle.
It could be a very bad thing, too.

Chapter Twenty-Four

Cheetah Luis watched the wheelhouse from inside the entrance to the bow stairwell, puffing away on a fat stick of ganja, getting his edge on.

Whether true or not, the Cajun was convinced that he moved faster and fought better after he'd dosed himself with crazyweed. The sense of calm that flooded over him provided him with a feeling of invincibility. It made him utterly fearless.

But not startle-proof.

The sudden torrent of blasterfire from the top of the tower set his heart racing. He took it to mean the bridge was under attack, and that the companions had at least gotten that far. The cannies on the deck took it to mean something entirely different. As the shooting on the tower ended, they hoisted their blasters in the air and sprayed blasterfire into the night sky.

That's why shooting wasn't the signal for the all-out attack, Cheetah Luis thought, squinting his right eye to keep the curling, pungent smoke out of it. The signal was going to be unmistakable, that's what the one-eyed man had told him. He said he would know it when he saw it.

And he was right.

After a minute or two passed, behind the windows of the wheelhouse, flames started dancing and flickering, low at first like a campfire, but rapidly growing higher and brighter. The cannies on the deck didn't seem to notice what was happening up there, either, because they were too preoccupied with celebrating, or they were too close to the tower and had a bad angle of view.

Cheetah Luis flipped away his weed and turned from the deck. "Hold this doorway!" he ordered four of his fighters standing just inside the entry. "Whatever you do, keep the bastards off the stairs!"

Taking the steps two at a time, he raced down to A Deck. He shoved his way through the fighters waiting for him there. "Come on!" he shouted, leading the charge down the corridor, toward the stern.

When they burst through the armory door, J.B. was propping up an armload of plastic stock AK-47s alongside the hundred or so others he had already prepped for battle. Piles of loaded mags lay at his feet.

"Now," Cheetah Luis told J.B. and the Cajuns. "We go, now."

J.B. grabbed up his pump gun and joined the Cajuns as they ran down the hall for the captive hold.

Cheetah Luis lifted the locking bar and swung the door open wide.

Inside the hold, the seated and standing prisoners looked toward the doorway in terror. None of them moved.

Under the circumstances they could hardly be blamed for expecting the worst.

"Come on!" Cheetah Luis shouted to the Cajun captives, stepping into the hold so they could see him. "It's a break-out!"

When the Cajuns rushed for the door, the other prisoners came to life, leaping to their feet. They charged the exit in a human wave.

J.B. pulled Cheetah Luis out of the way as they spilled out into the hall; otherwise he would have been trampled.

"Keep moving down the hall," J.B. yelled at the escapees. "Keep on moving!"

As the throng hurried by, a small, wiry man with shoulder-length white hair brushed past Cheetah Luis.

"Jak, Jak!" J.B. said. He reached out and grabbed his slender shoulder, pulling him nose to nose.

J.B. was greatly relieved to find the albino still alive, but he could read no comparable emotion in those strange ruby-red eyes. All he saw was hate. Bottomless hate that wanted out.

"Where's Mildred?" he asked.

"Took her away," Jak said. "While ago. Scarface cannie. Up to bridge, mebbe."

"The bridge is on fire," Cheetah Luis said. "Your friends captured it and set it ablaze."

"If she was up there," J.B. said with more confidence than he felt, "then she's probably free now."

Farther down the corridor, J.B. could see the other Cajuns guiding the released captives single-file into the armory. There, they were being handed longblasters and extra mags, and ushered back out into the hall. A smooth, quick operation. Anybody who could carry an AK got one.

A flurry of shots rang out in the hold to his back.

When he turned to look, stragglers were still running out. The shooting made them run much faster. Through the open doorway, he, Jak and Cheetah Luis watched helplessly as the cannies on the deck above systemically shot the few remaining prisoners in the hold. Those too weak or stunned to flee were riddled by streams of blasterfire.

One of the last out the door was a fat man. He glanced over his shoulder and froze. "Michelle!" he cried. Then he reversed course and started to reenter the hold.

J.B. saw a small, birdlike woman standing stock-still in the middle of the yawning space, her eyes closed, her hands at her sides, as if she were trying to make herself invisible.

It didn't work.

Blasterfire chattered and she was hit by dozens of high-powered bullets, and literally torn limb from limb.

"Michelle!"

J.B. and Jak caught the fat man from behind and dragged him out of the doorway. They shoved him down the hall toward the armory.

"Oh, my God! Oh, my God!" he moaned, holding his head between his hands.

"Go on, get yourself a blaster," was the Cajun's advice. "Make the fuckers pay."

All the prepped AKs were gone by the time J.B. and Jak got inside the armory. The last assault rifle went to the grieving fat man who clutched it to his chest like a life preserver.

The albino wasn't put out by the shortage. He picked a blaster at random from an open wooden crate, tested it, checking the barrel and action, and finally dry-fired it.

"Stamped steel crap," was his terse assessment of the weapon's quality, but he accepted the full magazine that J.B. handed him, slapped it into place and chambered the first round.

"Got some other goodies to take along with us," J.B. said. He directed Jak over to the rack of RPG-16s. "Grab yourself a launcher," he said. "I'll take one, too. Got a backpack for the HEAT rockets."

Out in the hallway again, when J.B. started to head for the bow, Jak stopped him and said, "Hold aft stairway on main deck."

"No, that route's got to stay open," J.B. told him. "That's where we're going to push the bastards. We start at the bow and sweep them toward the stern."

The albino gave him a hard look.

"We've already got a bunch of cannies locked in the crew quarters one deck down. We want to drive the rest of them belowdecks so we can jump off this stinking ship and blow it and them clean to hell. Get it?"

Jak showed J.B. a feral smile. He got it.

They moved through the ranks of the well-armed escapees to join the Cajun fighters at the head of the line. Cheetah Luis stood on the landing, ready to lead them up to the main deck and into battle.

As J.B. and Jak arrived at his side, angry shouting echoed down the stairwell, a dispute over who got to use the stairs and who didn't.

"Shit," Cheetah Luis said. "The bastards—"

His sentence was cut off by a horrendous barrage of blasterfire from the deck over their heads.

Outgoing and incoming fire, but mostly incoming.

The Cajuns up there were in big trouble.

Ricocheting bullets clanged and whacked the walls of the stairwell.

Cheetah Luis waved for his fighters to follow him. "Come on," he cried, "the cannies are breaking through!"

In fact, they had already broken through.

The shooting suddenly stopped. As it did so, the bullet-pocked bodies of two Cajuns tumbled down the steps, landing in a bloody heap at their leader's feet.

"Back!" he shouted to the others.

The head Cajun jumped into the hallway just as blasterfire rained down on the landing.

He was hit in the back by fragments of the shattering bullets, receiving minor wounds to his shoulder and neck. The fighter beside him wasn't as lucky. He took a metal splinter through the center of his eye. It had sufficient force to penetrate his brain. He dropped as if he'd been poleaxed.

The shooting from above stopped again.

"Wipe out time," the Cajun roared to his troops. "On the landing, massed fire, now."

Cheetah Luis led the way, heedless of the danger. From the hallway's end, he jumped to the right of the landing, to the side with the staircase leading down. Above him was the underside of the stairway leading up and the landing on the main deck.

Seven of his fighters crossed the gap in single bounds. Packed shoulder to shoulder, they pointed their blasters straight up and cut loose.

Eight autoweapons unloaded 240 rounds in less than three seconds. The din of sustained gunfire was deafening.

They shot holes through the landing, through the treads, up through the soles of cannie boots, through legs, through backsides, into spines. With the roar of blasterfire still ringing in the well, bodies began to slide and topple down the steps.

Cheetah Luis stripped out his empty mag, flipped it around and inserted the full one, duct-taped back-to-back. His fighters likewise dumped their empties and reloaded.

With the exit above cleared, the Cajuns ran up the steps, over the cannies' sprawled bodies. J.B. and Jak followed them up the well. As the companions reached the end of the first flight of stairs and were about to make the turn to the top, Cheetah Luis and the fighters on point opened fire again.

Cannies were trying to retake control of the access-way.

Bullets zinged and whined off the inside of the stairwell.

A gap opened on the steps above as the Cajuns ducked and dodged the ricochets. J.B. charged up stairs and onto the landing. Cheetah Luis and the others had their backs to the walls. They were reloading again. As J.B. made for the doorway, more cannies rushed through it.

He fired from the hip. The first cannie was blown backward, lifted off his feet by the power of the pump gun's high brass load.

J.B. fired again and a second flesheater went flying

in reverse out the door. As the Armorer advanced, he kept cycling the M-4000's action and firing at closer and closer range. It was too late for the cannies inside the entry to beat a retreat. They had overcommitted and they were caught dead. J.B. had all the momentum. The pump gun boomed and another cannie was hurled backward through the doorway, his chest erupting in a puff of red. Even after the last one went down, J.B. continued to shoot through the entrance, dissuading further intrusion with blasts of double-aught buck.

"Got it," Cheetah Luis said, clapping a hand on his shoulder.

The Cajuns had finished reloading their blasters. They took up the slack at the entrance, putting up covering fire while J.B. pulled a handful of shells out of his side pocket and started feeding them, one by one, to the M-4000's tubular magazine.

Cheetah Luis shouted down the staircase. "Time to move. Let's go. Let's go."

The rest of the Cajuns and the freed captives behind them began scrambling up the steps.

"Find some cover," Cheetah Luis told them. "Take cover."

Eager for revenge, the first five or so spilled out of the doorway onto the main deck.

Into a withering crossfire.

The Cajuns went down hard, without firing a shot in return. As they lay on the deck, bullets plucked at their clothes, sallying their bodies from the left and the right.

Cannies were waiting for them on either side of the bow. J.B. recalled the foredeck's layout. There was an anchor windlass and mooring winch. There were bitts, too—the solid steel, barrel-like posts that guided the anchor and mooring lines. All were matched in size to the enormous vessel. Solid, ample, bulletproof cover for staging an ambush.

Cheetah Luis rushed forward, blocking the doorway so no one else could step out.

"Let's clean house," he said, reaching into the pack of one of his fighters. He took out a pair of foot-long pipe bombs. Striking a wooden match on his thumbnail, he lit both fuses at once. As they sputtered in his hand, his lips moved silently.

He was counting down.

When there was about an inch of unburned blast cord the Cajun chucked both bombs out the doorway to the left, to the ship's high side. They clanked as they hit the deck near the bulwark, then they started rolling back down the slope, toward the center.

Somebody out there screamed a warning.

Cheetah Luis turned his back to the doorway and hunched over as the bombs detonated simultaneously. The rocking double boom shook the deck underfoot and sent hot shrapnel singing through the air.

As a cloud of smoke swept past the entrance, they heard moans, shouts and the sound of running boots.

J.B. poked his head around the steel jamb for a look-see. The explosions had put a sudden end to the cannie ambush. On the bombed side, behind the windlass, was a wide, blackened section of deck. Half a dozen bodies, whole or in parts, lay strewed there, smoking.

On the low side of the bow, cannies slipped away, low and fast, heading for the cover of the deck hatches.

"Get 'em!" Cheetah Luis shouted. "Don't let 'em get away!"

J.B. knew the Cajun wasn't talking to him, not with a short-barreled scattergun in his hands. As he pulled back, a pair of very eager released prisoners pushed by him. They opened up on the running cannies with their AKs, sending bullets zipping down the length of the ship.

It took sixty rounds, but they dropped five of the bastards. When their guns locked back empty, they jumped back to cover inside the entry, looking mighty proud of themselves.

From his position beside the door, J.B. could see the wheelhouse totally consumed by flames. The windows were all blown out by the heat. There was no sign of the companions.

Then blasterfire rattled from the stern and steel-jacketed bullets started slapping either side of doorway.

"They're regrouping," J.B. said. "Come on, Jak, let's do some damage."

He didn't have to ask twice.

The albino beat him through the doorway and they both bolted for the cover of the windlass, about fifty feet away, lugging RPG launchers and bagged rockets. Slugs skipped on the deck and whined around their ears as they slid in behind the massive machine.

J.B. was looking around for their next move when bullets clanged into the capstan beside his head. "Nukin' hell!" he exclaimed.

"Sniper," Jak said. "In mast."

The towering steel foremast stood in the center of

the canted deck, not twenty feet away. At its top was a crow's nest, turned sniper nest.

More high-powered slugs whacked the deck and the windlass on either side of J.B.

"What are you waiting for?" J.B. cried, screwing his fedora down on his head. "Chill him!"

Lauren popped up from behind cover, pinned the trigger of the assault rifle he'd appropriated from a dead Cajun and streamed a line of hot lead into the crow's nest. Some of the bullets pinged and sparked off the metal cage, some made wet smacking sounds. The cannie's weapon came down from the height, spinning. It bounced on the deck and clattered end over end into the scuppers. The cannie shooter came down next, in a straight, headfirst, forty-foot fall. He bounced, too, but he didn't clatter. He splattered.

Jak ducked back as fire from the hatches swept over the windlass and hammered the deck and bow behind them. "Mag!" he shouted, ditching his empty.

J.B. slid him a couple of full 30-rounders from his pack.

Cajuns pushed out of the doorway, shooting back as they spread out. They were putting up covering fire so the rest of the fighters could exit. More and more attackers poured onto the deck, moving to cover, advancing into the teeth of a feverish cannie defense.

The flesheaters had no intention of yielding the main deck. They held firing positions behind hatches, kingposts, cranes and oil drums. Their initial shock at the assault had turned into grim resolve. No way they could miss the burning wheelhouse to their backs. The flames were shooting thirty feet into the night sky.

They couldn't know for sure, but they had to suspect that their queen was either chilled or in big trouble.

Everything they had bled and died for was going down the tubes.

All or nothing.

Streams of bullets sawed back and forth down the deck. Ricochets sparked off the bulwarks. Gunsmoke hung over the ship like a caustic fog.

When J.B. looked back, the deck was littered with the dead and dying. Young and old, male and female. But at least they'd gone down fighting.

"Mag!" Jak cried, dumping another empty.

J.B. took out four more clips and shoved them across the deck. As he did, Cheetah Luis and three of his fighters joined them in the lee of the machinery.

"No blasterfire from the tower, yet," Cheetah Luis said.

That was a good thing. If the cannies climbed the tower and took up positions at the facing windows, they could control movement on the deck.

"Knock on wood," J.B. said.

The Cajun glanced back toward the bow. "That fat man's moving way too slow," he said.

As J.B. turned to look, the party in question was hit by at least thirty rounds before he dropped to the deck.

"The road trash are much better fighters," Cheetah Luis said.

It made sense to J.B. that they would be. The robbing, raping scum were skilled chillers. Coldhearts by nature. They had pushed to the cover of the bitts on the foredeck. One of them had pulled a pack from a dead Cajun's back and they were dividing up the pipe bombs it contained.

As they started lighting them and throwing them as far as they could, Cheetah Luis said, "That's more like it."

The pipe bombs landed behind the hatches, about 150 feet away.

J.B. and the others ducked as the explosions popped off, one after another. When they looked up, divots had been cut out of the ranks of the cannies. Blackened blast circles dotted with corpses.

Despite the destruction, the cannies didn't pull back.

They kept on firing.

"How about doing a little RPG number on the bastards?" Cheetah Luis asked the Armorer. "Blow 'em out of their socks."

"Not possible," J.B. told him. "If I had a vertical target to shoot at, it'd be different. I got nothing but horizontal targets here. An armor-piercing warhead might skip off a hatch cover or the deck. Fly right up into the tower. Pipe bombs won't penetrate that sheet steel. HEAT rounds will, big-time. Might chill our friends up there by accident."

"If they're still alive."

J.B. didn't say anything.

The road trash had recruited a new bomb chucker, a skinny woman with matted hair and raccoon eyes. From the short skirt she was wearing J.B. took her for a gaudy whore.

One of the road scum put a pipe bomb in her hand, then another one lit the fuse.

As she rose from cover to chuck the thing, something went wrong. The fuse was either faulty or too short. Or she froze as she watched it sputter in her fist. Or she was hit by a cannie 7.62 mm slug.

Bottom line, she didn't throw it. The bomb went off with a thunderclap. It blew her right out of shoes. Her high-top black running shoes and scorched leg stumps were all that was left of her on the deck. The steel shards and shock wave took out five of the road trash next to her, too.

"Lemme try one," Jak said.

Cheetah Luis handed him a bomb. When the Cajun offered to light it, he declined.

Jak hefted the pipe on his palm to gauge its weight, then eyeballed the distance downship. Almost nonchalantly, he lobbed the thing in a high arc. The foot of pipe made a solid clank as it dropped into the flames of an oil barrel near the right-hand kingpost.

"Damn!" Cheetah Luis exclaimed. "That was one sweet toss."

The cannies hiding around the barrel scattered in all directions.

But not fast enough to escape the tremendous blast.

The circular shock wave whipped across the deck, sending shrapnel from the barrel and the pipe flying, slicing into the flesheaters from behind as they ran.

As more pipe bombs exploded around the kingposts, the attackers, with Cheetah Luis in the lead, pressed forward to the second row of hatches, which cut the distance to the enemy front line by a third, and made for a much shorter lob.

The bursting pipe bombs quickly cleared the deck ahead, forcing the cannies to retreat or be blown apart.

The attackers moved to the third row of hatches and the bases of the kingposts.

The cannies had lost control of two-thirds of the main deck. The range for bomb tosses had dropped precipitously. Cover for the backpedaling cannies had fallen off, as well; they were trapped with the tower at their backs. Sensing imminent victory, Cheetah Luis yelled for his fighters to press on.

At that moment, the cannies broke and ran, fleeing for the stairwells at the base of the tower. From behind the hatches, their ex-prisoners poured fire into and around the doorways. The full-auto bursts sent slugs flying twenty or thirty feet off target.

"Single shots! Single shots!" Cheetah Luis yelled. "Aim the fucking things!"

The last of the cannies dived through the doorway and disappeared.

When all the shooting stopped, the initial silence was eerie. Gray smoke swirled above the deck. As the ringing in J.B.'s ears faded, he heard the hiss and roar of the burning wheelhouse and the moaning of the wounded. Spent brass was strewed everywhere. Bodies lay everywhere. More than a hundred were dead, by J.B.'s guess. It was impossible to sort out the ratio of cannies to norms.

Two of Cheetah Luis's men raced unchallenged to the stairwells the cannies had just entered. Each unshouldered his pack and took out a pipe bomb. After lighting its fuse, they threw the bomb back into its pack, then slung the pack down the stairs.

The explosions that followed made the deck ripple like a sheet flapping in the breeze. Rivets popped, metal buckled.

"That's it!" Cheetah Luis bellowed. "Regroup! Everybody, regroup! Pick up the wounded. Head for the ramp. We're out of here!"

The surviving Cajuns directed traffic, steering the jubilant prisoners and the injured toward the only exit. To protect their backs, they continued to rain fire on the two, smoke-belching doorways.

Before the first captive reached the bottom of the ramp, sniper fire clattered from the tower windows. As the freed folk streamed down the slope, they were chopped down. Some jumped off the ramp to escape. Some turned and emptied their autoweapons at the tower, others just dropped their blasters and ran.

"Can you do something now?" Cheetah Luis asked J.B.

J.B. pushed his spectacles back up the sweaty bridge of his nose. He figured Ryan and the others had to be off the freighter by now. Knowing them, they were waiting down by the cargo containers where they could give covering fire while the prisoners made their exodus. J.B. unshouldered his RPG, knelt on the deck and took careful aim up at the sniper's window. He pulled the launcher's trigger and the rocket whooshed away. A second later, a blinding white light flashed in the tower's fourth story, followed by an ear-splitting boom and a torrent of thick smoke. The rectangular window had been transformed into a ragged, blackened circle.

"That'll make the bastards think twice," the Cajun said.

Then he called out to his fighters who were herding the captives off the ship, "Hurry them up! Help the wounded! Pick up the pace!"

J.B. and Jak backed down the ramp with the last of the Cajuns, ready to fire back at the ship if anything moved. Below them, blasterfire roared. The captives who had kept their weapons and their ammo were using them on the cannie smoker tenders, either shooting them down like dogs or driving them off into the marsh for the gators to finish.

When they passed the cargo containers, the companions were nowhere to be seen. Cheetah Luis ordered them into a trot. The path ahead was choked with running people. For J.B. and Jak it was a hard slog. They were loaded down with more than their fair share of armament—two blasters, two RPG-16s and a bag of extra rockets.

"Where Ryan and others?" Jak asked J.B. after glancing over his shoulder at the deserted path behind them.

There was no sign of their friends in front, either. Certainly they would have shown themselves by now if they were really off the ship. J.B. felt the bottom fall out of his stomach.

"Don't know," he said. "But if they're still on the boat, they'll fight their way out. They always do."

He was trying to think positive.

After they'd gone about three hundred yards, Cheetah Luis stopped the file. "This is far enough," he told J.B. and Jak. "You've got to blow the ship now, before cannies break out."

"We're too close," J.B. told him. "Remember all that RDX in the armory? The blast perimeter is farther out. Most that hundred thousand tons of metal back there is going to go flying. About half of that is coming our direction. What doesn't go sideways and cut off our heads, will fall straight down and cut us in two. Besides, our friends might still be inside…"

"Let's go, then," Cheetah Luis said, waving his fighters on.

The refugees ran in a tight pack, filling the path from edge to edge. When they had retreated another three hundred yards, near the limit of the RPG's range, the Cajun stopped them again.

"Far enough?" he asked.

"Yep," Dix said.

"Good angle?"

They were parallel to the side of the grounded ship. It sat there, a big fat target, waiting to get punched.

He and Jak got their RPGs ready. They lined up extra rockets. Then they shouldered the launchers.

"Come on, Ryan, come on," J.B. muttered.

"What are you waiting for?" the Cajun demanded.

"Give it another minute. They could still be coming."

"They're either already out, or they're chilled and they're never coming out," Cheetah Luis said. "Time to let fly."

Bullets whined through their ranks, followed an instant later by sharp reports from the direction of the ship's tower. Cannies were firing on them with longblasters. The way the captives were jammed together on the path, the bastards couldn't miss, even at six hundred yards. A coldheart took a shot through the chest; the man beside him was struck in the leg. Farther down the line, people started to scream.

"If the cannies get off that ship before we blow it

up, this game is over," Cheetah Luis snarled. "And we lose. Fire, damn you!"

"Not yet, not yet," J.B. said.

Cheetah Luis shoved the muzzle of his M-16 hard against the Armorer's cheek. "If you don't shoot, little man, I will."

Chapter Twenty-Five

Her arm locked behind her back, Dr. Mildred Wyeth was hustled from La Golondrina's presence. The pair of Angels forced her down a narrow corridor, to the rear of the wheelhouse where a cramped, low-ceilinged, windowless room had been converted into a kitchen.

A big, cast-iron pot simmered on a predark all-electric stove, which had been crudely customized so it could burn wood. With the stove stoked up, the room's air temperature was well over 100 degrees.

Hanging on the wall beside the cooktop was a selection of cast-iron fry pans, from huge to tiny. On the shelves above the unfinished plywood-on-sawhorse counter were condiments looted from conquered villes and ransacked farms: coiled necklaces of red chile peppers; bundled thyme and rosemary sprigs; Mason jars full of black peppercorns and bay leaves; beakers of salt; blue antifreeze jugs of joy juice for marinades. Everything on the spice shelves was employed in the preparation of savory meats.

Despite her fear Mildred guessed that all of the queen's meals were cooked here by her Angels.

That included the slicing and dicing.

Next to the blazing woodstove was a two-foot-wide chopping block. Its upper surface was deeply dished out and splintered, from too energetic swings of the cleaver. It wasn't the kind of block found in a four-star restaurant. It was the kind of block found in a prison courtyard on execution day.

In the five-gallon pot on the front of the stove, a soup stock was bubbling and steaming. She could see a pile of gray rib bones sticking up from the foaming surface, bones cooking to mush and releasing their rich marrow.

One of the Angels picked up a wooden ladle and carefully skimmed off the thick skin of greenish froth, which he flung unceremoniously in a plastic slops bucket. Then he used the ladle to dip some of the vile bouillon into another, smaller cooking pot.

A head-size pot.

"Don't put in so much of that fucking broth this time," said the Angel who was holding Mildred in the armlock. "She likes it mixed with plenty of fresh blood."

And a sprig of bruised thyme, Mildred thought. The cannie Martha Stewart.

The Angel wrestled her over to the chopping block. When he tried to make her bend over it, she resisted with all her strength, stomping on his toes, firing elbow shots into his ribs with her free arm. The huge man hitched her arm up higher on her back, and when the spearing pain froze her, he kicked her behind the knees. Her legs gave way and she hit the floor.

"Nice and easy now," the Angel told her, leaning his full weight into her shoulders.

She pushed back as hard as she could, but she couldn't stop him from forcing her head toward the chipped and gouged hollow.

"Don't you struggle and make me miss my first swing," he said as he made her bend over even further, pressing down until her neck lay across the splintered block. "You don't want me to have to take a second cut, believe me. If I don't chill you on the first swing, it's gonna hurt like hell."

Mildred had no intention of giving him a first swing, no intention of going out nice and easy.

The Angel at the stove took hold of the heavy stock pot's wire handle, preparing to hoist it onto another burner.

At the peak of his lift, Mildred lashed out with her right foot as hard as she could. She caught him square on his weight-bearing leg just above the ankle. The kick didn't knock him down, but it knocked him off balance. He fell forward, onto the red-hot stove and the stock pot in his hands tipped over, sending blanched ribs and boiling water sheeting down this bare chest. With a piercing shriek he joined her on the floor on his knees, his mouth and outstretched fingers trembling in agony.

Startled by the turn of events, the Angel behind her relaxed for a second, letting the pressure off her back and arm. In this case, a second was long enough. Mildred wrenched loose of his grip and, once free, scrambled around the chopping block. As she lurched past the scalded cannie, she snatched his sword from its scabbard.

Instinctively, the wounded flesheater raised his hand to protect the side of his neck.

Mildred pivoted from the hips, putting everything she had into the sword slash. The blade passed cleanly through his forearm at the wrist, severing his hand without slowing. It hissed on, slicing at a downward angle through his throat from the hinge of his jaw to his Adam's apple. The edge stopped only when it came up hard against his spinal column.

As it turned out, there were worse things than a third-degree burn.

Mildred booted him in the shoulder as she jerked the blade free of his neck. The edges of the slash gaped wide. The clipped ends of the vessels looked like pink soda straws.

Eyes bulging, the Angel tried desperately to staunch the tremendous flow of blood. His efforts were in vain. He had only one hand to work with, and he had sustained two mortal wounds.

Blood squirted in all directions, from the stump of his arm and from his cut jugular.

In a second, his face went from furious-red to dead-white. Then his chin slumped to his chest. His brain was out of blood, but his heart was still beating. Blood continued to pulse from his severed wrist.

"You're in for it now," the other Angel told her. "I'm going to chop you up in little bitty pieces." With that, he took a practice cut with his sword, making the blade hiss through the air.

"You're more than welcome to try," she said as she backed away.

Mildred's adversary was much bigger and much stronger than she was. Not as agile, though. And because he was so tall and his arms were so long, he was handicapped by the confined space of the kitchen. The low ceiling and narrow walls would make it difficult for him to aim and deliver full-power blows.

The Angel came at her like a whirlwind, sword whistling as it slashed back and forth through the air. His blade tip knocked the iron pans off the walls and crashed through the collection of dishes and crockery.

Mildred was unable to return a single thrust. Under the horrific attack, all she could do was retreat while keeping up her guard.

They circled the cluttered little room again and again, the cannie's sword point scoring the ceiling and walls as he tried, forehand and back, to angle a chilling strike through her defenses.

The Angel's repeated blows on her cutlass hilt sent shock waves and pain rippling up her hand, arm and shoulder. She realized it wouldn't be long before all three went numb, making it impossible to lift the cutlass or maybe causing her to lose her grip on it altogether. It was a matter of physiology, not willpower or determination.

As she ducked away from him, he nicked the back of her left hand with the edge of his blade. There was a sharp tug, then a stinging sensation.

Mildred looked down to see the skin gone over the knuckle of her middle finger. For a second, she saw the exposed white bone, then the wound filled with blood.

The Angel laughed. "Little bitty pieces," he said.

Even though he'd cut her, she knew she'd lucked out. She had come within an inch or two of losing all the fingers on that hand. She couldn't stay lucky for long.

As she barely twisted out from under an overhead strike, she realized she was praying for a single chance, an opportunity to stick this pig while she still had the strength to run him through.

In other words, it was desperation time.

Dragging the sword point on the floor to rest her arm, she darted around the room's small worktable.

"Can't hold it up anymore?" the Angel said, grabbing the tabletop in his left hand and tossing the thing aside.

Mildred took her best shot. The cannie's arms were wide apart and he was momentarily rocked back on his heels. She whipped the blade point up and lunged.

It was a trick. A sucker's game.

The Angel neatly turned to make her miss, and as he did, he slashed down with his sword.

Again Mildred felt the rasping tug of steel on flesh and a burst of sharp pain. This time it was her sword arm that was struck. A long oval patch of skin was sliced from her tricep, the pink flesh beneath oozed red. Hot blood poured down her arm and wrist. Inside the cutlass's basket, her fingers were suddenly slippery on the grip.

"This is gonna be the death of a thousand cuts," the Angel said. "You're no match for me."

Mildred had to agree with that. Her legs were fine, but it was getting hard to swing the sword. She was moving the blade slower and slower, and she could feel her arm getting weaker. She didn't stand a chance with this particular weapon, under these circumstances.

When he charged her again, she managed to fend him off with the cutlass, but dodging was far preferable to parrying his powerful blows. As she skirted the perimeter of the room, she let the weapon drag again. She needed to recover the feeling in her sword hand before she tried Plan B.

Mildred made a point of not glancing directly at the two revolvers stuffed into the front of the Angel's pants, but she had already noted the way their butts and trigger guards hung tantalizingly over the waistband. Two very familiar weapons, both fully loaded when she last hefted them. She didn't want the cannie to guess what she had in mind until it was too late for him to do anything about it.

"I'd rather not die by inches," she said as she darted away from a sideways slash. It was the truth, oddly enough. A clean death had a whole lot of upside. "If you promise to chill me quick," Mildred said, "I'll throw down the sword and give up."

The Angel spread his arms in a transparently bogus gesture of magnanimity. "Sure, why not," he said. "Go ahead and drop it."

Mildred did so at once, letting the heavy sword clatter to the floor behind her.

"There," she said, holding out her empty hands. "I lived up to my part of the bargain. It's your turn."

Though it made her scalp crawl, when the Angel started to step up she forced herself to slip to her knees in front of him and assumed the classic, doomed prisoner pose. "Make it quick, now," she said, looking up, meeting his eyes and holding his gaze.

The cannie's expression twisted into an evil leer as he cocked back the cutlass, fully intending to finish her off with a single, terrible swipe. "Die, bitch..." he snarled.

Well inside his guard and the cutting arc of his long blade, Mildred lunged up from the floor. The Angel reacted just as she had expected. He jumped backward so he could bring his cutlass to bear. But he didn't move far enough, and certainly not fast enough. Reverse was his slowest speed.

Mildred kept coming at him full-tilt, driving with her legs, her arms outstretched toward his midsection. Before he could retreat farther or twist away from her hands, she grabbed the butts of both pistols at once.

In the next instant, the Angel realized just how fatally he had underestimated her skills.

Mildred didn't yank the blasters free. That would have taken too long, and perhaps given the giant cannie time to smash in the top of her head with his sword's pommel.

She simply turned the weapons' barrels and cylinders, twisting them around inside his pants. Grinding the sights and muzzles deep into his groin, she fired the weapons point-blank. The simultaneous reports were muffled by his shuddering flesh.

The Angel squealed as the crisscrossing through-and-throughs blew out the cheeks of his ass. He doubled over, clutching at his belly and his perforated bowels. He staggered backward a half step, then his knees buckled. No longer able to stand, he sat hard, his legs extended out straight from his hips, his heels drumming on the floor.

"That pretty much evens the odds, doesn't it?" Mildred said as she stowed the pistols in her belt and picked up the cutlass she had dropped.

The gut shot Angel gave her a look. Squinty. Hateful. It was supposed to be defiant to the last, like a wounded tiger. It came across more like a wounded jackal.

She wiped her bloody hand on the back of her trousers, then delivered a backhand slash across the front of the cannie's undefended throat that nearly took off his head.

Cutlass in one hand, Python in the other, she returned to ship's control room on the run. She fully expected to meet more Angels head-on, either in the narrow corridor or in La Golondrina's suite, but there was none in sight. She was kind of disappointed.

The smell of sandalwood incense still hung heavy and cloying in the queen's chamber. Behind the drooping folds of brown muslin, backlit by the oil lamps' weak glow, a slender figure suddenly moved for the wheelhouse door.

"Hold it right there," Mildred warned. Then she hacked down the intervening gauze curtains.

La Golondrina found herself caught in midstep. She lowered her pale, scrawny arms to her sides.

"There's been a slight change of menu," Mildred informed the cannie. "Soup's off."

"I don't know how you managed to get away, but you have accomplished nothing," La Golondrina assured her. "You have earned yourself a few more meaningless moments of life, that's all."

"Maybe I can think of something to make them meaningful."

"No matter what you do," the queen said, "you will still end up on my plate. Beneath a sauce made from your own marrow, I think."

"But will you be around to enjoy it?"

La Golondrina scowled at her.

"I think you know what's going to happen next," Mildred said.

She did.

The freezie hag filled her withered lungs and lifted her head to cry for help.

In a blur, Mildred thrust the cutlass forward, stopping its keen point against the front of La Golondrina's throat. The blade neatly pricked the wrinkled, parchment skin. Instead of screaming, the queen let out an agonized yip and jumped back, clutching at her neck with a skeletal hand.

"Shouting won't do you a bit of good," Mildred informed her. "It sounds like your lackeys have problems of their own."

They both could hear male voices heatedly arguing on the bridge outside the wheelhouse.

"No help is coming," Mildred said. "At least, not in time."

La Golondrina bent with a speed that took Mildred by surprise. Out from under a tasseled pillow, the queen pulled a long, silver dagger. The first two inches of its needle point gleamed iridescently in the lamplight, making Mildred think it had been dipped in poison.

Jabbing weakly with the slender knife, the cannie queen began to circle her fellow freezie. In that baggy black dress, she looked like a doll made of sticks, one leg long, one leg short.

"Spicy," Mildred said, turning the insult back on its author. Then she swung down with the flat of her sword, knocking the dagger out of La Golondrina's hand.

The blow made the hag screech in pain.

"You broke my wrist! Oh, you broke my wrist," the queen cried, cradling one bony hand with the other.

"If you're looking for pity, you've got to know you're looking in the wrong place," Mildred said. Then she dropped the sword on the floor and shifted the .357 Magnum revolver to her strong hand. A gesture with unmistakable meaning under the circumstances.

"You can't chill me," La Golondrina snapped. "Not if you're really infected with oozies. I'm the only thing that can keep you alive. You need me in one piece with my immune system pumping up a storm."

"Because your blood is the only cure?"

"That's right. I have enough antibodies in me to save a hundred thousand cannies from the Gray Death."

"I'm not a cannie, yet."

"But you will be, soon enough. Nobody escapes the virus."

"You're wrong about that. I think there is a way."

"You're kidding yourself, my dear."

"Maybe so, but it's worth a shot."

Mildred scooped up one of the plush pillows. With her left hand, she jammed it against the stunned woman's face.

Not as a courtesy to the queen, rather to avoid coating Jak's favorite blaster with cranial back splatter.

Mildred rammed the Colt's muzzle into the middle of the pillow and fired. Big hunks of cheddar-colored foam stuffing blew out the other side. La Golondrina's head jerked backward, her long, dyed hair on fire, her skull flying apart like a dropped teapot.

In the same instant blasterfire erupted from the bridge wing behind her. A barrage escaped five or six longblasters, and strings of bullets pounded on the side of the wheelhouse. Stray slugs crashed through the windows, plucking at the sweltering room's brown muslin veils, then slamming into the opposite wall.

Mildred leaned down, out of the line of fire, over the frail, twitching body. As she did so, she took a detailed inventory of her every sensation. Her right hand and wrist tingled from the Magnum revolver's powerful recoil. She smelled burned cordite and coppery blood mixed with sandalwood. She could feel a river of sweat sliding down the hollow of her back, between her buttocks. Her heart was beating like mad, but the unholy desire that Junior Tibideau had tortured her with wasn't there.

Perhaps she didn't need to do anything more, she thought. Perhaps the infection hadn't taken hold, after all.

Perhaps she was safe.

The scientist in her answered with cold, irrefutable logic. There was no way of knowing, one way or another, until the full array of behavioral and physiological symptoms showed up. In other words, until it was too late.

The real question was whether she could live out the rest of her life with something so horrible hanging over her head.

There was only one way to make sure she had nothing to fear.

The irony of the situation wasn't lost on Mildred. But she knew exactly what she had to do, and she steeled herself for it.

Mildred made her mind go blank before she started. She didn't let herself think. She didn't let herself breathe through her nose or mouth. She closed her eyes. She didn't let herself feel anything. She knew if she hesitated for a second, she could never go through with it.

She so detached herself from the act that she was able to view it as a disembodied spectator, an apparition floating along the ceiling of the room. She recognized the woman below her, but it wasn't really her because she wasn't there.

Before she was finished, the gunfire outside the wheelhouse ceased. There were more full-auto bursts, scattered and erratic, but they came from the deck below. Then she heard the heavy tramp of boots coming her way.

She hurried.

Ryan burst into the wheelhouse, blaster in hand.

He was a sight for sore eyes.

"Mildred are you—" He stopped in midsentence when he saw the blood dripping from her mouth and hands.

Then he looked down at the shriveled old woman on the floor beneath her. The top of her head was gone. Her skull plate and the attached hair had been tossed aside. The cranial vault had been emptied.

It was a moment frozen in time.

A moment that should have spanned an hour.

But didn't.

When Mildred opened her mouth to speak, Ryan cut her off with a chop of his hand.

"Mildred, you know I always keep my promise," he said.

Ryan's face twisted in sorrow. He pointed the SIG-Sauer at her heart and tightened his finger on the trigger.

Chapter Twenty-Six

"No, Ryan, don't!" Krysty shouted at his back.

A fraction of an ounce short of trigger break, Ryan caught himself. This wasn't an act he cared to perform in front of an audience, particularly an audience that included his lover. Ryan was certain that Mildred didn't want it done in front of the others, either. That wasn't her style. He released the trigger and lowered his SIG-Sauer.

Doc and Sprue entered the wheelhouse behind the tall redhead. Doc looked as startled and concerned as she did.

"Good grief, my dear Dr. Wyeth!" he exclaimed. "What has happened? Are you injured? Have you been shot?"

"It's not her blood," Ryan informed them as he holstered his weapon.

When the awful truth sank in, shock, anger and betrayal replaced the concern on the companions' faces.

Of the three companions, Doc the Victorian was without a doubt the most hurt and the most outraged. "Well, Dr. Wyeth?" he demanded angrily.

"Ryan's right," Mildred said, "it isn't my blood." She picked up an embroidered pillow from the floor and wiped her hands and mouth on it. Tossing the cushion aside, she pointed at the supine, emaciated body. "It all came out of her. That was La Golondrina, the cannie queen. I shot her dead with Jak's blaster."

"The means by which the killing was accomplished is of no importance," Doc said. "I think I speak for everyone when I say that what you did after you shot her is our only concern."

"It was the last thing I ever wanted to do, believe me. I know what this looks like. But really, it isn't what you think."

"Evidence to the contrary is smeared on that pillow and clotting under your fingernails," Doc said. "I understand why Ryan was prepared to immediately dispatch you to hell. I commend him for his initiative, and second the motion."

"She asked me to do it, Doc," Ryan said. "Right after she got dosed by that scarface Tibideau. She said I was to put her down, no questions asked, if she ever showed any signs…"

"I think what we have before us constitutes more than a mere indication or a potentiality."

"I haven't turned cannie," Mildred insisted. "What I mean is, I'm not the pawn of some infectious disease. I chose the act. Consciously. Rationally. In full possession of all my faculties. It was the only way I could think of to cure myself."

"But you're not sick," Krysty said.

"That's right. I don't have any concrete symptoms. I felt lousy for a while, but that seems to have passed.

Nearly getting your head cut off tends to clear the mind. Maybe what I felt was the power of suggestion. Junior's suggestion. By all accounts, the disease should have kicked in by now. And it hasn't."

"If you are not sick," Doc said, "pray tell why did you subject yourself and your victim to this abomination?"

"Mildred, haven't you risked an even bigger chance of infection?" Krysty asked.

"Not from La Golondrina," Mildred said. "She could never infect anyone. After she came out of cryosleep she no longer had the virus, she just had the antibodies to it—the virus killers her body manufactured. It seems logical to assume that if one drop of her blood can save a hundred cannies from the Gray Death, a massive dose of her antibodies will keep an early stage infection from ever taking hold. I wanted to make certain that I never got the oozies."

At least one of those present wasn't willing to let it go at that.

"I concede that you were forced into the vile act against your will in the first instance," Doc said, "but this time is different. You perpetrated the deed all on your own."

"I had no choice."

"All you are giving us is conjecture and speculation," Doc said. "What proof do we have that you are really cured of anything? All we have is your admission to what you have done. Perhaps you have already succumbed to the disease and don't realize it yourself."

"That's where I puked it all up the first time," Mildred said, indicating an opaque, pinkish residue on the floor beside the corpse. "Ask yourself, Doc, if I had already turned cannie, would I have thrown it up? Or would I have wolfed it down and be out looking for seconds?"

"I find that argument less than convincing," Doc told her. "As we used to say in my day, 'A cannibal is as a cannibal does.'"

"That's a catch-22, Doc," Mildred said.

"I beg your pardon?"

"A no-win situation. You're saying a person is defined by his or her actions, ignoring his or her intent. By your yardstick, I became a cannie the instant I was forced to swallow brains in that cave."

Doc reflected on that for a second. As he did so, his anger seemed to abate. Then he looked chagrined. "Yes, yes, I do see the problem. The logic is circular and absurd. An elementary confusion of case and class. Aristotle would be horrified. Please accept my sincerest apologies. I let emotion sway my reason. It was both unfair and unseemly."

"No apology needed, Doc. It's like that old predark joke—when I occasionally cook up some dinner, you don't call me Mildred the Chef. When I happen to shoot a rabbit, you don't call me Mildred the Rabbit Killer. But just eat one little brain…"

"At least you've still got your sense of humor," Krysty said, obviously relieved.

"I never heard of a cannie cracking a halfway decent joke," Sprue chimed in.

Neither had anyone else.

"You really ate the whole thing?" Sprue asked her.

Mildred nodded. "If a brain can make me sick, a brain can make me well. Sad to say."

"Two brains in as many days," Doc remarked, his face completely deadpan. "I sincerely hope you are not acquiring a taste for it." He hadn't lost his sense of humor, either.

"If you knew how absolutely gross they were, you would never say that, my friend."

"I believe I shall take your word for it, if you do not mind."

"What are we going to do with the rest of her?" Krysty said, indicating the body on the floor.

"She has to be completely destroyed," Mildred said.

"Let's check those lamps," Ryan said. "See how much oil they've got left in them."

There was oil aplenty.

For a funeral pyre.

At Ryan's direction, the companions gathered, then heaped all the cushions in the middle of the room, piled on the ripped-down gauze. Ryan and Sprue lifted the frail corpse by ankles and wrists and deposited it on top of the mound. Mildred bent and snatched up a hank of long black hair to which part of the skull plate was still attached. She tossed it into La Golondrina's lap.

Doc and Sprue poured the lamp oil over everything. Pillows. Gauze. Black baggy dress. Anorexic form.

"Our Cajun friends are waiting for our signal to start the attack on the main deck," Ryan said. "This should do them just fine."

He struck a wooden match on the back of his pants and tossed it onto the heap.

With a whoosh, the oil ignited. Brilliant blue flames licked around the queen's pallid form; they threw off tiny sparks as they leaped from the fine gauze to the saturated pillows. As the flames jumped higher, fed by cloth and flesh, they turned vivid orange. The fire quickly spread and grew in intensity. In seconds, the entire mound was ablaze and the flames shot up to the gauze-draped ceiling.

Behind the curtain of fire, the freezie's parchment skin crackled as it blistered, peeled and blackened; her blood hissed as it turned to steam.

The firelight danced in the reflection of the wheelhouse's windows. It flickered off the walls, casting wild shadows over the grisly ceremony.

The signal was duly noted on the deck below.

Shooting started up almost at once. Automatic weapon fire clattered from the bow.

Ryan and the others moved to the windows for a look.

The cannie defenders were trying to hold the bow, and the attackers were trying to seize it. A wicked crossfire from the flesheaters scythed down the first group of fighters as they rushed from the stairwell entrance onto the deck. The total wipeout produced a momentary stalemate.

An explosion in the midst of the ambushing cannies put an end to it. The blinding flash and powerful shock wave rattled the glass in front of the companions' faces.

"Better stand back from the windows," Ryan said.

They moved away, but not before they glimpsed the Cajun's considerable reinforcements. Dozens of escapees spilled out of the entryway and joined in the pitched battle. The fighting quickly spread to encompass the entire length of the huge ship. Flurries of blasterfire seesawed back and forth.

"They're pushing the cannies this way so they can trap them belowdecks," Ryan explained to Mildred. "The ship's already set to explode. We want them inside when that happens."

"Shouldn't we go down and help the Cajuns?" Sprue said. He was clearly itching to get into the fray with his Desert Eagles.

"You guys go on ahead," Mildred told them. "I'll catch up. I'm not leaving until she's completely burned."

"We'll all wait," Ryan said. "The Cajuns are doing fine on their own. They don't need our help, now. Getting the job done here is more important."

"Besides," Krysty said, "we don't want to get split up again. Not under these circumstances. We're sitting on a very big bomb that's about to go off."

As the ceiling's drooping fabric channels caught fire, the heat at the room's center became almost unbearable. The companions were forced back from the pyre, their hands clamped over their mouths and noses—a small measure of protection from the lung-scalding high temperature and the choking black smoke given off by the burning cushion foam.

At their backs, more pipe bombs exploded, making the window glass shiver. Sustained blasterfire rattled on and on. As the fight moved inexorably in their direction, they stood silent witness to La Golondrina's incineration.

The baggy cocktail dress was long gone. The queen's blackened skin had withered to ash. Her internal organs had shriveled and charred. Her skeleton glowed red as air sucked in through the open door and broken windows fed the flames.

Sweat rolling down their faces, Ryan and the others let her cook to a turn, until there was not a single drop of her juices left. Until the ligaments and sinews that held her bones together gave way. Until her skeleton collapsed in on itself, throwing up a shower of bright sparks.

"She's done, let's go," Ryan said. "I got the impression Cheetah Luis isn't going to wait for us to show up before he blows the ship. He's going to demolish it the first clear chance he gets, whether we're off it or not."

With Ryan in the lead, they left the wheelhouse. Outside, the air felt cool against their sweat-soaked clothes and skin. They stepped around the dead Angels on the deck, retracing their route across the bridge wing to the staircase entrance.

Ryan looked down from the top step, SIG-Sauer in hand. There were four flights and two hallways between them and the break in the staircase just above the fourth floor. He couldn't see any farther than the next landing down where the steps doglegged left. He couldn't see what was going on out on the deck, either. But he heard more sharp explosions. Shrapnel rattled against the outside the stairwell, streams of bullets sparked off it.

"Hold at the first landing," he told the others over his shoulder. "I'll go down and check the door to the next hall."

As they began their single-file descent, they had a

new problem. Or rather, an old problem exacerbated. With Mildred's additional weight, the staircase was under even more strain. It quaked and swayed, steel groaning on steel.

It was like walking on a suspension bridge—or a tightrope.

"Shit on a stick," Sprue moaned, no doubt reliving in vivid detail what he had already been through. The way his legs were trembling wasn't helping the situation one bit.

"Not so fast," Ryan cautioned. "Take your time."

When they stopped on the first landing, the shaking subsided.

Ryan continued down the flight of stairs. As he was about to step off onto the landing, the hallway door opened inward. A big man in pigtails and chin beard looked up, very surprised to see him.

So many questions.

All with the same answer.

Ryan clocked the Angel in the middle of the forehead with a steel-jacketed 9 mm round. The bullet impact sent the cannie flying through the doorway in reverse. As the Angel toppled onto his back, rag-doll limp, the spring-loaded door automatically swung shut.

It slammed with finality, but the action was far from over. Almost at once, autofire burst through the outside of the door. Thirty or forty rounds blistered the sheet steel, slamming and shattering into the staircase wall, ricocheting around the well. Ryan retreated up the stairs as the others descended, their weapons ready to back him up.

"Don't fire!" he shouted at them. "The bastards can't hit us from here. They don't have the angle. Let them waste their ammo."

Abruptly the shooting from the hallway stopped.

"How many do you think are in there?" Mildred asked Ryan.

"Three, mebbe four, if the blasters are anything to go by."

"They're joining the party on deck a little late, don't you think?" Krysty said.

"Mebbe they thought their pals had it under control," Ryan said. "Plenty of numbers. Plenty of blasters. No need to ruffle their skanky little braids. Doesn't look that way to them now."

"If the bastards were heading down the steps to help their cannie kin, you changed their minds in a hurry," Sprue told Ryan. "They saw you blast that Angel from above, mebbe even heard us coming down. They'll be desperate to go the other way, to get up to the tower and see to their queen."

"He's right," Mildred said. "The Angels' mission is to protect La Golondrina. They probably don't even know the wheelhouse is on fire. They can't see it from here. They're thinking about making a last-ditch stand. There is only one way up to the wheelhouse, and it's defendable."

"You know they're gonna beat feet up the steps to check it out as soon as we're past," Sprue said.

"And your point is?" Doc asked.

The convoy master put a hand to the wall to brace himself and bobbed his weight on the staircase, making it screech in complaint. All became clear.

"Mr. Sprue would have us thwart their efforts by rendering the tower approach certain death."

"Yeah, what he said," Sprue agreed.

"We sure don't want to leave these guys with access to the tower windows," Ryan added. "Don't want them potshotting at us while we cross the deck. But we don't have time to bust through the door and take the hallway room by room."

"Sounds like Sprue has the best option," Mildred said.

"The only option," Krysty corrected her.

"Get busy, big man," Ryan said.

Sprue started bouncing up and down, getting a good rhythm going. The entire staircase began to flex. The others fell into swing of things, adding their weight to his efforts. The stairs' upflex levered the lagbolts from the walls. The downflex did same thing. In fractions of an inch, with the staircase creaking like rusty bedsprings, the retaining bolts backed out of their holes. The risers and the treads separated.

"Enough!" Ryan ordered. "Sprue, you and me will put up covering fire while the others slip past the door. Keep on going until you reach the fourth floor. Don't wait for us. Don't stop for anything."

The convoy master stepped carefully down beside him and unlimbered both of his semiauto blasters. "Ready," he said.

"Now," Ryan told Sprue as he descended the stairs, cutting down the firing angle. Sprue did the same. When they were shoulder to shoulder on the landing, they both opened fire on the door, pumping round after round through it and down the hallway beyond.

If there were Angels on the other side, they were either shot to pieces or ducking for cover.

Behind them the others slipped safely past. As Krysty, Doc and Mildred raced down the steps full-tilt, the weakened landing shuddered sickeningly under Ryan and Sprue.

The Deathlands warrior grabbed hold of the big man's shoulders and pulled him away from the door. They hurtled down the swaying stairs three at a time, hearing the lagbolts popping free.

Then the door above slammed back hard. Angry voices shouted unintelligibly. The Angels were having a bit of a confab.

"Go, go, go!" Ryan urged the convoy master as they rounded the last turn. Below them, the gap in the staircase loomed; below that was the fourth-floor landing. To Sprue's great relief, jumping down proved a whole lot easier than had jumping up. In unison, the two men leaped from the stairs to the small, grated platform. It groaned under them, it buckled in the middle, but it held.

At that moment, with an ear-splitting shriek, the stairway above them collapsed.

Sprue shoved Ryan through the hallway's open door where the others waited. As he ducked in after, it all came down.

Ripped loose from the walls, the staircase treads were no longer connected to the risers; there was nothing to hold the structure together. It fell in an avalanche of twisted scrap steel and boiling dust. The Angels toppled along with it, yelling at the tops of their lungs.

One after another, their bodies hit the fourth-floor landing like 250-pound bean bags. Poom. Poom. Poom. And on the third poom, with a guncrack snap, the landing was ripped away from the wall. Seconds later, a crash roared up from the bottom of the stairwell.

Ryan didn't bother closing the door.

It led nowhere.

The companions were crouched on either side of the fourth-floor hallway, weapons ready. At the other end of the corridor, cannies stood in front of the windows with longblasters and armfuls of extra mags. A few looked over at the newcomers in alarm, others were preoccupied with the job at hand, getting ready to rain down death on the deck.

Outside the bridge, the pipe bomb explosions had ceased, but blasterfire continued to rage.

Ryan waved the others forward, intent on sweeping the hallway clean of hostiles.

They had run only forty feet or so when really big bangs from directly below jolted the entire superstructure. The floor jumped so violently under them that they either fell to their knees or were slammed into the walls. Dust cascaded from the ceiling and rose from the floor.

The attention of all the would-be snipers immediately turned to the battle on the deck, and the threat it posed them. They knelt in front of the glassless windows and shouldered their AKs.

Cawdor dashed ahead, closing the distance to the first shooter. He didn't realize it was the horse-faced woman until he was almost on top of her and she half turned his way. She smiled at him, then squinted back down her rifle's sights.

She still thought he was a cannie.

"Get yourself a blaster," she said as she cut loose with a short, aimed burst. "From up here it's a fucking turkey shoot."

There were several AK-47s on the floor at her side, along with a pile of loaded magazines.

Ryan picked up one of the assault rifles. He checked the chamber for a live round, stepped between her and the cannies down the hall and shot her once in the head.

With all the firing going on, the other bastards didn't even notice.

At Ryan's direction, the companions gathered up the other blasters and mags. Fanning out, they turned the appropriated weapons on the cannie shooters, peeling them away from the windows with hot lead.

Only the two snipers at the far end of the corridor managed to pull back and return fire.

With high-powered slugs streaking past, Sprue grabbed Doc by the waist and carried him through an open doorway on the left.

Over the clatter of blasterfire, Ryan heard the piercing scream of a rocket motor. He launched himself into Krysty and Mildred, knocking them to the deck, shielding them with his body.

The RPG warhead detonated with a brilliant flash and mind-numbing concussion. The explosion tore the door Sprue had ducked through off its hinges and sent it cartwheeling down the hallway.

The HEAT warhead did a lot worse to the snipers.

Their pulped remains were sprayed like red stucco over the walls, floor and ceiling. Dark smoke billowed from the four-foot-wide hole in the metal wall where the rocket had exploded.

Gathering themselves, Ryan and the companions charged through the smoke to the door that led to the only stairway down. They had three floors and six more flights to go.

Everything went smoothly until they passed the second floor, when they heard the sound of many boots, then felt the vibration. The staircase shook and groaned.

"Bastards on the steps, coming this way," Sprue said, "retreating from the main deck."

If he was correct, Ryan knew the cannies were forewarned. They had already seen the flames shooting from the wheelhouse. They knew trouble was above them. They would be advancing with weapons up, ready to shoot anything that moved.

Ryan took another AK from Mildred, dropped both weapons' selector switches to full-auto. An assault rifle in either hand, he charged down the stairs to meet the cannie wave head-on.

The one-eyed man knew that fighting downhill was a lot easier than fighting up. He didn't have to take his eye off his targets to keep from tripping. He was already looking down.

The oncoming cannie wave broke over an immoveable object. Firing from the hip, Ryan stitched bullets through their heads and shoulders, sweeping them aside. He riddled their backs as they turned to run the other way. Some of them jumped the rail to keep from being shot.

When his weapons locked back empty, Krysty took over with another of the appropriated AKs, firing short bursts into the last of the fleeing flesheaters. Few of the cannies had the clarity of mind to fire back, and when they did, their aim was hasty and off target.

The companions clambered over the shambles of heaped bodies Ryan and Krysty had left in their wake. They ignored the wounded. Even if mercy had occurred to them, there was no time for coups de grâce.

As Ryan reached the main deck, he saw smoke boiling up from the stairwell that led to the next level down. The steps were black, twisted ruins. Cannies could still climb them, but with difficulty. He could hear them coughing, but no targets appeared out of the smoke.

Ryan hurried the others into the open, into the lee of the bridge tower.

Blasterfire echoed from the second and third floors above. The cannies assembled there weren't shooting at them, but at something—or someone—farther off on the island.

The deck in front of them was littered with bodies and parts of bodies, and scorched with thirty-foot-wide blast rings.

Nothing moved.

"Where is everybody?" Mildred asked.

Nobody had an answer to that.

"Time to leave," Ryan told them. "They still think we're cannies. They won't shoot their own kind."

The companions crossed the deck at a measured pace. Not panicked, but focused. As though they had business to attend to.

At the head of the ramp they looked out at the desolate marshland.

"I can't see anyone," Doc said.

"Look, out on the path," Krysty said. "See? Way off in the distance? Someone's waving."

"Damn, they sure are far away," Sprue said.

Ryan added, "I don't like the look of this."

Chapter Twenty-Seven

As rifle fire from the ship's tower continued to fall on the path, the Cajuns and former cannie prisoners took to their heels, trying to get out of range.

Some made it, some didn't.

Those who didn't, dropped in midstride, either howling and thrashing in pain or silent and still in death. Slugs smacked the salty puddles and flicked the blades of marsh grass.

A sparse leaden rain, whizzing to earth.

"Face it, your friends are all chilled," Cheetah Luis snarled down at J.B. "There's only one way on and off that ship. There's only one path leading to it. And you're looking at it. There's no other place for them to go. If they aren't here with us, they're goners. And you're about to join them. A lot of brave fighters gave up their lives tonight. A lot more are gonna die if you don't shoot."

J.B. said nothing in response. He continued to scan the side of the distant ship, but with failing hope.

"Either fire that rocket, or hand it over," the Cajun said. "If you don't, I'm going to blow your head off."

J.B. reached up and shoved the M-16's flash-hider away from his face. "You want the HEAT, you got it, Chief," he said.

As J.B. lurched to his feet, he jammed the pointed nose of the warhead into Cheetah Luis's flat stomach. His finger rested on the launcher's trigger, ready to rock.

The Cajun looked down at him, shook his head and said, "You don't have the balls, little fella."

"Got any last words?" J.B. asked him.

"If you fire, you'll die, too."

"In case you're interested, mine are 'fuck you.'"

"Look!" Jak cried. "They come!"

The albino's sharp eyes had picked up movement at the top of the freighter ramp.

In the light of the main deck's oil drum fires, J.B. could make out Krysty's red hair and Mildred's dusky skin. He couldn't identify with certainty the two tall men with them, but he figured they had to be Ryan and Doc. Sprue, the fat man, was unmistakable, even at six hundred yards.

"You are one lucky crawdad-eating son of a bitch," J.B. told the Cajun as he lowered the RPG-16.

"No luckier than you are."

Jak grabbed a torch from one of the fighters and started waving it overhead to get the companions' attention.

It worked. The five of them came barreling down the dirt ramp.

For a short distance after they reached ground level their backs were protected by the height of the ship's hull. The shooters in the tower couldn't see them below it. But as soon as they appeared on the path, heading at an all-out sprint to join the retreating attackers, the cannies figured whose side they were really on.

Blasterfire chattered from the second and third floors of the tower, no longer aimed at the Cajuns and former captives, but at the companions.

J.B. knew the cannies had the wrong weapons for the job. He had seen the limits of their arsenal, and there wasn't a real sniper rifle in the lot. What they had was raw firepower. Great for shooting ducks in a barrel. Great for "human wave" assaults. Piss-poor for hitting scattered, running targets.

The raw firepower quotient took an upward jump as more and more cannies appeared on the deck, lining the rail with their assault rifles.

It was clear to J.B. that his side had hardly made a dent in their numbers, this while suffering high losses, particularly among the skilled Cajun fighters.

J.B. was sure he could see somebody storming around on the deck, no doubt whipping up and organizing the pursuit.

It felt as though everything was about to fall apart.

"They're coming down the ramp, dammit!" Cheetah Luis cried.

Indeed, the cannies abandoned ship in hordes, chasing after the fleeing quintet. The bastards who remained along the rail and in the tower continued to fire at the companions' backs.

J.B. and Jak could do nothing to aid their comrades. They knew firing on the pursuit was a waste of ammo. They couldn't hope to hit running cannies with assault rifles at six hundred yards.

The Cajuns didn't share that pessimism. Several opened up with their long blasters.

"Dark night, no!" J.B. shouted as he turned on them. "Don't shoot! From this angle you're just as likely to hit my friends!"

Behind them, the escapees had taken advantage of the targeting shift. They were already two hundred yards farther away, and well beyond the accurate range of the tower guns.

J.B. knew the cannies couldn't have cared less. They planned to run down the captives long before they reached the other side of the island.

Under a torrent of blasterfire from the ship, Ryan and the others ducked between the cargo containers-smokers.

"They're clear now," the Cajun growled in his ear. "Fire the fucking thing!"

"They're still too close to the ship!" J.B. shouted back. "The shock wave would chill them!"

Ryan had to have realized that, as well, because after a few seconds he and the others burst from cover, dashing along the path, trying to put more distance between themselves, the freighter and the pursuit.

There was another thing that J.B. was sure had registered in his old friend's mind. The farther they got from the ship's burning oil drums, the less light there was for the cannies to shoot by. It was bright enough looking back at the vessel, but looking away from it was like looking down a deep, dark well.

J.B. knew it was coming up on crunch time. The companions were about three hundred yards away. The cannies trailing them were about 150 yards beyond that, and closing rapidly. If he and Jak waited until the companions got completely clear of the blast zone, it was going to be too late. The cannies coming up behind would have already shot them in the back.

"Get set," he told the albino.

Jak shouldered his launcher and peered through the sight.

"About fucking time," Cheetah Luis said.

J.B. ignored him. "Gasoline is in a hold on the first deck just forward of midships," he said to Jak. "It's on our side of the ship.'

"Got it."

"Clear behind!" J.B. shouted over his shoulder. He acquired the target and adjusted his aim for the distance. The bull's-eye was big, but it was a half mile off. When he tapped the trigger, the rocket launched with a roar.

Jak's rocket was away a second later.

The twin tracks of the exhausts glowed orange as they streaked over the marsh, arcing up to the maximum height of their trajectory then dropping down the last thirty yards. They made what seemed like pip-squeak flashes and booms against the freighter's steel skin. The primary, shaped charges had exploded on impact, boring holes for the secondaries to slip through. A fraction of a second later, the bigger payloads detonated, blasting huge rips in the side of the vessel.

That was it.

No subsequent explosions.

No chain reaction.

"Try a little more to the left," J.B. said as they hurriedly reloaded their launchers.

The rockets sailed away with a blistering whoosh. Again, J.B. followed the glowing embers of the tailpipes as the warheads closed on their target.

Both warheads detonated, tearing holes in the hull's sheathing.

Again, no cigar.

"I thought you knew what you were doing," Cheetah Luis said.

"I do," the Armorer said as he sighted and again fired.

Jak had his reloaded launcher up, but he never got the shot off.

The fifth burning ember was the charm. J.B. scored a ten-ring hit on the hold with the gasoline, which was right next to the armory with the RDX. Both were above the ten-thousand-gallon oil bunker.

The explosion was much, much bigger than J.B. had expected.

Quasi-nuclear.

In a split second the vast ship became a dome of light from one end to the other. A light so bright it seemed to turn the steel translucent. The sides of the vessel peeled open under the awesome pressure. The deck and superstructure were launched upward in billions of fragments.

The blast's concussion sent a hundred-foot-high wave of dust rolling outward, a doughnut of churning black propelled by a thousand-mile-an-hour tailwind.

J.B. watched in astonishment as the pursuing cannies were engulfed by the racing cloud. An instant later, astonishment turned to horror as the companions were swallowed up, too.

Ryan, Krysty, Mildred, Doc and Sprue vanished.

Even though J.B. could see it coming right at them, he wasn't prepared for what happened next. The shock wave and the sound of the blast hit him like a battering ram. For a moment, he blacked out. When he came to, he found himself twenty feet up the path, flat on his rear end.

If he had underestimated the power of the blast, he had also underestimated the diameter of the blast zone. Parts of the freighter began to fall all around them: sections of steel railing; hunks of three-inch-wide wire rope; anchor chain links; eight-inch rivets. Other items, too. Unidentifiable things, but definitely on fire. All of it thudded to earth.

Junkyard hail.

A mooring cleat landed on a Cajun standing right next to Jak. The cleat weighed three hundred pounds if it weighed an ounce. It crushed the poor bastard like a grape.

J.B. and the albino did the only thing they could.

They ran like hell.

Chapter Twenty-Eight

It took a full minute for all the debris to come down through the swirling dust. First came the heavier objects. They screamed to earth like meteors. Hunks of the ship the size of semi-tractor-trailers splashed into the marsh's pools. The debris fell in ever-smaller waves, peppering the ground with impacts.

When the deluge finally ended and the dust began to settle, a pall of noxious black smoke started to pour from the burning oil bunker. It spread like the densest fog over the landscape, obscuring everything, even the roaring blaze that spawned it.

J.B. and Jak didn't speculate on the odds of finding their friends alive. They didn't speculate on anything. Without a word, they pulled rag masks over their noses and mouths, and after borrowing a couple of torches from the Cajuns, they moved back down the path in search of their companions.

The torch lights barely penetrated the thick smoke. To view the ground, they had to hold the crackling flame a yard away. They followed the trail by feel and by stepping on things. When they stepped in water they knew they were veering off the path.

They found other things by feel and by stepping on them. Human body parts were mixed in with the scrap iron and steel, the remains of cannies from the freighter's main deck, blown four hundred yards from the epicenter of the explosion.

"Do you see anything?" J.B. asked, his voice already hoarse from the smoke.

"Nope," Jak said.

They both dreaded the prospect of finding their friends in pieces, but they had to look. They owed Ryan, Krysty, Mildred and Doc that. On either side of the path were thousands of small, scattered fires from objects hurled far out onto the marsh. They cast a ghastly wavering light through the curtain of smoke.

As they proceeded to search, minor explosions popped off from the direction of the ravaged ship. J.B. and Jak couldn't see the vessel itself, but the yellow glow of its blaze reflected dully off the banks of low-hanging clouds.

They found their friends three hundred yards down the path, roughly where J.B. had seen the dust wave overtake them. They found Krysty Wroth first. She was facedown, unbloodied but still.

She looked dead.

J.B. gripped her by the shoulder and gently turned her over. Then he leaned down and held the torch close to her face. As its heat radiated against her skin, the long strands of her prehensile, mutie hair coiled into tight ringlets of alarm.

"She's alive, Jak!" the Armorer said.

"Mildred's over here," the albino said.

J.B. shook Krysty back to consciousness and got her to sit up.

"Oh, my head," she moaned.

"You're going to be all right," J.B. told her. "Just stay still for a minute. Get your bearings."

When he moved to check on Mildred, he found her already recovered and kneeling beside Ryan, who was coughing violently.

Even with a filtering rag, it was difficult to breathe through the smoke.

"Is he okay?" J.B. asked her.

"Don't know, yet," she said.

Mildred quickly checked Ryan for broken bones and flash burns, and found no serious injuries. "Jak's still looking for Doc and Sprue," she said as she stood. "They could be in much worse shape. We'd better help him."

About twenty feet away, the albino was standing over the seated old man and Sprue. Even in the weak torchlight, J.B. could see their hands and faces were coated with soot. He guessed the shock wave had to have landed them on their backs.

Both men coughed rackingly.

"It's smoke inhalation," Mildred said. "Get them on their feet. Get them moving."

As they did so, she took the Colt Python from her belt and handed it to Jak. "You've probably been missing this," she said.

He reholstered his weapon without thanking her.

Miraculously, no one had been hit by falling debris. Aside from the smoke they'd breathed in, their injuries amounted to little more than contusions to the hands and face.

They all regrouped around Ryan and Krysty.

"What about the cannies?" the one-eyed man asked, glancing back in the direction of the freighter.

If there was anything moving closer to the ship, they couldn't see it for the smoke. There were no sounds of life, either. No moans. No cries for help. Just the roar of the bunker oil burning out of control.

"They were a lot closer to ground zero than you were," J.B. told him. "Shock wave probably blew them apart."

"Lot of gator food 'round here, then," Sprue said.

Doc broke into another fit of coughing.

"Got to get you some fresh air," Mildred told him.

"Good luck finding some," Krysty said.

The burning ship had managed to wreath the entire island in smoke.

"How are we going to get off this hellhole?" Mildred asked.

"Same way we got on," J.B. told her. "Cheetah Luis sent some of his fighters ahead to capture the barge."

Doc suddenly doubled over, hacking his lungs out.

"Let's get on with it, before Doc drops dead," Ryan said.

They crossed the flat, featureless island like penitents, shuffling along the path, filthy, bloody, faces wrapped to the eyes in rags, bone-weary from the exertions of the last two days.

After what seemed like hours of trudging, they sighted a row of dim lights through the smoke ahead. Then they heard the water lapping at the shore.

The barge emerged out of the shifting smoke, torches lining its deck. There were few people aboard, the sole survivors. As the companions stepped aboard, the Cajuns were dumping the dead cannie skipper and crew over the side.

Cheetah Luis greeted them. He seemed subdued. "You were the last ones to make it out?" he said.

"Looks like it," Ryan said.

"Mighty expensive victory," the Cajun said as he looked around the boat.

Cheetah Luis had lost two-thirds of his kinsmen fighters in the battle and subsequent explosion. Some of the freed prisoners looked shellshocked. They couldn't believe what they had lived through. Some openly wept, their faces buried in their hands, mourning the loss of loved ones.

"Way better than an expensive defeat," Ryan told him.

"Back home we still got a fight on our hands," the Cajun said. "Got to hunt down the rest of the bastards before we can start fixing things like they used to be. Gonna be a long, hard road."

"You'll find your way," Ryan assured him.

Across the deck, Harlan Sprue was already laying the groundwork for a fresh start. He was buttonholing the survivors, trying to recruit himself a new convoy crew.

The barge backed out of the narrow cove, piloted by one of the Cajuns. He steered it over the black water toward the mainland, leaving the foul stench of burning oil behind. With the clean salt air rushing over them, the companions stripped off their rag masks.

Mildred took a seat beside Ryan on the bow. To the east, dawn was breaking a bloody red.

Cannie red.

"We didn't get all of them," Ryan said.

"Got a lot though," Mildred said. "Put a serious dent in them."

"How long before the cure wears off and the bastards start to die back?"

"No way to predict that," Mildred said. "The important thing is they won't spread any further."

"Couldn't there be other cure carriers like La Golondrina out there?" Ryan asked. "The whole thing could start all over again."

"Anything is possible, Ryan. We don't know what caused her to be source of cure in the first place. We don't know how she became a cannie, either. Even she didn't know that."

"How much of her is inside you?"

"You're thinking I might be carrying the cure?"

"It crossed my mind."

"Ryan, just because I harvested her antibodies doesn't mean I have the capacity to store them, or to make them for myself. The cure La Golondrina produced was the result of a complex set of unique biochemical processes. The genetic changes behind those processes were created by a series of events that cannot be reconstructed, even if we knew what they were."

"So you're saying it's over?" Ryan said.

"I'm saying it's over for now," Mildred said. "Enjoy the sunrise."

James Axler
Outlanders®

SKULL THRONE

RADIANT EVIL

Buried deep in the Mayan jungle amidst a civilization of lost survivors and emissaries of the dead, lies a relic that hides secrets to the prize—planet Earth. In sinister hands, it guarantees complete and absolute power. Kane and the rebels have just one chance to stop a rogue overlord from seizing glory, but must face an old enemy to stop him.

Available May 2007, wherever you buy books.

NEUTRON FORCE

The ultimate stealth weapon is in the hands of an unknown enemy...

A grim presidential directive comes down to Stony Man: an unknown entity is in possession of one of the deadliest weapons known to man, and the death toll across the globe is mounting. It's a silent murdering machine, killing with no heat, no noise, no radiation—just silent, invisible slaughter from ultrafast, subatomic particles. With no nation able to defend against it, Stony Man's only option is to destroy it. But first, they must find it....

STONY® MAN

*Available
June 2007
wherever
you buy books.*

JAKE STRAIT
THE DEVIL KNOCKS
BY FRANK RICH

HELL IS FOR THE LIVING

It is 2031, the hellscape of the future where chemical and biological cesspools have created everybody's worst nightmare. In the corner of hell known as Denver, Jake Strait must face a bounty hunter turned revolutionary in a flat-out race for the finish line, where even victory will place him in double jeopardy.

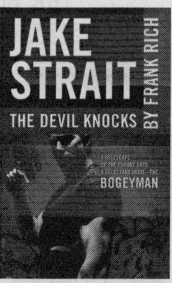

Available April 2007, wherever you buy books.

GOLD EAGLE®

GJS2